DEATH ON THE
NIGHT OF LOST LIZARDS

A HUNGARIAN TEA HOUSE MYSTERY

Death on the Night of Lost Lizards

Julia Buckley

THORNDIKE PRESS
A part of Gale, a Cengage Company

LIBRARY OF CONGRESS CIP DATA ON FILE.
CATALOGUING IN PUBLICATION FOR THIS BOOK
IS AVAILABLE FROM THE LIBRARY OF CONGRESS.

ISBN-13: 978-1-4328-9186-2 (hardcover alk. paper)

Published in 2021 by arrangement with Berkley, an imprint of Penguin Publishing Group, a division of Penguin Random House, LLC.

Printed in Mexico
Print Number: 01   Print Year: 2022

For my father and mother,
in gratitude for Christmases past

Our snow was not only shaken from whitewash buckets down the sky, it came shawling out of the ground and swam and drifted out of the arms and hands and bodies of the trees; snow grew overnight on the roofs of the houses like a pure and grandfather moss, minutely ivied the walls and settled on the postman, opening the gate, like a dumb, numb thunderstorm of white, torn Christmas cards.

— DYLAN THOMAS,
A CHILD'S CHRISTMAS IN WALES

Take this cap, which has magical properties, and if thou dost put it on, and say, "Fog before me, fog behind me," thou wilt instantly become invisible.

— NÁNDOR POGÁNY,
THE HUNGARIAN FAIRY BOOK

CHAPTER 1
THE MAN IN THE SNOW

My grandmother once told me that snow is friendlier than rain.

"Why?" I asked.

"Because rain wants only to soak you and leave you shivering. Snow sits on your shoulder and tells you the truth: that life is cold, but it warms us with beauty."

"And *then* it soaks you," I added.

"Not if you brush it away. But more than that: snow is magic."

"Why?"

"Because it reminds us of the Land of Dreams."

This struck me as poetic, especially when she assured me that the snow that fell upon her as a girl in Békéscsaba was nothing like the snow that fell upon us in Riverwood today. I had therefore always associated Hungary with surreal and beautiful snows.

The snow falling now, as I trudged down Andrews Street, did hold a touch of magic in that it resembled something inside a glass globe one shakes to create a Christmas scene, but it also had a diagonal quality, and seemed bent upon landing directly on my eyeballs. I reached my car and made haste to stow my packages in the backseat, then ran around to the driver's door, flung it open, and dove in. "Ah," I said. I brushed the "friendly" snow from my shoulders and got the car heater going. Then I leaned back for a moment to study the snowfall.

It did look more dreamlike from a warm, dry place; I marveled at the lacy flakes that sat briefly on my windshield, allowing me to appreciate their perfect symmetry before transforming into moisture and sliding away.

I sighed and closed my eyes for a moment. What magic would this dream snow bring to me?

My phone buzzed twice in a row. I picked it up and checked my texts. One was from my neighbor, Paige, who was seven months pregnant and quite bored, she had recently assured me. You got a package, she wrote. It's huge!

This was exciting. I didn't tend to get much mail beyond sales flyers and holiday cards. "Ooh," I said aloud.

The other text was from Detective Erik Wolf of the Riverwood Police. It said, Your mother has informed me your birthday is approaching. Surprised that Haniska did not tell me this herself, since she and I are pretty close these days.

I grinned, then typed, I didn't want to make a big deal. Of course you can buy me presents if you want. Or celebrate me in kisses.

I will do both, he wrote, and sent about twelve heart emojis. Erik Wolf had struck me early on as an aloof person, but I had found instead that he was just socially awkward and was in fact an utter marshmallow beneath a hard exterior.

I put my phone aside, wondering why my mother had been talking to Erik in the first place, unless she called him especially to talk about my birthday. This possibility seemed likely, and I experienced a burst of embarrassment. Still, it was good that Erik knew.

My car was toasty now, and I buckled in, ready to make the ten-minute drive home. A young man emerged from an alley, his dark clothing a sudden surprise in the white landscape. He wore black jeans and a dark sweatshirt that said "Riverwood" and bore the stately crest of Riverwood University, located a couple of blocks west of where we were. The boy (that was how he seemed, although my mother would laugh and say he was less than a decade younger than I was) seemed slightly agitated. He slid his hands into his pockets, pausing for a moment under the warm, twinkling lights in the window of Stones by Sparkle, a new shop that I'd been meaning to investigate. His face told me that he was cold and miserable.

"Wear a coat, silly," I murmured. I had inherited my mother's horror of seeing someone not dressed for the weather. The young man hesitated for a moment; he turned toward a large pine tree outside Sparkle's store, and I laughed because it looked as though he intended to walk into the tree itself, his hands plunged in his pockets, like a child entering Narnia. He turned back, his hands visible again and bereft of gloves; he was a lost soul in the snow, and briefly his eyes seemed to meet mine. *I know him,* my brain said, and then he loped away, turning eventually at Wood Street.

A thought lingered at the edge of my consciousness, something elusive and distant, and my Uncle Zoltan's face shimmered before me for no reason at all. I sighed, putting the boy and my uncle out of my mind. I pulled away from the curb, wondering what Erik Wolf would get me for

12

my birthday, now that the cat was out of the bag. I really would be happy with an evening of kisses, since that was how we tended to spend our evenings anyway . . .

My phone rang, and I poked it with my right hand while I steered with my left. Then I grabbed it and put it against my right ear. "Hello?"

"Haniska," said my grandma's voice. "Did you find something good?"

She meant for tomorrow's Christmas party at the tea house. We were hosting no fewer than fourteen holiday events before Christmas Day, and tomorrow's was for the employees of a local medical group.

"Yes, something awesome. We want to celebrate medicine, right? I found little stethoscopes that can go on cupcakes, and first-aid-kit business card holders. We can put the tea house cards in there, and then they can use them at work."

"Good. Your mama and I did the Christmasy part. And we'll use the white Christmas tea set with holly berries and greenery edges."

"This was supposed to be our day *off,* Grandma. We've got back-to-back events tomorrow."

"Yes, yes. Now we are all done. Your parents will go see a movie, and Grandpa and I will be home with Netflix. Do you want to come over? I make *pörkölt* and dumplings."

"Mmm, sounds good, but I think Erik is coming over tonight."

"Ah, the wolf. Always lurking around my little lamb." There was laughter in her voice, though. She had come to terms with Erik Wolf's "unlucky" surname by reading his tea leaves and determining that he was actually a shepherd who dressed as a wolf to catch wolves. That, she said, was the nature of police work.

"Yes, he lurks, and I like it. Your lamb is safe if he's around."

"Ya. Okay, see you in the morning."

"I wouldn't turn down some *pörkölt,* if you have leftovers. Erik would like that, too."

"Ya, okay, I make extra," she said, sounding distracted.

"Grandma! Are you watching TV?"

"No, no. Just a show on Netflix. Grandpa and I are on season three. We keep trying to stop, but then something happens, and we have to watch one more."

I stopped at a light, a winking red eye in the flurry of snow. "You're binge-watching, Grandma. That's what they call it. Bingeing on Netflix."

"No. Just to the end of this season, as our

14

little treat. Then we stop and play cards or something."

I laughed. "Good luck with that. See you, Grandma. Enjoy the show."

I set the phone aside and watched my own show as I drove — the beautiful snowfall that was beginning to accumulate on roofs and lawns. Riverwood donning its winter white.

It was a relief to pull into my parking lot at last because the snow had made the roads slick, and I had already seen a couple of cars slide unexpectedly into an adjoining lane or into an intersection. No collisions, thank goodness, but a sight to make one cautious.

I grabbed my packages and purse, climbed out of the car, and moved carefully toward the door. It was opened for me before I got there by my neighbor Paige and her daughter, Iris, a bright five-year-old who had become our unofficial doorman.

"Hi, guys," I said. "Iris, that is one terrific sweater."

It was: a bright blue number covered with white reindeer joined together by their spectacular antlers. She wore this with a tiny pair of jeans. "That looks like something from the Ulveflokk children's line," I said.

Paige brightened. "It is! After you told me

15

Erik's sisters run that company, I had to get something for Iris."

"It looks fantastic on her. I do love their winter stuff."

The two Gonzalez women, mother and daughter, looked at me expectantly.

"What's going on?" I said.

"Can we watch you open your package? It's just so big. We've been dreaming about what could be inside."

"Oh my gosh, I forgot! Yes, yes! Where is it?"

"I had the guy carry it to your door."

I smiled at them, their rosy cheeks and hopeful expressions. "Let's hope it's not been misdelivered, now that we're all excited about it."

We climbed the stairs to my floor and I saw the box immediately: it was indeed big. I jogged down the hall and peered at the information. Yes, addressed to Hana Keller at 444 Abbott's Lane, Apartment 2-5, Riverwood, in beautiful calligraphy-like writing very similar to my grandmother's. "Oh, this is great," I said, my eyes flicking to the return address. "It's from Uncle Zoltan! See the California return address? This is so weird, because I was just thinking about him . . ."

Paige nodded. "I wasn't sure about that

name, Horvath."

"Hor-vott," I corrected automatically. "It's my mom's maiden name. Zoltan is her brother. He's sent Domo and me birthday presents since we were tiny. I should write and tell him he can stop, but I just love that yearly tradition. I should have known it was from him, but I keep forgetting my birthday is coming."

"I would never forget my birthday," Iris said, her little fingers on my package. She was unconsciously picking at it, an act born of innocent desire and curiosity. I laughed.

"Let's get this inside and see what he sent me! Iris, how strong are you?"

I tried the package. Not impossible, but, yes, heavy. We decided to push it in with our hands and feet. Eventually we transported it into the kitchen, where I had tools for opening it. Iris helped me slice open the tape and remove some tissue paper, beneath which we could see bubble-wrapped bundles.

"Oooh, it looks like china. Maybe that Hungarian stuff you love so well," Paige said. "Oh no, I'm too excited. Hana, can I use your bathroom?"

"Of course," I said, laughing.

Iris gave me a wise look. "Mommy has to pee all the time."

"Yes, well, she has a little person in there leaning on her bladder. Can you imagine?"

"No," Iris said, her eyes on the package. My cats, Antony and Cleopatra, had joined her and were expressing a similar curiosity about the contents of the box.

"Okay, it's always polite to read the card first. Let's see which words you can read, Iris."

This excited her; she was in kindergarten, but she could read at a second-grade level, her mother told me.

I opened the little blue envelope on top of the wrapped things and pulled out the greeting card, a glitter-covered old-time European holiday greeting.

I opened it and handed it to Iris. "Do your best; I'll help."

Pleased, she said, "Dear Hana."

"Good."

"I canow —"

"Know."

"I know it is your *birthday* — that's a big word, but I can read it!" Iris said.

"Go on, my little reader."

"I know it is your birthday, but I know" — she said it right this time — "you like dese cards."

"Very good! Let me try the next sentence."

"Okay." Iris handed me the card with

some reluctance and some relief. Her cheeks were bright above her reindeer sweater.

I peered at Zoltan's perfect handwriting. "I discovered this set quite by chance, and I remembered how enchanted you were with this design a long time ago — remember when I stayed with your family in River-wood? The memory of your sad little face has stayed with me through time, so this gift had Hana Keller written all over it."

"What?" Iris asked, amazed.

"He means he knew I would like it. Not that there was actually writing there."

"Oh."

I continued to read to her. "I hope that the reclaiming of a lost porcelain treasure is a good birthday treat." Iris leaned in to see how porcelain was spelled, and I stole a quick hug. "Have a happy birthday, my dear niece. I hope to see you sometime in the New Year."

I set down the card, not daring to hope about what might be in the box; Iris gave me a no-nonsense look. "Let's get to the opening," she said.

I laughed, and Paige returned just in time to see Iris and me unveiling a beautiful teacup with a pinwheel of bright yellow, blue, and white, and hand-painted art inspired by Chinese designs. "Oh, my

gooooosssshhhh," I said. "Oh, my lost lizards!"

Paige's eyes widened. "What?"

"This is unbelievable. It's wonderful."
They stared at me blankly, and I said, "Back
when I was nine or ten, Zoltan stayed with
my family for a while. I don't remember
why he was here, but it was fun having him
at our house, my handsome uncle. Even
then I loved looking at porcelain, and my
mom would take me to antiques shops and
teach me about the different makers. While
we were at a local shop with Zoltan, we saw
this set. I thought it was beautiful, and I
was fascinated by the design — see the little
twin lizards, the way they twine together to
make a handle? I wanted it, and Zoltan said
he would buy it for me, but my mother said
no, I had to save up for it. The set was quite
expensive. Well, even before I had saved up
the money, the set disappeared. I'm sure I
was devastated at the time. And then I never
saw something like it again."

I lifted one of the cups and touched its
delicate rim. "This is Herend. From their
Yellow Dynasty collection. It's not even
available in the United States anymore.
How did you find this, Zoltan, you wonderful, sweet man!"

Iris ran a tiny, reverent finger over the

handle. "Look at dis," she said.

"Oh, Iris — yes, the lizards are definitely the best part. They go along with the Asian-inspired artwork, like these bending willow trees and all that gorgeous flower work."

We all bent to study the cup, resplendent with glittering gold dots that added a touch of magic to the beautiful and colorful detail. "I can't believe this," I said. "This stuff is so expensive. Either he found a vendor who didn't know what this is worth, or he spent a small fortune. Either way, he was right about one thing. What is it, Iris?" I pointed at her.

She grinned and said, in a voice that was minuscule but mighty, "It has Hana Keller written all over it."

"Exactly!"

Paige laughed, and I got a high five from Iris.

"And now I have to know just how many pieces are in there," I said. "Let's unwrap. Iris, I'm going to put a cushion under you in case something falls."

Nothing fell. Iris was as careful as an archaeologist, and the three of us un-wrapped a total of six teacups, six saucers, and one beautiful serving plate of the same Yellow Dynasty pattern.

"Gorgeous," I said, running a finger over

the bright yellow glaze of the plate, then turning it to admire the Herend maker's mark underneath. "But too small a set to use at the tea house. This one is going to live here."

Iris had run to the window and informed us that her father was home. "Oh, Paul is going to want a late lunch," Paige said. "Iris, can you go down and tell Daddy I'll be right there?"

"Okay," her daughter said. "And I'll tell him we're having spaghetti."

Paige shrugged. "Sounds as good as anything. Do not run on the stairs."

Iris waved to me and darted out my door. I turned to Paige. "It's hard being seven months pregnant."

"Not every day. But lately, with the holidays, and my lack of energy — it's kind of a bummer, yeah."

"How would you like to attend a girls' night out?"

"No booze for me," she said, holding up a hand.

"No, not that kind. A tea party! Hosted by Hana. Tonight."

"Oh my gosh, I would love that!" Paige's blue eyes grew wide and bright. "I'll bring a dessert."

"Great. I just need four other ladies, and I

am already making a list in my mind. You go make your spaghetti, and I'll call you with the details."

"Awesome. Thank you so much. I might even summon the energy to put on some makeup."

"Just be you. We'll have so much fun! I haven't had a tea party in years, not one for myself."

"I'm excited, Hana. Call me when you know the time of your gathering." Paige made her way to the door and said, "I'm so glad you live in this building. Otherwise we never would have met."

After she left, I considered that for a moment, appreciating the whims of the universe. I plugged in the cozy lights all around my apartment. This month they were multi-colored Christmas lights, both on my fireplace and on my tree, as well as a set lining the window of my bedroom. I sat down on my couch and took a deep breath. This was a special December for many reasons. First, because I would turn twenty-seven on December 18, a mere week away. Second, because this Christmas holiday was the first I would spend with my new boyfriend. Third, because I could not recall a snow quite like this . . .

I looked at my cats, who were gazing up

at me. "Okay, time for decisive action. First: I feed you. Second: phone calls."

The cats seemed to appreciate this ordering of things; they were already on the couch and bathing their paws when I picked up my phone.

I made a quick call to Erik before I got down to tea party business. He sounded busy, as he generally always did.

"What time do you think you'll be here tonight?" I asked.

"Bad news about that. I'm on my way to a scene. I might be late. It depends what we find there . . ."

"Okay. Be careful. I'm having some friends over, just so you know. So don't come in and throw off all your clothes."

That was supposed to make him laugh, but something distracted him, and all I got was a terse, "Gotta go. Talk to you later."

He ended the call; I shrugged and dialed my first party guest.

Ten minutes later, at the end of my efforts, I felt gratified. Despite my last-minute invitations, no one had declined. In addition to Paige, I had four other visitors on the way, including Erik's two sisters, Runa and Thyra, my brother's girlfriend, Margie, and my best friend, Katie. They had all agreed to bring a little something for our table, so all I had to focus on was decor and tea.

I started with the table covering: a plain white holiday cloth with a red border. I set out some white cake plates that looked good beside the Yellow Dynasty set, then laid out the cups and saucers from Uncle Zoltan. I put the decorative plate in the center; when the time came, I would fill it with *kiflis.*

I went outside and snipped some evergreen fronds from a tree near our front stairs (our landlords had given me permission for this at holiday time) and brought them back to my table, laying them around the plate in a fragrant and festive wreath. I put out two fat white candles and two white teapots. I would fill these with some standard Earl Grey and some flavored cinnamon tea.

I gazed at my modest Christmas tree, bright with multicolored lights and ball ornaments, along with various European treasures that had been given to me as gifts over the years. My eyes traveled to the faux fireplace, already lit and glowing festively; I moved to the mantel and lit my snowball candle, which added a quiet glow to the main room.

Pleased with the aesthetics of my kitchen and living room, I went to the counter and began gathering tea things — not just *kiflis* my grandmother had made, but a dip of my own invention, chips and crackers for tasting, and a box of chocolates that Erik had given me.

By the time people arrived two hours later, the tea was hot, the room glowed with pretty things, and I was ready to celebrate.

One by one, my guests set things on the table. Runa and Thyra, Erik's twin sisters, had brought Ulveflokk scarves for everyone. "Something from the new winter line," Thyra said proudly. We squealed with delight, chose scarves from the bin Thyra held out, and wrapped them around our necks. Thus warmed, we studied the treats on the table. Katie, my best friend, had brought her long-famous fudge bars, one of which was missing because I knew how good they were and had pounced early. Margie, my brother Domo's shy girlfriend, had brought gingerbread dogs, made in the (sort of) likeness of her amazing wolfhound, Boris. Paige, who had in fact put on makeup, had come bearing a banana Bundt cake, which she efficiently sliced and served to those who raised a hand.

"All right, everyone, grab your sweets and choose your tea. That's Earl Grey, that's cinnamon," I said, pointing to the two teapots. "Then we'll get down to business."

Runa, wearing an emerald-green turtle-neck and no other adornment except a blonde braid coiled on top of her head, looked lovely and contented. She was pregnant, too, but among the people at the table, Thyra and I were the only ones who knew that, for now. She sipped her tea and smiled. "Getting right to business. This sounds good. Are we in a girls' club? Are we spies, like Nancy Drew?"

Margie took a raspberry *kifli.* "Nancy Drew wasn't a spy; she was a detective. This feels more like a tree-house meeting."

I laughed. "It *is* a girls' club. First, I think I introduced you all, correct?"

My guests nodded.

"Okay. Second, I want to point out the star of my show: a gift from my dear Zoltan. Your teacups came today from my uncle, by way of some California antiques shop. They are Herend pieces, very rare and expensive, and you'll note the twin lizards on the handles."

"Oooh," Thyra said, genuinely intrigued.

"I had seen this set once when I was a child, and I wanted it, but someone bought it. Zoltan saw my disappointment and seventeen years later he sent me this treasure."

I held up a teacup, and the assembled women nodded their approval.

"I was so smitten with the set, I realized I had to have a party, and we had to drink out of them and share sweets and tell tales. So, on this night of lost lizards, I want you to tell me the most magical thing that ever happened to you. Because my grandmother says that weather like this" — I pointed at the now-dainty snowfall — "is magical."

"This is so fun! You do know how to set a mood, Hana!" Katie said. "I'll start."

"Oh, I forgot one rule," I said. "No boyfriends."

Katie snorted. "I wasn't going to talk about my boyfriend. He's great, but he's not *magical.* Just super sweet and good-looking."

Thyra pointed. "That's a cheat. She's talking about her boyfriend."

We laughed, and Katie waved us away with a casual movement of her hand. "Anyway. The most magical thing that ever happened to me occurred when I was about ten years old. I was hanging out in my house, waiting for dinner like always. Probably bickering with my brothers. And suddenly I just wanted to go outside. This was weird for a few reasons. One, I didn't take solo walks; two, it was raining; three, I was hungry and dinner was almost ready. I felt really urgent about going, though. So I went to the porch and got an umbrella and told my mom I was just going to walk around the block to use up some energy. She was probably relieved; we always drove her nuts before dinner.

"I went outside and started walking. It was a gentle rain, no thunder, but it was coming down steadily. I lived on a suburban block, so there was nothing spectacular to see, just other people's houses. I turned onto the next street, ready to make a big square and come home again, and I passed the mailbox. It had been there my whole life; I mailed my mom's bills in it every week. It shouldn't have caught my attention at all, but it did. I couldn't stop looking at it. I moved closer and closer to the mailbox, wondering why it looked such a bright red and blue. When I got really close, I heard the cries. Really tiny cries, of a small creature. I threw the umbrella aside, bent down, and peered into the darkness under the box; there was a kitten underneath. All alone, soaking wet, so pitiful. I reached under and picked it up, and it wiggled into my coat.

"I saw that it was a boy, and I said, 'You

are Charlie.' And then we walked back home. My family saw my face and they knew not to complain. And that was how I got my sweet Charlie."

"Oh, that's beautiful!" Paige said. "How long did he live?"

Katie grinned. "He's still alive. Sixteen years old and dominating my parents' house. He's their cat, too, and they would never part with him now."

"That's a wonderful story," Margie said. "Somehow you sensed his distress. I think we can all do that, if someone is sending strong vibrations. Right? It's how we know when someone needs us to call them, or that they need a hug."

Katie shrugged. "I've really never had an experience like it since. That's how I know it was magical."

Margie smiled and nodded. "I'll tell you the most magical thing that ever happened to me." I was proud of her. Going second! Margie was an introvert, and she didn't tend to speak until spoken to. I gave her a thumbs-up and sipped my tea, enjoying the visual of the Yellow Dynasty design. "I used to sing in high school. I was selected to sing a solo for one of our school shows, but I got sick and lost my voice. My director asked me that night if I thought I could do it. He said, 'Don't talk, just shake your head. Keep gargling and drinking tea with honey. We'll try to make this work.' "

I couldn't imagine Margie singing alone, with a spotlight on her.

"So I didn't talk all day, and then that night, when it was time to do the solo, I opened my mouth and sang, and it turned out beautifully. My director was very happy, and so was I. And then after the show, I couldn't speak a word. Total laryngitis. I just got my voice for the two minutes that I had to sing."

"Wow — that's a good one," Katie said.

I stood and replenished everyone's tea. Paige said, "The most magical thing I ever felt was my baby kicking inside me. Little Iris — she's five now. At first, I didn't even know what it was. It's so tiny, that first feeling. Like fluttering wings. Or like little bubbles floating in there. When I realized what it was, I cried." She smiled and patted her stomach. "And now I can feel it again. How lucky am I?"

I stole a glance at Runa, who looked fascinated and slightly envious. Thyra saw it, too, and put an arm around her sister. "I'll tell you mine. I was a teenager, lying in bed at night and looking at the stars out my window. And it just hit me all of a sudden:

31

that we all will die. Not just other people, but me, too, and that I would not be Thyra anymore, at least not on earth."

We stared at her solemnly, but she smiled. "That revelation actually made me feel wonderful. Because I realized what a miracle it was to be alive at all, to be this beating heart, lying in this bed, in this house, in this town, country, hemisphere. It's all so unlikely but so miraculous. That moment has guided my thinking ever afterward."

I stared at her, my fork between my plate and my mouth. "You know, in the Hungarian tales, the shepherds believe that every man and woman is represented by a star in the sky. And when that star falls, they die."

"You and your tales," Katie said, staring into her teacup with a little smile.

Runa looked at me with her startling blue eyes. "Erik told us that you tell him stories every night. Like *The Arabian Nights.*"

I shrugged. "He asks to hear them. Anyway, that was beautiful, Thyra. And it's a hard act to follow."

"I can follow it," Runa said. "My magic moment came when I looked into the eyes of her grandmother." She pointed at me. "You all know she reads tea leaves, right, Hana's grandma? But did you know it's not an act? Did you know that she really knows things? She looked into my eyes and that was suddenly very clear to me. Her wisdom, and her power. It flows out of her. She told me things about myself that no one could have known — yet she knew them, just from holding my hand. She is magical. If you haven't talked to her, you should."

Everyone rustled and murmured, familiar at varying levels with my grandma's psychic ability. I stood and refilled the *kifli* plate and the dip serving dish.

"What about you, Hana?" Margie asked. "There must be a reason you asked us all that question."

Scanning the table and finding it well stocked, I sat back down. "Not really. It's just the snow." I told them what my grandmother had told me, all those years ago. "It put me in a magical mood, I guess. It did have a fairy-tale quality, didn't it?"

"Not in the city," Thyra said. "More of a sleet and slush situation there. But here, yes. It's very pretty."

"Yes. There's just something about this snow," I said, my gaze drawn to the window. "And this surreal thing I saw. For some reason I can't stop thinking about it."

"You must tell," Katie said, poking a cracker into the dip.

"I was sitting in my car this morning,

33

escaping from those big, fat snowflakes. Inside it was much cozier, and easy to understand why people find snow beautiful. So I was thinking of my grandma and her hometown, and this guy just appeared. Maybe eighteen, twenty years old."

"What do you mean, appeared?" Runa asked.

"I guess he came out of the alley. Margie and Paige, you'll know the one I mean — between Stones by Sparkle and the Bedford Bagel Company."

They nodded.

"He came out of the alley, and he was wearing dark clothes — black jeans and a dark Riverwood University sweatshirt. He looked cold and miserable."

"Lots of people look miserable in the snow," Thyra said.

"Yes, but he had no coat. I know, often people refuse to dress for the weather. But — he looked like he wished he had something warm to wear. So all of a sudden there he was, looking kind of lost in a snowstorm. He stood in front of the tree by Stones by Sparkle. Like he was an animal seeking shelter. And then he turned and looked at me for a second, I think, and I felt like I recognized him. But then he walked away and just disappeared into the white world."

34

Paige took a sip of tea; her cheeks were rosy and her eyes were bright. She had needed this night out. "What makes it stick in your mind, Hana?"

"I don't know, exactly. Maybe because it is like a folktale. There's a story in one of my books called 'The Prince and the Snowflakes.' A young prince is caught in a snowstorm one day, and a beautiful fairy appears to help him find his way home."

"Okay," Thyra said, her face confused. "So — you looked at this boy and thought he looked like a prince?"

"No. But it reminded me of the legend of the prince in the snow, and the way he falls on hard times. And it was just mysterious, you know?"

"So, what's the mystery?" Katie asked. "Do we need to determine why the man was without a coat? Or where in the world is the coat that has lost its man?"

We laughed.

"He could have just been a dumb college kid who doesn't know hot from cold. I saw someone in shorts the other day," I murmured.

Runa studied my face. "But if that were the case, it wouldn't be bothering you. As your grandmother's progeny, you have a sixth sense. So we should go on the assumption that something was wrong. Where does that alley lead — the one he came out of?"

Margie leaned forward. "It's a dead end. There's nothing there but a big sewer grate and a dumpster." Her phone rang at the exact moment that mine buzzed. We exchanged a smile and I glanced at my text, from Erik: Might not come at all, or be there after ten. Lots to do here.

Margie was turned away, talking into her phone in a low voice. Then she said goodbye and turned back to us. "That was my mom. She was just checking in on me because she heard on the news that there's been a murder in Riverwood."

"Ooh, that's weird," Paige said.

Margie's blue eyes were wide. "It happened at the university."

The table was silent for a moment. I sipped my tea, then set the cup down and ran a finger over the charming handle. "Did she say what time it happened?"

"The news didn't reveal that, but my mom said it was some professor who got murdered, and that someone had seen him still alive early this morning."

"Erik was driving to a scene this afternoon. He told me over the phone."

Thyra and Runa, who had trained to be cops before they changed their career trajectory, exchanged a glance.

Katie said, "Well, we might have stumbled on a mystery after all."

The only sounds in the room were the clinking of teaspoons and the slight howling of the wind behind the kitchen window.

I leaned back in my chair. "We could reason it out. Like a logic problem."

"I'll get a pad from your desk drawer," Katie said. She was very familiar with the layout of my apartment. She jumped up and left the room.

Paige took a Boris-shaped cookie. "If we're playing Nancy Drew, I'll be Bess. She was the chubby one, right?" She set her free hand on her pregnant belly.

Katie returned. "And I'm George, because I have dark hair."

Runa said, "Does Nancy have three more friends?"

"She does now," I said.

I remembered that moment much later for its paradoxical nature.

On the one hand, I was very happy. The room looked cozy and beautiful, the tea set was sublime and everyone admired it, and my cats were curled up in feline companionship on my windowsill. The women around me were all real friends, and I still recall their bright faces as we joked about mysteries and childhood adventure novels. We were high on togetherness and the imminent holidays.

On the other hand, a feeling I knew well was growing in my stomach, a gray feeling that I had once dubbed "the misery." It emerged from my very cells and into my physical consciousness.

Even then, I knew that something was wrong.

Chapter 2
The Land of Darkness

Katie sat across from me, her pen poised over her pad. "Okay. So just call out reasons. Why might the kid have been in the alley?"

Thyra said, "He was hiding."

"Or he was waiting," Runa added.

"He was throwing something in the dumpster," Margie said.

Paige leaned forward. "Let's say he was involved in the murder. He wasn't far from campus, it was within hours — or minutes? — of the poor guy's death, if in fact someone saw that professor this morning, and Hana said the kid was acting strangely. So — would he be disposing of a weapon?"

I chewed my lip for a moment, then said, "I can't forget about the coat. He looked as if he missed having one. What if he threw his *coat* in the dumpster?"

"Why would he do that?" Margie asked. "Do you mean because it had blood on it?"

"Maybe."

"Could a coat be evidence for some other reason?" Runa asked. "Or perhaps he was just worried that he had been *seen* in the coat!"

We all rustled with approval at this theory.

I glanced at my phone. "But this is hypothetical. We don't have enough to give to Erik, right?"

Thyra lifted her cup to study the lizards' faces. "Hypotheticals are what the police work with much of the time. I think it's worth telling him about boy, coat, and dumpster."

The other faces at the table nodded at me.

"Okay." I grabbed my phone and stood up. "Give me a minute."

I took the phone into the next room and dialed Erik.

"Erik Wolf." Even after two months, I still felt an electric thrill when I heard his voice.

"Erik, it's me."

"Hey." His voice softened, but it held on to some officialness. "Listen, babe, I'm working. I can't talk right now —"

"This is *about* your work. Something I saw this morning."

"What?" Genuine surprise now, and a dose of interest.

"This morning on Andrews Street I saw a kid, a young man, who wore a Riverwood

40

University sweatshirt. He had no coat, even in the snowstorm. He looked cold."

I could feel Erik's effort at patience. "Hana —"

"I couldn't forget about it. I was talking with my friends tonight at a tea party, and we decided that given all the details — the dead man at the university, the boy's shirt, his proximity to campus, and his lack of a coat — were strange."

"Why is that?"

"Because he looked cold. And he was just feet away from a dumpster. He had come out of an alley when I saw him."

I could almost picture Erik scratching his head. "Well, that adds up to nothing at all, unless you witnessed something in particular."

"No."

"Or unless you had — some very strong feeling?" Erik knew about my newly awakened psychic impulses, and he trusted them, for the most part. "Is that what you're telling me, Hana?"

I closed my eyes so that once again I experienced the snow, the dark figure, the surreal feeling . . . "I think you should investigate the dumpster," I said. "It's on Andrews, in an alley between Stones by Sparkle and the bagel place."

"I know it. Okay. I have to go — I'll talk to you later."

"Bye."

I was never offended when my calls to Erik at work ended abruptly. He had lots of things going on and he really had no time for personal issues. Especially not if someone had been murdered.

I walked back into the kitchen, a place filled with cats and friends and teacups, and forced a smile, suppressing the gray feeling. "Who wants a refill?" I asked.

Each woman thanked me separately for the impromptu tea party; despite the strangeness of the evening, we had managed to enjoy ourselves immensely.

I gave Runa a hug when her sister went to get their coats from my bed. "How is the baby?" I said in a low voice.

Runa shrugged. "Everything feels fine so far. Andy and I have an appointment tomorrow. Another ultrasound. We'll know more then."

My grandmother was the one who had told Runa she was pregnant; a store-bought pregnancy test had proved Grandma right. She had also told Runa she was having a girl, and that this baby girl would need to be strong because she had a fight ahead of her. She had implied that the baby was sick, but "a warrior." The news of the baby girl had entranced Runa, but the other part of Grandma's vision weighed heavily on her, and she and Andy made regular trips to her doctor to make sure things were progressing smoothly.

"I'm glad. Take good care. And thank you for this wonderful scarf," I said, wrapping a red, purple, and pink–knit woolen around my neck.

Thyra approached and handed Runa her coat, then hugged me good-bye, as well.

Then they moved down the hall together, tall and blonde and elegant. Paige followed, thanking me for an "escape" into a carefree evening, and then Margie, looking sleepy but pleased in her new blue scarf. Katie appeared behind me and touched my shoulder. "Fun party, Han. Let me help you clean up."

Together we cleared the table and carried the dishes to the counter. Katie wiped down the wooden surface as I started hand-washing teacups.

"So, tell me more about this Uncle Zoltan," she said. "What an amazing name."

"Yes. He's my mom's older brother. She's the middle child, and then there's Aunt Luca. She's crazy, in a good way."

"So you said this uncle lives in California?"

"Yeah. He usually comes out to visit every year or so, because Aunt Luca lives in Wisconsin, so they all meet up in Riverwood and hang out at Grandma and Grandpa's house. They lived there from the time Zoltan was fourteen and Mom was twelve, until they both moved out and got married."

"Wow. You have a pretty close family, right?"

"Yeah. I wonder —"

"What?"

"Well, I only just realized, back in October, that Grandma had something. A gift, you know? And that maybe Mom does, too. And I'm wondering if Zoltan knew. Or if he has it. Or if Luca does. I wouldn't be surprised *at all* if Luca did."

"Why? Does she act like a psychic?"

"She's just a real free spirit. She always has been. My mom says she's a spoiled baby, but she says it affectionately because of course she was one of the people spoiling her. Luca was like her little doll since childhood. Four years younger and always wanting to go everywhere with Mom. There, that's the last one. Now I can dry them."

Katie grabbed a towel and helped me. "Where do you want these?"

"See that corner cabinet with the glass door? I want to put them in there so that they're visible. There's room on the second shelf."

"Perfect. So back to Uncle Zoltan. Is he married?"

"Yes. To a woman named Paula; they met at Berkeley. They have two sons. My cousins. I don't know them very well; usually when Zoltan visits, he comes alone."

"Oh? Why is that?" Katie began arranging yellow teacups in the corner cupboard.

"His wife is a lawyer. She's always on some case when he wants to travel. The boys historically just stayed with her, and it became a habit. I don't think there's any ill feeling. Just people being busy. Although they did separate once, for a few months. My mom was afraid they would divorce, but they worked things out. Zoltan always says my parents finally told him to go home and apologize to his wife."

"What for?"

"Taking her for granted. So they say. I was a kid at the time."

"Huh. And your aunt, Luca?"

"No children. She's had two marriages that both ended in divorce, much to Grandma's chagrin. But they were both amicable divorces. No one can stay mad at Luca, not even ex-husbands. They get together at the holidays — sometimes all three of them. It's hilarious."

"Your family is eccentric. But so is mine. And Eduardo's family is downright bizarre. They're all so emotional; they weep at the drop of a hat."

I giggled. "Good luck with that."

"Give me another one of those fudge bars. They're so good."

"They really are." I took one, too.

We stood and chewed in a companionable silence. I looked out the window; the snow had died down to a flurry. "I was thinking of Zoltan today, too, when I saw the snow. Before I even knew he had sent me anything."

"Yeah? How come?"

"When I was a kid, a teenager, he came out to visit and stayed for a while. I didn't know him that well, but of course he won me over immediately because he's a very warm person, and he paid attention to me. It was winter, and there was this big snowstorm, and Zoltan said to Domo and me, 'Why don't we have a snowball fight?'

"We said sure, of course, and we dressed up in our snow clothes and met him outside, where he immediately pelted both of us with snowballs he had premade. And then it was an hour of snow and strategy and laughter and terror and fun. I don't think I've really had a snowball fight since then — not the kind we had with him. He's like that. He spent time with us when we were kids, not just to kill time or do his duty, but because he liked us. He found ways to connect to us." I laughed, musing. "Zoltan in the snow. He was handsome, too. I had a crush on him then, even though he was my uncle."

"Weird," Katie said. "But I know what you mean. I once told my cousin Denny that I would marry him and live with him in Paris. I was, like, seven at the time, so it's cute and innocent."

I sighed, leaning back against the counter. "My grandma has this friend, Mrs. Kiraly. She made us gorgeous doilies for the tea house. Anyway, people hire her to make family tapestries. She makes them look like Old World antiques, and she embroiders little figures that represent all the people in a family. Sometimes many generations. She charges a lot of money, but they're worth more than she charges."

"Wow."

"But whenever I see one, I think — you really couldn't weave an authentic tapestry, because all of us have such complex associations. Family, friends, friends of friends, friendly acquaintances. If we made a list of all the people who were somehow important in our lives —"

"Then it would be a really crowded tapestry," Katie joked.

"But a beautiful one."

Katie studied me. "You're in philosopher mode. I'd love to hear more of your Confucius-like musings, but I have to get going." She went into the other room to get her coat, then came to hug me. "I'm really glad you're on my tapestry, Hana Sofia Keller."

I smiled. "Even Erik doesn't know my middle name."

Katie pumped a fist in the air. "I win!"

We laughed, and I followed her to the door and watched her walk down the stairs.

"Be careful," I said.

I turned back into my room, appreciating the quiet glow of Christmas lights. "Ah, peace," I said.

Antony and Cleopatra twined around my legs. I filled their bowls with kibble and flipped on my television, ready for a holiday movie.

It was eleven o'clock when I heard a key turn in my apartment lock. I was in my pajamas and sitting on the couch, watching the silent white landscape through my picture window, but at the sound of the door opening, my eyes drifted toward the entrance. Erik came in, looking tired. He set down his keys on my hall table, toed off his boots, removed his coat, and hung it up on a silver hook on my wall.

Then he saw me watching him and smiled. He walked over to the couch and sat down beside me, bundling me immediately into his arms. "Hello," he said into my hair.

"Hello. Sorry to hear about the murder."

He sighed. "It's always shocking."

"Did you —"

"Yes, your instincts were right. The boy had no coat because there was a coat in the dumpster, wrapped around, uh — evidence. We'll know tomorrow if it's related to the murder."

"Oh my. Oh wow. So when I saw him . . . he was concealing a crime. That's so odd."

"I'll have a picture from a security camera tomorrow, too. I'll need you to identify him."

"Okay." I smoothed some of his hair from his forehead. "Would you like anything to eat or drink?"

He shook his head. "Too tired to eat." He stroked my cheek. "Tell me one of your Hungarian stories."

I smiled at him; his green eyes reflected the Christmas lights. "I don't have an endless supply, you know."

"So far, you *have* had one."

I nestled against him and looked out the window. "It's so dark out now, you can't see the snow. Did I ever tell you about the young man whose true love was captured and taken to an invisible kingdom? And he tried to find her by traveling all over the world. Eventually he came to what was called the Land of Darkness, which was really the land of the witches. He knew he had reached it because he entered a forest so dark he couldn't see the path before him, but he felt things swooping past his shoulders, this way and that. He thought it was owls, flying through the trees, but it was the witches, flying in silence on their broomsticks."

"Creepy," he said appreciatively. "What happened then?"

"I can't remember. I know he ended up befriending a giant, who helped him conquer the witches and cross the Eternal Sea. He eventually found her, of course, but only with magical intervention. Because it was through magic that she had disappeared."

He thought about this, then sighed. "Every case I try to solve is the Land of Darkness.

I can't see the path before me."

"But you always find a way, because you're very smart. You will this time, too."

"Thanks for your confidence in me."

I stood up. "I think I'll go to bed."

He smiled. "Good idea. I'll be right behind you."

I brushed my teeth in the bathroom while Erik checked my locks and turned out the lights. The cats had long since tucked into their little condominium, snuggled together against the winter draft.

Erik eventually climbed under the covers with me, clad in a T-shirt and some sweat pants from a drawer of clothing he kept at my house. I rested my head on his chest, and he said, "Tell me about your day."

"I had a tea party with some girlfriends."

"That's nice. You don't get to do things like that very often, do you?"

"No, but I just had to today." I told him about Uncle Zoltan and the tea set.

"You'll have to show me tomorrow. It sounds striking," he said.

I lifted my head to look at him. "Oh, it is. So guess who I had over? Your sisters."

"Really." His eyebrows went up, but he was smiling.

"And Paige and Katie and Margie."

"And this is the group that helped you realize that what you saw in the snow was significant."

"Yes. We worked together like girl detectives."

"Huh."

I looked again out the window, where the last white drifts were visible from our dark room. "I'm glad it snowed. At least the soul of this poor dead man could rise to heaven through gentle flakes. My grandma says snow is friendlier than rain."

He adjusted his head on the pillow and closed his eyes. "You have a sweet way of looking at the world. Not one person I worked with today was thinking about the soul of the dead man."

"Well, I suppose every time someone dies, it's an opportunity for us to consider our own journey, when the time comes. To empathize, because we share that fate. Did you study John Donne? Ask not for whom the bell tolls."

"It tolls for thee," Erik said. He opened his eyes and studied my face. "You're very philosophical this evening."

"Katie said that, too! I guess I must be."

"Do you always become profound when your birthday approaches?"

I found that question interesting. "I don't know. I *was* thinking about my birthday today, a little bit. It turns out I can't really think of one thing I want or need. I have the best gift in the world."

"Your new tea set?"

"No. My Erik Wolf."

A small smile. "He's kind of annoying, isn't he? Always hanging around, mooching food, wrapping his long arms around you like some kind of ape."

I laughed. "No, he's wonderful." I snuggled against him.

His lips touched my hair. "Haniska. I can't remember how I spent my days before I knew you."

My eyes met his green ones in the dark room, lit only by some magical sparkles on the wall, created by the snow that fell in front of the streetlight outside. "Me, neither."

Then he was kissing me, and my thoughts about the anonymous dead man floated far away.

But later that night, when Erik Wolf lay sleeping at my side, I looked out into the darkness and wondered at the fact that three people had been killed in my little town in just two months' time. My grandmother would undoubtedly suggest that this was a bad omen, perhaps because someone had angered the *sárkány,* the dragons of Hungarian mythology.

I sighed and stared at the ceiling. Dragons and fairies and witches were all very good as entertaining folklore, but these were real murders, real deaths.

Real souls.

I hoped that Erik and his partner, Greg Benton, would find the perpetrator quickly and bring some peace to Riverwood for Christmas.

I sighed and drifted back into the memory of my long-ago snowball fight with Uncle Zoltan and Domo. Zoltan in a white world, dark haired and vibrant, laughing as he packed snow together between gloved hands, shouting as he fired his cold missile toward my brother and me, both of us screaming with laughter.

Zoltan in the snow. Dark hair and surreal white landscape.

And then the image of another man in the snow, another face, but this one wasn't laughing.

I sighed and wondered — why wrap evidence in his coat? Was there no better plan he could have come up with, and no better location for disposing of whatever it was?

The combination of the coat and the dumpster made me think that he had acted on impulse. Perhaps it had been a crime of passion?

The silent room offered no answers. I curled against the man beside me and closed my eyes.

CHAPTER 3
THE WORLD TREE

In the morning Erik Wolf was gone, but he had left me a note: "See you at the tea house later." Then, to my gratification, he had drawn about twenty hearts and signed his name. This was surprisingly emotional for my very reserved lover. I smoothed out the piece of paper and slid it into a kitchen drawer where I kept things I wanted to save.

The cats were doing their traditional milling around my feet but hadn't yet started squalling because they, too, were still tired; I fed them their breakfast and they ate with sleepy expressions. A glance out the window told me that the sun was bright, and yesterday's snow had already begun to melt.

"Time for me to get going, guys," I said to them. I took a shower, ate a quick omelet, and dressed in my tea house uniform: white blouse, black skirt, and apron with Hungarian embroidery. Then I pulled on black tights and donned low-heeled black shoes.

I blew kisses to the cats, threw on a coat, and wrapped my new Ulveflokk scarf around my neck; then I whisked out of my apartment, sailed down the stairs past the home of Paige, Paul, and Iris, and out the door. My purchases from the day before were still in the car, ready to unpack. I climbed inside, letting the heater warm up for a minute.

The drive across town usually lasted about ten minutes, but today it took twenty because drivers were still tentative about the snow. I was relieved when I finally pulled into the lot of Maggie's Tea House. Laden with yesterday's purchases, I marched toward our attractive front entrance, missing the happy clacking of the "Alpine train" that my father sometimes had running in nicer weather. I struggled with the front door but managed to get it open and proceed to the main room, where I was struck by an odd image: my mother and my grandmother, dressed in outfits just like mine and looking like versions of me at various points in my future.

My mother didn't resemble me in obvious ways; she had golden blonde hair, while mine was auburn; her eyes were blue; mine were brown. But often people told us we had the same smile, and I occasionally thought that, as well, especially when I caught my reflection unexpectedly and glimpsed, for a moment, the essence of my mother, Magdalena (the "Maggie" of Maggie's Tea House).

My grandmother, Juliana, might have looked more like me when she was younger; her hair had been a similar color, as had her mother's hair. In fact, it was *her* mother, Natalia, that I was said to resemble most of all. I had been given a picture of Natalia when she was my age, and I did in fact resemble her, thanks to the reliable patterns of heredity. I had framed the photo, and I kept it on a shelf in my bedroom.

Now the matriarchs of my family scuttled from table to table, putting real Christmas greenery in the center of every white-clothed surface. My grandma looked up and said, "Hana, good. Let's see your toys."

I brought my bags over to them and dug around for samples of my wares. I took out one of the tiny stethoscopes.

My mother clapped in delight. "Oh, those are adorable. I think they should go right in the center of the plates, don't you, Mama? Maybe with a red napkin underneath."

"Ya. Perfect," my grandmother said.

Then I produced the little business card holders that looked like tiny first-aid kits.

"How are these?"

My grandmother nodded, pleased. "We were saying things look bare. This will fill it out nicely. Then just the pine branches and candles, and of course our tree."

We all looked at the huge, real Christmas tree that my father and my brother, Domo, had wrestled into the tea house for us. It was a beautiful balsam fir that we'd strung with tiny white-gold lights, red glass balls, and various European ornaments, along with faux cranberries and straw stars. Every year there were some guests who came just to see our tree, and this year we felt we'd outdone ourselves. The Riverwood *Review* had put a feature about us on the front page of their Happenings section, and we had actually been forced to decline some event requests. Before we knew it, we were booked through the spring.

My mother had put on some Christmas music — a gentle Austrian CD she'd gotten as a gift one year — and at the moment a choir was singing to some gentlemen, assuring them they could be merry because someone had saved them from Satan's power . . .

"Here, Dreamy." Grandma appeared beside me and handed me some Maggie's Tea House business cards — cheerful yellow rectangles with fleurs-de-lis around the names — and I began inserting one into each little first-aid kit, then tucking them next to the teacups at each place. My phone buzzed, and I glanced absently at the texts. I had a new message from Falken Trisch. Falken was a friend of mine who owned a business called Timeless Treasures, a beautiful antiques shop that I frequented and from which I had obtained much of the Hungarian porcelain in my personal collection. His note today said simply, Call me!

Curious, I finished the table I was working on and then dialed Falken's number.

"Hana?" he asked, rather breathlessly.

"Yes — what's up? I have something amazing to tell you," I said, thinking of how much Falken would love Zoltan's teacups.

"And I have an amazement, too — a wonderful find. Can I stop by the tea house?

"We're preparing for an event that starts in two hours. But if you make it quick, maybe."

"I'd love to show this to your mom and grandma, too."

"Oooh. Now I am intrigued."

"See you in a few." He hung up, and I turned to my tea house doppelgangers, toiling once again in their pretty aprons.

"Falken's stopping by for a minute. He

60

wants to show us something."

My mother, normally calm and perfectly coiffed, brushed a stray hair out of her eye and looked at her watch. "Okay, but we can't indulge him for long."

"I know — I told him." I studied her more closely. "Are you okay?"

"Yes, yes. Fine. I just — an old friend of mine is vice president of the Riverwood Medical Group. I recognized her name. We were always rather competitive in school."

I stared at her. "You? Competitive? I would never have described you with that word."

She nodded. "It was something about our particular chemistry. When we were around each other, we compared achievements. It wasn't a healthy thing, and we lost touch after high school. But I occasionally see her name in headlines. And I suppose she saw mine — when we opened the tea house, and when the murder happened here." She paled slightly, and we silently contemplated the terrible shadow that hung over this pretty room — the memory of tragedy.

With a glance around the tree-twinkling, white-clothed, holly-bedecked room, I said, "She won't find anything amiss here. She'll be jealous, if she still bothers to compare."

"Yes, right," said my mother. She actually

looked nervous; it was disconcerting.

I patted her shoulder and moved swiftly to the remaining tables. My grandmother had finished with the tiny stethoscopes and was now working on our big tea urns. We were serving two flavors today: a standard black tea and a spicy holiday blend we'd purchased at the Riverwood Tea Merchants. We got a discount there, thanks to our mutually beneficial relationship. We went from table to table with actual pots of tea, but customers could go to the urns for refills if they wished.

The door opened, and two people came in. The first was François, our pastry chef, and the second was Falken Trisch. As always, François looked young, handsome, and mysterious in his French way. I suspected that many of our customers, of all ages, were secretly in love with François. He waved and shrugged at me and slouched his way to the back room — his kitchen and domain — to prepare today's sandwiches and pastries. He had done much of the work on the previous day, baking a large cake that he would now frost and cut into tiny petit fours. He would ice the sides and embellish the tops with holiday-inspired artistry. We really never had to give François any particulars other than the day's theme. My grandmother had learned that the more latitude she gave him in the kitchen, the more splendid were the results that he wheeled out on his pastry carts.

Falken, in comparison with the younger man, looked tall and gray and rather rumpled; his glasses were still slightly fogged from the cold. He set down a bag he was holding and took off his spectacles, polished them on his scarf, then put them back on. His eyes roamed the room, and when I approached, he said, "It looks enchanting here, as always."

"Thanks, Falken. We've got a big group coming in today, so we want everything to be perfect. But I have to tell you what my uncle sent me: a partial tea set from the Herend Yellow Dynasty collection!"

Falken's brows rose. "Oh my. I must see that."

"Come for tea next week sometime. Bring Elise. I'm sure your better half would enjoy a nice tea party, right?"

"Sure. We'll have to compare calendars. Okay, my turn." He grinned at me, then bent to retrieve his bag, which he set on the table next to us. Slowly he lifted something made of velvet — no, silk — and unrolled it for me. My jaw dropped.

"It's definitely Hungarian," he said, as my

63

fingers reached for the delicate material, the tiny, impeccable stitching. "A silk tapestry, perhaps from the turn of the century? I still have to get it dated. But you would know more than I about the details depicted here. Something mythological, I would say?"

"It's the World Tree," I breathed.

"Like the Tree of Life?"

"Yes. In Hungarian lore, it's called Világfa. You see here, how the artist created all of these beings in the foliage? It's just like other standard mythologies that have a higher, middle, and lower world. You know, like Zeus on Mount Olympus —"

"Yes, sure," Falken said.

"So the foliage represents the upper world of gods and spirits. The trunk, the middle world, is people, but also mythological creatures. And the roots are the underworld. The place of bad souls. Oh, look how they stitched the miserable faces down under the tree!"

The tapestry was clearly a work of great art; the top of the tree glittered with shimmering threads and shiny beads, so that it seemed to glow with the light of heaven; the middle world, the bark, contained threads of all colors, showing perhaps the vibrancy and possibility of life. At the root of the tree, the thread was dark — grays and blacks to indicate the darkness of corrupted souls. The tapestry was about four feet square, and the silk was faded. The bottom left corner was stained and slightly stiff, and the top right corner was missing about an inch of material.

"It's not in the best shape," Falken admitted.

"It's unbelievably beautiful," I said.

He nodded. "I knew you would think so. Here comes your family. Let's see what they think."

My mother and grandmother approached; Falken laid the tapestry flat on the table and beckoned them toward it. Grandma reached it first, and her eyes grew wide. Her fingers touched the beaded heavens and hesitated over one face in the foliage. "Boldogasszony," she breathed.

"Who is that?" Falken asked.

My mother's eyes were also locked on the tapestry. "She's the goddess of women and motherhood. She's also sometimes called 'Dawn Mother.' She's a figure of great power. And here is Isten, the god of all." The two deities sat side by side in the foliage at the top of the tree, serene in their love for each other and all humanity.

"Ah."

"And look in the middle world — here's

Szélanya and Szélkirály. Wind Mother and King of the Wind. Mama, look how they made the thread look like blowing wind. What is that stitch?"

My grandmother said something in Hungarian, and then they were talking in their native tongue, their heads bent over the tapestry with rapt attention.

I sighed. "It must be worth a fortune."

Falken shook his head. "It could be. But it's too damaged. Those two battered corners mean its value is greatly diminished, from a collector's perspective."

My mother's head whipped toward him; her blue eyes were bright. "Where did you find it?"

"At an emporium in the Loop. A world market. I go there once every month or so and come home with a car full of stuff."

My mother moved closer to him. "Falken, may I speak to you for a moment, over by the door?"

He looked surprised but intrigued. "Uh — sure." He walked to the entrance with my mother; she spoke animatedly to him the entire time.

"What's that about?" I said.

My grandmother's eyes were still on the tapestry. "Ah," she said. "So powerful. Such knowledge in the fingers which made this."

Her own fingers hovered over the roots, where the bad souls could be glimpsed in various anguished or cruel faces. Some of those anguished faces hung out of a huge cauldron, stirred by a humanlike creature with goat horns and cloven hooves. "Ördög," she said.

I looked closer. Ördög was a devil-like creature who ruled the underworld. He was said to continually stir the cauldron filled with sinners, increasing their suffering. But he could come up to earth, too, wearing a disguise. His goal was to challenge people's faith and see if they could be corrupted; he made bets with them, and if they lost . . . then they *were* lost.

"They really captured his evil," I said.

"Yes. This is powerful. All of that ancient belief, in one place, one visual. So beautiful, yet so terrifying. Potent. That is the World Tree."

My mother returned, her face flushed. She was smiling widely. "It's ours, Mama! I bought it from Falken."

Grandma and I stared at her. Of the three of us, my mother was the most frugal and sensible. I had never seen her so over-whelmed by a piece of art. "That's great!" I said. "It's an amazing thing."

"Where shall we hang it?" she asked, still

67

jubilant with the joy of her purchase.

I hesitated. "Here, you mean?"

She nodded, her expression firm. "I have this strong feeling that it belongs in the tea house. I felt that since I saw this beautiful tapestry."

I glanced around the room. "There's that small blank white wall right by the kitchen. Everyone can see it, and the square wall would be like a frame."

My mother and grandmother stared at this spot and said things in Hungarian. Then they nodded their agreement. "Good choice, Hana," my mother said. "First, I'm going to the fabric store to see if I can find something in this same pale green silk. I won't touch the original, but I might cover the damaged corners."

Falken, who had been talking on his phone, approached now and clapped his hands. "Well, I knew I could find a good home for it here." He looked at me. "Your mother is a shrewd negotiator."

I knew this, but I also knew that whatever she had agreed to pay Falken was a fair price. I felt pleased; like my mother, I had a sense that the tapestry belonged with us, here in the tea house; perhaps the magical fingers that had stitched that story a hundred or more years ago had some link to our family. At the very least, we shared a powerful cultural connection.

Falken's face creased with an unrecognizable expression — something between amusement and awe. "What?" I asked him.

"For a minute there — the three of you bent over the table, wearing your matching outfits — you looked almost . . . mythological."

I laughed, and my mother shook her head with a wry expression, but my grandmother pondered his words, her eyes somber. "Strong connection," she said. "Between art and the human soul. And we three have power to read connections."

"Ah — ?" Falken looked at me, and I said, "Grandma is psychic. For real. And Mom and I — well, we're discovering in little ways that it might be hereditary."

His eyebrows hitched up to his hairline, but then he looked at his watch. "Okay, Miss Hana. When we have tea in your Yellow Dynasty cups, you can explain this to me in more detail." He turned to my family. "Ladies. Always a pleasure."

They thanked him sweetly, and he strolled to the door, adjusted his coat and scarf, and went out into the white world.

My mother sighed, still high from art. "I love that he brought it to us, like the peddlers used to do in the Old Country. He matched the piece with the owners. There's something beautiful about that," she said.

"Now you understand, don't you, Mom? Why I get so excited when I find things at his store? Why I was over the moon when Uncle Zoltan sent me those teacups yesterday?"

Her blue eyes contained a new wisdom, and a great deal of affection. She hugged me. "Oh yes, my little Haniska, I think I do understand!"

"Wolf," my grandmother said urgently. For a moment I thought she was actually telling us that a predatory animal was loose in the tea house. Instead, I looked up to see my boyfriend, tall, blond, and rather rumpled, despite my efforts at ironing his suits, or getting him to iron them. He walked toward us, handsome in a dark coat and a red flannel scarf.

"Good morning, ladies," he said.

"Hello, Erik," my mother said, her voice warm. "Look what I just bought."

We all stepped away from the tapestry so that Erik could see it. The genuine shock on his face pleased me. "What is *this*?" he asked, moving forward and, like us, delicately touching the beaded silk.

"The World Tree," my grandmother said,

and she explained the concept to him, of the upper, middle, and lower worlds.

"So far," he said, studying it, "Hana has taught me about the fairies and fair ladies, and about the dragons and the witches. So where do they all land on the tree?"

My mother's eyes actually seemed to be sparkling. "They're all in the middle world, with us. In this mythology, we move through the world with the supernatural creatures who make life happen around us. Only the gods live in the upper world, along with good souls. Those who have died, just like our idea of heaven."

"Interesting. And the lower world is just this horned devil —"

"Ördög," Grandma said. "He tries to bring souls down with him, down to his cauldron where he stirs them forever." The souls looked genuinely tormented, severed from what was good. The cruel mother turning her back on an evil-looking child; a pair of lovers with their hands around each other's throats; Judas-like brothers facing off with knives behind their backs. And Ördög, smiling at them all.

"His tail is a blade," I added. "See it there? A knife that can cut." We all looked down upon the sinister Ördög, smiling as he stirred, a snake slithering near his feet.

Something turned in my stomach, and I clutched my midsection in surprise. No one noticed; the tapestry held their attention.

"Wow," Erik said. "So you bought this?"

My mother hugged him, and Grandma and I exchanged a surprised glance.

"Yes, yes, I bought it, and we'll hang it here!"

"Congratulations," Erik said, hugging her back.

My mother stepped away and adjusted her blonde hair. "Okay, girls. Now we really have to get going." She waved to Erik and bustled away.

Erik looked at my grandma. "I just need to borrow Hana for a minute. I have a picture, and I want to know if she can identify someone."

"Oh?" She moved closer.

I patted her arm. "Yeah, a boy I saw yesterday, a college student. He — had a wrong look about him, Grandma. So I called Erik and told him to search the area, and they found some evidence related to the murder of that professor. Did you hear about that?"

She nodded gravely.

Erik took a picture out of a folder he was holding and showed it to me. It was a security camera shot, but I recognized both the posture and the clothing of the person in the frame. "Yes. That's him. That's the boy with no coat."

"No coat?" This seemed to particularly offend my grandmother, who peered at the picture over my shoulder. "Oh, it's Ferenc," she said. "No sense, that one."

"What do you mean, *FEDentz*? You know this guy?" Erik asked, eager and leaning forward.

Grandma shrugged. "Ferenc." She pointed at me. "You call him Frank."

I stared at her for a moment, then felt a burst of horror and regret. "No, *Frank*? Oh my gosh, he's such a nice kid!"

Erik turned to me, impatient, and I said, "Frank's dad has a window-washing company. Frank works for him. He washes our windows and always does a good job. He's actually very sweet and funny. I thought I recognized him yesterday, but he looked different because of that weird expression on his face . . ."

It was Detective Wolf studying me now, not my boyfriend, Erik, and he was thinking this over. "Today," he said. "I know you have an event. But I'm going to need Frank's contact information."

"You don't need it," my grandmother said.

Erik's expression was stern. "Juliana, I do,

because if this boy —"

"No, I mean you can talk to him right now," she said, pointing.

We spun around and saw that Frank and his father were at our large front window, working with their giant squeegees, applying the liquid that they assured us would not freeze on the window.

Erik was gone on long, swift legs before I could say a word. We watched through the window as he spoke to Frank and his father, flashing his police ID with a quick and efficient gesture. He looked both official and grim.

Frank's face was pale with shock and a palpable guilt; he put his squeegee down and looked at his father; then the two of them followed Detective Wolf back to the front door of the tea house.

"I'm borrowing your back room," Erik said, pointing to the door so that both men would head in that direction.

"François is going to *love* that," I said under my breath.

My grandmother shrugged. "Might not be so bad. It's exciting sometimes, to see the police."

Frank didn't look excited; he looked miserable. And as he trudged toward the back room of the tea house, I sensed that he had a very good reason for feeling that way.

CHAPTER 4
THE CAULDRON OF BAD SOULS

Under the pretext of retrieving something from the large refrigerator in the back room, I wandered in and found Detective Erik Wolf sitting at the table, facing Frank and his father. François stood at his work island, staring unabashedly at the scene before him with wide, fascinated eyes, his frosting bag still clutched in his right hand. He had told my policeman boyfriend that he, as the chef, could not leave the kitchen; he was under a deadline and he needed all his time.

Erik had guided the window washers to the far corner of the room, where he spoke to them in a low voice. I rustled in the refrigerator, looking for the cream.

Out of the corner of my eye, I saw Erik hold up the photograph. "Is this you, Frank?"

Frank pretended to examine it closely. "Um — I don't know. It could be. I have a shirt like that."

His father stared at the picture, then at his son, his expression quizzical. "Of course it's you. Your face is visible. Where are you, anyway?"

Frank's complexion was white now. "I don't know. Why was someone taking pictures of me, anyhow?"

Erik said, "It's a security camera image from Andrews Street, right where it intersects with Wood. About two blocks from the university."

"Okay." Frank stared at the table.

"Witnesses have said that they saw you there yesterday morning. You can also see the time stamp here on the picture. It's eleven oh two."

"Okay." Frank's gaze stayed on the table, but Frank's father's gaze was on him.

"What were you doing by that alley, Frank?"

He shrugged. "I don't know. Just hanging out, I guess."

Frank's father did not look nervous as much as aggravated. He glanced at his watch, then said, "What do you need from my son?"

Erik leaned in. "I need to know why he was there, wearing no coat, at this time of day."

The father's head swiveled to the son. "Well?"

Frank shrugged again. "I guess I was just walking. I guess I forgot my coat."

"What if I told you we have video footage of you putting something into that dumpster?" Detective Wolf asked. I doubted that Erik had this, but then again, he hadn't said that he had.

Frank's eyes widened. "I — it's not what it looks like. It's not my gun."

His father sat up straight. "Gun! What gun?"

I was glad to see that Erik saw the young man's terror and spoke gently. "Why did you throw it away, Frank? Why was it wrapped in your own coat?"

He shook his head. His voice was almost a whisper. "I went to the university offices before class; I got there early because I wanted to see what I got on my final, and Professor Balog was going to go over some things with me. I saw him on the floor; I just panicked. The gun was lying there."

His father gasped. "Oh my God! You saw Sandor *dead*? Frank, are you okay?" He slung an arm around his son, who shrugged.

The green of Erik's eyes grew darker; he was deeply intrigued. He ignored Frank's father and said, "And what would make you, shocked and frightened as you must have been, take a weapon from a crime scene and throw it in a dumpster several blocks away? Are you telling me you killed Professor Balog?"

"No! Oh God." Tears rolled down Frank's face, and I felt moisture building in my own eyes. "No."

"Then why? Instead of reporting the crime, you took away the gun, wrapped in your coat — was that to prevent fingerprints? — and threw it away. Why?"

"I can't tell you."

Frank's father tightened his grip around his shoulder and gave it an encouraging shake. "Tell him," he said. His face was eager; he clearly hadn't even considered that his son could have done anything wrong.

Frank's voice was a whisper again. "Because I thought I knew who did kill him."

Erik nodded. "And you wanted to protect this person?"

"Yes." Frank gulped, and I saw his Adam's apple bulge up and down.

"Who did you want to protect, Frank?"

He shook his head. "Someone who works there. Someone who had a big fight with him the day before."

Frank's father looked stunned. Apparently, he knew the person to whom Frank referred.

"What was the fight about?"

"I guess he had one with the whole department. I don't know, I wasn't there."

"And how are you, as a student, privy to the arguments in the World Languages Department?"

Frank's father sat back in his chair with a shell-shocked air. His hand slid off of Frank's shoulder. "My wife works there. Professor Sarah Dobos. She teaches Spanish." He pronounced the family name the Hungarian way: *DOE-bohsh.* "We've all known Sandor a long time. He and I had some shared interests, including a Hungarian football club — here we would say soccer team. Budapest Honvéd FC is the one we like . . ." His voice tapered off as he looked at his son.

Erik studied him for a moment, then turned back to Frank. "Why would you assume your mother did it, Frank?"

Frank shrugged. "She was complaining about him at home. I had never seen her so angry. It made me nervous; she didn't — seem rational."

His father, recovering slightly, almost laughed. "Your mother didn't commit murder, Frank. Your *mother,* who rescues baby squirrels and rabbits. She was venting to us because we're her family. That's all it was. Venting. Balog was her friend." He turned to Erik. "They were friends, all of us were friends. She was just angry because he said he was going to cut one of the languages from the program. They didn't know yet whose job was on the line."

"Would Balog's death change that?"

He looked uncomfortable. "Well — maybe. It was Balog's call. Sarah was upset because Balog taught Hungarian. It wasn't exactly a popular choice with students, but *that* course he was keeping because he taught it. Sarah thought it was unfair."

"Everyone did," Frank said. "Everyone in the department thought it was unfair."

Erik thought about this, then beamed a green gaze at Frank. "Why did you think the gun was your mother's?"

His father held up a hand. "I own a gun. I have a license." He turned to Frank. "Was it ours?"

Frank shrugged. "I don't know. I panicked. It looked — similar. And she had been acting so weird. I heard her talking on the phone, and she was just — angry and different. Saying that if that was how he was going to be, he didn't deserve this life, or something like that."

"That was taken out of context," his father

said, his eyes darting to Erik.

"Of course," Erik said.

Frank crossed his arms and held his elbows. "I guess I could have heard it wrong."

His father's face went blank. "It's easy enough to check. You can come home with me, Detective Wolf. I can assure you our gun will be in the safe."

"I'll do that," Erik said. "And whether it is or not, I'll be paying a visit to your wife. Is she at work today?"

"At some point. The campus is closing soon for the holidays; just some last people hanging around, grading exams. And some students who live too far to go home, or kids like Frank, coming to see how they did before the exam results are officially posted."

Erik stood up. "Frank, I understand that you were afraid, but you took a weapon from the scene of a crime; I'll need you to come to the station, right now, to make a formal statement." He looked at Frank's father. "You might want to consult a lawyer."

When they were gone, I sat feeling guilty, unready to return to the main room to face my mother and grandmother, who both doted on Frank. François stole little glances at me while he shaved a red pepper into tiny curls that would sit atop his chicken salad sandwiches. "Your boyfriend is quite forbidding."

"It's his job."

"I would not want to face him, in the interrogation."

"I assume you'll never have to."

"Yes. I am peaceful. The pacifist. I only love," he said softly, setting the peppers aside and pulling a bowl of cream cheese toward him so that he could soften it with a fork.

I smirked at him. "Unless someone comes back here and touches your workspace."

His face hardened, and then he smiled at me, admitting defeat. "Yes, then I could murder. You have caught me. And your lover would catch me, as well."

I was about to complain about him referring to Erik Wolf as my lover, but the appellation was in fact accurate and I realized that I sort of liked it.

François added some spices to the cream cheese with his deft hands. "I texted Claire. She went one year to Riverwood before leaving for the culinary institute. She knows of this man."

"Professor Balog?"

"Yes. He was her sponsor. No, not. The one who guides you —"

"Her advisor?"

"Yes. That. She's going to come by later. It is her free day."

"Uh — we're going to be so busy —"

"Just for a moment," he said, with a yearning expression.

"Fine." Then, on a sudden impulse, I said, "Ask her to bring her Riverwood yearbook."

He raised pale brows but nodded. "Yes, all right." He pulled out his phone and sent a text with rapid thumbs. Then he returned to the mashing of the cream cheese.

I left him to his creations and went back into the main room. My grandmother frowned at me as she tucked napkins next to plates. "The wolf attacks," she said.

"Grandma, the boy took a murder weapon from a crime scene!"

She paled and clutched her pile of napkins to her chest. "Why?"

I shook my head. "I shouldn't have been listening. Hopefully Frank's dad will get a good lawyer and they'll be able to — I don't know. Work it out somehow."

My mother appeared and looked at her watch. "We only have a short time left. Hana, would you go over our checklist and make sure we haven't forgotten anything?"

"Sure, but I know we haven't," I said. I retrieved a clipboard from one of the tables and began checking off items. "Yes, yes, yes. Everything looks good. Your friend will be impressed."

She nodded but didn't look convinced. Suddenly, I was distracted from my thoughts of the murder and poor Frank, the boy in the snow. Now I was focused on my mother's old nemesis. Who *was* this woman, anyway?

I knew her instantly. Her name tag, obtained at the front entrance, read "Alessandra Spencer-Malandro." She had managed to jam all three names on the small tag. She was tall, dark haired, and attractive; she wore a great deal of eyeliner that made her face dramatic. As she approached, her expression a query, I sensed a strong blend of both insecurity and vanity.

"Hello? I'm Alessandra Spencer-Malandro," she said. "I'm a little early, I know. I scheduled today's event."

She smiled at me and nodded slightly, as though I had just given her a compliment she felt she deserved.

"Hello, Ms. Malandro. We're ready for you. You can choose any table you like, and —"

"I brought place cards for the tables. I thought it would be fun." Her face drooped in a dramatic faux frown. "Oh, but I don't see table numbers anywhere."

"It's a simple system," I assured her. "That's one and two by the kitchen. Then three, four, and five by the tree, six, seven, eight, in the middle, and nine, ten, here by the doorway."

She nodded, thinking about this. "All right, I suppose that will work. I have numbers on the cards themselves, so . . ." She pulled some little holiday place cards out of her purse.

"Would you like me to help you set them out?" I asked.

Her expression was cool. "Well, that is your job, isn't it?"

"It is today," I said with a bright smile. My father had long ago taught me how to deal with people like Alessandra Spencer-Malandro. *Kill them with kindness* was his motto, and it tended to work for me, as well. "If you'll hand me some, I'll put them out at the proper tables."

She held a pile out to me. "Leave them exactly in this order. I planned the seating very carefully."

Yikes. So much for a carefree holiday party. I whisked away from her, wondering if she planned to retrim the tea sandwiches after François brought them out. I grinned; that was a confrontation I would pay to witness.

My mother emerged from the back room, holding a teapot, and our visitor's voice cut through the air, loud with feigned affection. "Maggie, my dear! I am so glad to see you!" Still wearing her fur-trimmed coat and clutching her purse, she glided toward my mother, who looked for an instant like a trapped animal, then switched on a welcoming smile.

"Alex, it's good to see you," my mother said. "I suppose you've met my daughter, Hana?"

More drama, in the form of Alessandra Spencer-Malandro putting a hand to her forehead, as though she might faint. "Oh my goodness! I thought she was just some waitress." Her eyes flicked to me. "I'm so sorry, dear! I'm afraid I didn't see a resemblance, so it didn't dawn on me that you might be Maggie's child."

"No problem," I said. I had finished setting out cards on table one and had started on two. I flicked the little cards down with a bit more intensity.

My mother's voice was smooth. "Hana helps me run the place, as does my mother.

87

You'll see her in a moment. What are we working on here, place cards? Let me help." She set her teapot on the sideboard and took some cards from her old school friend.

Alessandra, or Alex, as my mother had called her, looked stiff and embarrassed. "Uh — no one has told me where I should put my coat," she said, as though we'd been guilty of a terrible faux pas.

My mother refused to engage. "I can take it, if you'd like, or you can hang it by that little sign that says 'Coats.' " She pointed to the hallway near the kitchen, where we had a tiny but cute coat rack painted with Hungarian flowers.

"Ah, I see. How quaint," said Alessandra. She walked swiftly to the back of the room and hung up her coat, making a point of checking for dust on the wooden rack. My mother moved past me on the way to her second table.

"She's a real treat," I murmured so that only she could hear.

"A paying customer," my mother said. But even she seemed to be gritting her teeth.

Alessandra returned, and I said, "We've finished tables one through five. Would you like to give me the remaining cards?"

She handed them to me and said, "Thanks, dear. Now your mother and I can catch up. How have you been, Maggie? You look wonderful; still like a girl, really. A tiny bit tired, but I guess a job like this takes its toll, doesn't it? Standing all day and serving people."

My mother kept her smile. "I love my job. We all do. We get to meet new people and be around beautiful things all day long." She swept her hand around the tea house, which glowed with holiday splendor. "How about you? Are you enjoying working for the medical group?"

She had looked rather bored while my mother spoke, but now she brightened. "Oh, of course. And that's where I met Antonio; you probably saw our wedding announcement, back in the day. It was the talk of Riverwood at the time, or so they tell me. I was just caught up in it all — trying to focus on planning my wedding — poor Antonio couldn't be much help because he's so in demand as a surgeon that he has no regular schedule. And then of course trying to get our honeymoon together. But it was so worth it — the Amalfi Coast. We're going to return for our thirtieth anniversary next year."

"That sounds great, Alex."

"And your husband is noteworthy, as well, isn't he? A professor or something?"

"Jack teaches history at Riverwood High."

"Oh, yes. A *high school* teacher." Her expression said that she found this career barely worth mentioning.

"Yes. I'm very proud of him. He's received several awards, and accolades from his peers and his students. He wouldn't want to do anything else." My mother wasn't just saying this; her face glowed when she spoke about my father.

Alessandra sniffed and looked around the room. "Well. Who would have guessed that two girls from Riverwood would still be in town, happy and thriving, all these years later? I always thought you'd go back to Hungary."

My mother's blue eyes looked cold, despite her smile. "Why is that?"

"Oh, I don't know. You always seemed sort of — foreign. In a good way, of course. And I figured you longed for your homeland."

My mother's smile stayed in place. "I think your guests are starting to arrive."

Alessandra turned to look at the entrance, where a few tentative people had wandered in, stamping their feet on the carpet. "Oh my goodness! So they have." She strode toward the newcomers, saying, "Hello, and welcome to my tea party! Merry Christmas to you all! I think you know me, right? I'm

Alessandra Spencer-Malandro. I'm the one who sends you all those administrative e-mails!" She laughed at her own joke and swooped in on the guests.

"I'm Alessandra Spencer-*Malandro*," I mimicked near my mother's ear.

She grinned and said, "Grandma is struggling with that cart — go help her, Hana."

"We're not done talking about this," I whispered, and rushed across the room to help my grandmother.

The tea was well underway when I noticed that my grandmother, too, had formed an impression of Ms. Spencer-Malandro, and it was not a good one. I caught her studying my mother's old friend with narrowed eyes. At one point I passed her near the kitchen and said, "I can't believe Mom was friends with her in school."

Grandma nodded. "She was at our house a few times. I remember; she didn't like Hungarian food."

I stared. I had never met anyone who didn't like Hungarian food.

Grandma paused there in front of the kitchen, looking at me. "Do you feel it, Haniska? Are you starting to feel these things?"

"What things?" I asked.

"Go near her, and you'll feel it strong. She wants something." She went back into the tearoom, stopping here and there to ask what was needed, and I looked back at my mother's old friend, who was dominating the conversation at her table. I moved closer, pouring tea into empty cups along the way.

I closed my eyes for a moment and tried to become a blank receptor. Something hit me hard, like a strong wind, or an inky black river that swirled around me. My eyes flew open, and I walked back to the kitchen on rapid feet.

My grandmother had been right: Alessandra wanted something, and her avarice was so strong it felt as burdensome as a clinging vine. But underneath the want I had felt traces of something else, something I recognized and for which I felt a spurt of sympathy.

Beneath the greed, there was pain.

When the event was over, Alessandra stood with my mother at our little billing podium and handed her a check with predictably dramatic gestures. "Thank you, Maggie. I've received many compliments about this place and the quality of the food," she said. "Obviously, I chose well."

"I'm glad they liked it," my mother said. Her usual placid demeanor was back in place. Her agitation about meeting her old friend had succumbed to her perpetual equanimity.

"I've included a tip there for your servers," she said, her eyes sweeping the room and landing on me. "You did a fine job, dear," she said.

"Thank you," I replied. "Mom, I'm going to help François clean up in the back. Nice to meet you, Alessandra."

"Yes, yes." She turned to my mother. "And now that we're back in touch, Maggie, we really must stay in touch. What if you and I had lunch sometime soon?"

My mother was far more professional than I. The only reason I could tell she hated the idea was that her hand went up instantly to smooth her blonde bun, something she did to maintain order when she was agitated. Her face remained serene and pleasant. "That sounds wonderful, but I'm afraid we're booked up until spring. It's rather a relentless schedule, believe it or not."

Alessandra clearly didn't believe this. "Oh, I'm sure you can make some time. I took one of your little cards here, and I'll send you an e-mail with some possible dates. I can even come to you. We can meet here in this splendid room, and I can bring you all some dinner when you feel weary after an event. Won't that be nice? Oh, I'm excited about this plan!"

My mother's smile was growing thin. I had almost reached the back room, but then I pretended to get a phone call. I pressed my turned-off cell phone to my ear. Now it was I who was dramatic, murmuring things and waving my hands in fake consternation. Then I plowed toward my mother and her clingy friend, my phone in my hand. "Mom, I got a call from Mrs. Peterson. She's requesting that we change the theme for tomorrow's event, and she wants you to call her ASAP."

There was no Mrs. Peterson, and tomorrow's event was the gentlest of things: a prayer retreat for a group of Catholic nuns. My mother grabbed at my lifeline, however. "Oh, darn it! She is adding a lot of stress to my life." She turned to her visitor. "Alex, I'm sorry, I have to make this call before this woman ruins everything. I'm sure we'll stay in touch."

"Yes, I'm sure we will," said Alessandra. She waved as I ushered my mother to the back room like a grim security guard. I turned back once and saw that she was leaving, but reluctantly so, with slow and plodding steps, as though her own execution awaited her on the other side of the door.

"She's odd," I said.

My mother nodded. "She was an only child, and there was always a neediness about her. But she's genuinely talented, and sometimes she was very kind."

"But I'll bet that didn't make her easier to deal with on a day-to-day basis." I know I sounded suspicious, and my grandmother's expression suggested she felt that way, as well.

My mother shook her head. "No. But as evidence of her generosity? The 'tip' she gave us is four hundred dollars. I tried to give it back, but she waved my protests away. So — a nice little Christmas bonus for each of us."

François perked up at this. "Including me?"

My mother laughed. "Yes, François! We would be lost without you, and I heard many compliments about the food."

He exhaled. "Ah. What a relief. I have started to Christmas shop for everyone, and my account is empty. *Joyeux Noël.*" His smile was wry, and suddenly he looked older than his twenty-three years.

"Don't forget that Maggie's Tea House will give you a Christmas bonus, too," she assured him. "A holiday gift for a valued employee. I'll give those out on the twenty-third, after our last event."

At that moment, Claire, François's pretty blonde girlfriend, walked into the back room. "Hello, everyone," she said with a dimpled smile. François had been wiping down a counter, but now he spun around with a beatific smile.

"*Bonjour,* Claire," he said, moving forward to kiss her cheek.

"*Bonjour,* François." She lifted a tender hand to straighten his hair; she was clearly still smitten with him after more than a year.

I waved to Claire. "Happy holidays."

"Yes, merry Christmas to you all!" she said. "Hana, I brought my Riverwood yearbook." She lifted her tote bag and removed a large leather-bound book that said *Riverwood Role Call.*

"Ah — thank you," I said, practically pouncing on it. "I just want to take a peek at the faculty section."

I sat down at the table and paged through the big book full of student faces. I found a section labeled "Faculty," and scanned through the various disciplines of academia. The World Languages introductory page was filled with flags and the word "learning" in various languages, including Hungarian: *"Tanulás!"* Then I was flipping through the pages and seeing professors of French, Italian, Spanish. I found a large picture of Balog on the *Magyar* page, where he was identified as a professor of Hungarian and the chair of the World Languages Department.

"Hana, are you okay?" Claire asked, her pretty face concerned.

"I know him. I *know* this man."

"How?" François asked.

"We share a passion." I had met him, more than once, poring over the treasures at Falken's store. We had chatted amiably, on several occasions, about Hungarian porcelain, Hungarian history, the Hungarian language. I had never even asked his name, beyond "Sandor." I figured he was one of the many Hungarians in Riverwood, and that, like me, he enjoyed collecting pieces from his homeland. And yet I had learned a great deal about him. I had just talked with him, perhaps a week earlier.

Now I studied the picture and saw some of those treasures he had purchased. He was posing at his desk, presumably in his university office, behind which was a floor-to-ceiling shelf filled with books and statuary. I recognized several Herend pieces that were obviously some of his best finds, really expensive things, and found myself wondering what would happen to them. Would someone in his family know how he had treasured them, and keep them in his memory?

Balog grinned at the camera with slightly crooked teeth. The misery rose in me; something was not right, something in this picture . . .

"Do you need to keep that?" Claire asked, still studying me.

"Yes, please. I'll return it, I promise. Mom, this is him. The man who died." My mother leaned in and sighed at the sight of the man. "Does he look familiar to you?"

"I'm not sure," she said. "Maybe. He has a very Hungarian face. Where do you know him from?"

"Falken's store. He was there as often as I was. We chatted all the time. I didn't know his profession, but I knew he was a collector. Remember that Herend statue I was pining for, the Hadik Hussar? I never could have afforded it, even with Falken's price, but this guy, this Balog, bought it. See? It's behind him in the picture. Really valuable, I'll bet. And so beautiful!

"And I see other Herend stuff there, too. Look at the dragon! And that gorgeous orange snake, with the white flowers. I think

I saw it on eBay once. It's all lovely."

"It is," she said, studying the picture. "Which reminds me. I want to get to the fabric store so I can repair our World Tree. It's going to be amazing."

I sat up straight. "Oh! And I need to show you what your brother gave me. I took pictures." My grandmother walked in holding a broom, and I said, "Grandma, you look, too."

I pulled out my phone and brought up a picture of the Herend tea set. "This is what Uncle Zoltan sent me!"

They leaned in and oohed in unison. "Look at the color," my mother breathed. "This is the day of beautiful art."

Grandma nodded. "Perfect for you, Haniska. Zoltan is a good boy. I hope he come to visit soon."

"Me, too," I said.

We went out with our carts into the silent tearoom and gathered teacups, leaving François to his Claire, and thinking our own thoughts. The gentle clinking of china was reminiscent of Christmas bells.

My eyes settled on the windows, still streaked with wintry grime after Frank and his father had been interrupted by what my grandmother called "a wolf attack." I wondered what had been determined at the police station, and whether poor Frank would have to go to jail for what he did.

People and their behavior remained a mystery to me — even that of my mother and grandmother, who had paused near the tree to speak in a language that I had heard all my life, but which, to this day, I could not understand.

CHAPTER 5
GRACE AND GOOD SOULS

Sister Mary Celine stood before a silent room, leading the assembled women in prayer. They had bowed their heads for private intentions, and I tried to make my tea cart silent, too, as I wheeled it back toward the kitchen. We had just put out the sandwiches and poured hot tea when Sister Celine rose to bless the meal. Now I moved through the tables of praying women and found it calming, like riding on a gentle wave.

"Finally," Celine's soft voice said, breaking the quiet, "let us thank the Lord, to whom we owe all things."

A quiet acknowledgment of this, and then Celine said, "Enjoy your tea, everyone. We'll begin with our speakers in about half an hour."

A quiet humming sound meant that women were starting to chat as they sipped their tea and tasted François's sandwiches, which today were made of cream cheese–cucumber, turkey, egg salad, and Swiss cheese. I went into the back room and found my mother studying her phone. She looked up at me, surprised.

"You know that booking we had for tomorrow? I just had it written down as 'university event.' Apparently the appointment was made by the murdered man. He was going to bring his department and the language students to a tea. Now I've just heard from his assistant. The other professors want to go ahead with it, but they're turning it into a memorial luncheon for him."

"Oh wow. Well — we've done memorials before. No problem. We'll just tone down the decorations and create a sort of muted environment."

"Yes, I suppose." She looked thoughtful.

"So — his whole department is coming?" The people who had been angry with him . . .

"I assume so," she said. "I'd better get back out to the nuns. Isn't it sweet, and kind of refreshing, how *quiet* they are? It must come from a life of contemplation."

I nodded, and she left the room with a basket of sugar packets.

François was putting the finishing touches

on his petit fours — white iced cakes topped with green fondant Christmas trees. He looked over at me. "Frank will be invited. If your boyfriend releases him from prison."

I sniffed. "He's not in prison. He went home that same day; my grandmother called his father and he told her so. I just don't know if — he'll have to go back for more questioning. It's none of my business."

François shook his head. "He wanted to protect his murderous mama. Poor boy. We would do anything for our mothers."

I moved closer to him. "Don't tell anyone that. We were eavesdropping on a privileged conversation."

He shrugged — his French response to just about everything — and said, "They were in my kitchen."

I sighed. My phone buzzed on the sideboard, and I picked it up to see a text from Runa. I have to talk to you. Coming to the tea house now.

The gray feeling rose in me, and I leaned on François's workspace for support.

"Something is wrong?" he said, setting aside his fondant smoother.

"I don't know. It's odd. Erik's sister wants to see me right away."

His brows rose. "The Viking woman? The one who tackled the groundskeeper last fall?" He grinned at the memory, then sobered. "Is something wrong with Erik?"

"I don't think so." I waved vaguely, and he nodded his farewell as he started placing tiny cakes on a platter. My heart felt heavy as I went into the next room, where one of the nuns was speaking in a flutelike voice about the importance of prayer as a way of keeping in touch not only with God but with one's own virtuous intentions.

My grandmother appeared at my side. "What's wrong?"

"It's Runa," I said. "She's coming here."

She looked concerned, but one of the visitors was waving a tentative hand, so she darted off to see what was needed.

I checked on tables as I moved toward the door, then went to the front window to see Runa pulling into the lot; even from a distance her cloud of blonde hair was visible. I went outside and waited under the awning over our front entrance. She moved toward me, elegant in a camel-colored coat and winter-white pants tucked into saddle-brown boots. She reached me, and we exchanged a brief hug. I felt it then — a wave of sorrow that made my eyes fill with tears.

"The baby?" I said.

She nodded. "Let's go inside."

I led her into the tearoom, and we tucked into the farthest corner, sitting at a table that had not been used for today's event. We spoke in voices so low no one would even know we were there. Runa sighed and ran a hand through her hair. "We went to the doctor yesterday. They looked at the baby, and then they immediately ordered more sophisticated imaging."

"What did they find?" I whispered.

Runa cleared her throat. I could tell she was fighting tears. "It's her heart. It has a defect. They want to operate."

"Oh, poor baby! How soon after she is born do they want to do this?"

She shook her head. "They want to operate *now*. The sooner the better, they said. They want to operate on my tiny girl in utero."

I reached for her hands, and she clutched mine. "They can't wait?"

"They say there's a risk she could — die in the womb. Your grandmother was right, about everything. She knew about my baby."

"Is there a risk to you?"

She shrugged. "I guess so. And I would never be able to have a child naturally after it — they all would have to be delivered via cesarean, apparently. I just want to make sure that it's the right thing for her, you know? She's so tiny. So alone."

"I'm sorry you have to face this, Runa." I looked at the hand holding mine, on which a large diamond glinted. "That's an engagement ring."

She managed a smile. "Yes. Andy proposed to me two weeks ago. We just got this back from the jeweler yesterday. Isn't it pretty? He's such a good man. I'm so lucky, and we're very happy. Even if — we lost her — I know we'll be happy together. But I can't bear to think of losing her now, Hana."

"I know."

"I need to talk to your grandma. She's the one who —"

She stopped, and we both looked up, surprised, because my grandmother stood beside us. I hadn't heard or seen her approaching.

"Hello, dear," she said to Runa. "You have some news?"

"The baby has a defect in her heart," Runa said. "They want to operate on her now, in here." She put her hands protectively on the small bump at her middle. "I'm afraid," she said.

My grandmother pulled up a chair and sat with us. She took Runa's hands and looked into her eyes. It was a strange and fluid moment in which I was conscious of nothing but her. I don't know how long it lasted, the three of us sitting there, Runa and I with our eyes locked onto my grandmother's face, and the gentle murmuring of a nun in the background.

And then the spell was broken; my grandmother smiled. "She is so funny. Fierce and demanding. But it weakens her, the heart." She squeezed Runa's hands and leaned even closer to her. "Do it now. As soon as you can. Your daughter is ready."

Runa nodded, her eyes glistening with tears. We sat in our linked circle: her hands in my grandmother's, my hands on her arm. Suddenly the words of the woman at the podium became audible and floated over us like a comforting mist.

"When we think of grace," she said, "we think of something that allows us to regenerate, to sanctify, not just what we feel within, but what we see without. We seek our moments of grace, and we find reward in them. And in its most powerful form, grace gives us the strength to endure any trial. I wish for you a Christmas filled with holy grace, and a year filled with opportunities to bring that feeling to others."

Runa closed her eyes, and I saw by her expression that she had made her decision; that in fact she had made it before she had even come to the tea house, but that my grandmother had validated her choice.

After work I found a message from Domo on my phone: Can I eat at your house? Margie's at some family thing.

Heaven forbid that Domo, at twenty-nine, might learn to make his own food. Since I enjoyed his company, though, I texted back that it would be fine. I stopped off at Fair Price Grocery to get some ingredients; they carried some good authentic Hungarian spices in deference to Riverwood's large Hungarian population.

I shopped around for a while, humming along with Neil Diamond as he sang about his loneliness. I took my wares to aisle two, where my friend Maria waited to ring me up. She and I had been through a recent shared trauma; I had identified her grandmother as a murderer and the woman had gone to prison, but my friendship with Maria had emerged intact. I waved at her. "Happy holidays," I said.

"You, too. Guess what?" she asked as she ran my paprika across the scanner. "I got into a master's program."

"That's wonderful! Is it nearby?"

"Yeah, at Riverwood. It's a good school. I went there yesterday to meet with my advisor, and the campus was crawling with police. I guess one of the professors got killed. So weird."

"Hmm." I didn't want to talk about the murder anymore. The gray feeling hadn't quite left me since it happened. An image of Ördög, stirring his cauldron of souls, came unbidden into my mind. "That's great that you got what you wanted. Now the sky's the limit."

"I hope so." She looked at me under her lashes. "My grandma is helping me pay for it. We had a nice little visit the other day."

"That's good to hear. How is she?"

She shrugged. "She's actually pretty great. My grandpa visits her twice a week. They see each other more now than when she was free. She got a job in the prison kitchen, and that has made her really popular. She said now every Thursday is Hungarian night."

I'm sure my smile held some sadness. "I'm glad, Maria."

"She's sorry, of course. She says she looks back and she can't believe what she did. That it was like someone else took over her mind, her life. She misses her friend."

"I believe that." I thought of the fact that a murderer now roamed Riverwood once again. "I'm glad she's back to herself."

Maria shrugged and shook her head. "Speaking of Hungarian, looks like you're going to make some chicken *paprikás.*"

"Yeah. My mooch of a brother is coming for dinner."

"Your brother is gorgeous. I suppose he's dating someone, right?"

"Yeah. Margie. I think they'll get married."

"Figures. If you ever meet a handsome guy who's looking to date a nice Hungarian girl, let me know."

"I will! I will keep that in mind. Thanks, Maria! And if I don't see you again, merry Christmas!"

"You, too." She smiled and waved, tucking a lock of dark hair behind her ear.

I made my way back to the car. The snow had stopped for the time being, and the roads were neatly plowed. I got home quickly, and there I fed my cats, put away my groceries, and began to chop an onion for the night's meal.

My phone rang, and I picked it up. "Hello?"

"Hey." Erik Wolf's voice, intimate and sexy, could make my bones turn to Jell-O with just one word, and it had that effect now.

"Hey. What's happening? Do you want to

come for dinner with Domo and me?"

"I'm not sure when I'll be leaving. Maybe I'll catch the end of it. But I need a favor from you."

"Sure." This was interesting.

"The man who has been killed taught Hungarian. His office has various Hungarian artifacts. If I bring a photograph, can you see if you can identify any of them? I just want the big picture. The cultural significance." I assumed there was more to it than that, but the picture would help me know more.

"I saw some of the pieces today. In last year's yearbook."

"Oh? Do you still have it?"

"Yes."

"Okay, great. We can compare."

"I'll be happy to try. I don't know how much help I'll be with identifying things. Maybe Mom and Grandma can look, too. Even Falken can probably be helpful."

"Let's keep it in your family for now."

"Erik — have you talked to Runa?"

A pause. "Yes. It's scary. But Andy is a great support, and we will be. And my parents, and even Felix, our out-of-town sibling. I think he'd come to Chicago if she needs him."

"That's good. Family helps. You know what?"

"What?"

"I like it when you call me, even if it's for police stuff."

There was a pause; I had probably made him go shy again. Erik Wolf was generally an introvert, and he had barely managed to indicate that he was interested in me on the day we had first kissed. I found this reticence unbelievably attractive. "Me, too," he said. "Your voice always lifts my spirits."

"Imagine what my body could do," I said, only half joking.

"I *will* imagine that. I often do."

I sighed into the phone. "Well, I hope I see you later. I'll have *paprikás* waiting."

He whispered something that I didn't quite catch, and then he was gone. I tried to picture him in his newly ironed gray suit (an ironing task we had done together), moving carefully through his crime scene and taking the occasional sip of his Diet Coke, making notes in his ubiquitous notebook, and murmuring to himself while he worked out his puzzle. He tended to say "hmm" without realizing it, over and over, and that was yet another thing I found adorable about him. But it was his blond hair that had drawn me to him at the start and continued to capture my imagination: blond as the golden caps of the princes in Hungarian fairy stories; so blond it was like the color of summer wheat in the sun; so blond that to me it had been as compelling as the green-gold light I generally saw around him these days. In fact, I would have seen light around Erik Wolf the day we met (as my grandmother and mother had done with their beloveds) except that I had not learned to see, as my grandmother put it, "with my inner eye." Now I was learning how to do that, and the light around Erik Wolf was almost always visible, his blond hair like a shining halo.

I shook my head, realizing that I was gazing at nothing with a smile so stupid that Domo would have teased me mercilessly. I got to work making chicken *paprikás* and dumplings. Antony and Cleopatra stropped around my legs and I sang "Winter Wonderland" to them. They seemed pleased, eventually settling in front of the stove, tucking all of their legs beneath their fuzzy bodies. I kept humming while I chopped my onion.

I was still feeling musical when I finished my task. My iPad sat nearby, so I washed my hands, opened it up, and found one of my cooking playlists. I selected the one with songs that were vaguely food related and also fun. The first was "Honey, Honey" by Abba, and I sang along while I sautéed onions in butter and pulled the chicken from my fridge. Soon enough I was singing "Strawberry Wine" by Matraca Berg and belting out the refrain about the girl who falls in love at seventeen and never forgets it.

I had been "in love" before, but I hadn't felt something deeply, in my very psyche, until Erik Wolf walked into our tea house . . .

Domo burst in moments later and caught me with a stupid smile on my face anyway. "What's your problem?" he said.

"Nothing. Hand me that paprika and set the table."

CHAPTER 6
THE FISHER WOMAN

Domo and I had a rather hilarious dinner, mostly because Domo had a raft of stories about eccentric people at his workplace. My favorite was the computer programmer who hummed while he worked but denied making any sound at all. Then he was surprised when Domo was able to identify the song he had been "thinking about."

"Every day I surprise him," my brother said, his mouth full of dumplings.

I pointed at him. "Gross."

He swallowed, unbothered, and said, "And every day he insists that he does not hum the music. So I just *happened* to know that he was thinking of the theme song from *Friends.*"

"That's crazy. You've got to be getting tired of all those eccentric programmers. You need to look for a new job. Something where you make even more money and can buy Margie a house."

Domo's expression softened, as it always did when someone mentioned Margie, and he shrugged. "I've got résumés out."

"Do you need help shopping for engagement rings?" I said. "Because I already think of Margie as my sister-in-law."

He shrugged. "That's fine. I know she's the one for me."

This was a first — Domo admitting his devotion to Margie. "So?"

"So that's in the works, too. Ouch. Your cat is sharpening his claws on my jeans."

"Antony, stop." I pushed the fuzzy black feline away with my stockinged foot. He always wanted extra attention from Domo.

My brother took his last bite and patted his tummy. "Delicious, as always, little sister. Thank you. Now I will take pity on this guy, who is clearly looking for some male bonding."

He scooped up Antony and held him high in the air: Antony's fuzzy face looked smug. Then Domo ran into the next room with him. "We're going to have some mouse adventures, buddy."

I laughed, and the door opened to reveal a slightly disheveled but ever-handsome Erik Wolf. He had a messenger bag slung over his shoulder and his phone in one hand. He used his free one to shake the hand of Domo, who still held Antony in his other hand. "Hey, man, how's it going?" Domo asked.

"Not bad. Your sister keeps me fed. I think I've gained five pounds since I started dating this talented woman."

"Working on another murder, though, huh?"

Erik nodded. "It never seems to end."

This made us all glum. "Come and have some food," I said. "I can look at your picture while you eat."

Domo went back to his cat play, and soon I saw Antony chasing and retrieving the mouse for Domo's amusement. Eventually, Cleopatra joined them, but lazily and without much interest.

I installed Erik at the table, handed him a plate of hot food, and poured him some wine. "Thank you," he said, his expression heartfelt. "Now let me show you this."

He opened his bag and retrieved a file folder, which he handed to me. "The pictures are just of his office. Nothing gory."

I'm sure I grew pale. "So — it was a gory scene?"

Erik's brows furrowed. "He was shot, Hana."

"Right." I gulped and opened the folder. I recognized the same shelves from the yearbook photo, photographed from several angles. Unlike the yearbook shot, these pictures were in color, and I could see the rich tones of the Hungarian porcelain and pottery on his shelves. I bent to study them.

"Mmm. So good," Erik said to his plate.

"I should tell you, I knew this man. I didn't realize it until today when I looked at the yearbook."

His head came up sharply. "Knew him how?"

"He was a collector, like me. I saw him a bunch of times at Falken's store; I just knew him as Sandor. You know Inspektor, the store cat? He loved Sandor. Sandor would pick him up and stroll up and down the aisles, petting Inspektor and enjoying the hunt. He loved finding great pieces. And of course, Falken always has Hungarian stuff; he had at least two customers who were always looking for it. Probably more."

"Huh. When did you see him last?"

"Just a week or so ago. I was there looking for a butter dish, because *someone* broke mine."

"Sorry!" Domo called from the next room.

Erik grinned as he buttered his bread.

"Anyway, I saw Sandor and said hello, and merry Christmas and stuff. He was holding Inspektor, as usual, and he said he was looking for a Herend dragon, one to match a piece he already had. It's another Chinese-inspired Herend series, just like my Yellow Dynasty teacups. They made these amazing dragons. Falken didn't have any — they're pretty rare and expensive — but he said he'd keep his eyes open. He's always going to estate sales, and as you have learned, there are a lot of old Hungarians in Riverwood."

"Uh-huh. What else did you talk about?"

"I'm trying to remember. He said he was glad to have some time off soon for the holidays — that should have clued me in that he was in academia — and that he was thinking of taking a short trip."

"Hmm." He forked some chicken into his mouth, then grabbed for his notebook and wrote this down.

My eyes moved back to the picture. "You know — these are really expensive pieces. He was collecting at a more serious level than I am. See this? The Medieval Dragon. Probably the one he was talking about. Look at the color! So rich, and such detail. I saw this in the Herend catalog. It costs more than ten thousand dollars."

Erik raised his brows and wrote this down, too. "So that whole shelf there behind the desk —"

"It's worth hundreds of thousands. I'm amazed that he was willing to bring all of this to work. I mean, how secure are those university offices? This is treasure, real treasure. Look at that beautiful orange snake — do you see it? Not as expensive a piece, but so lovely."

"How can you tell?" he said, peering at the pictures.

"Here — I'll pull it up on my phone. See? The snake costs four hundred fifty dollars. Not too crazy a price, but still out of my range. This one you're looking at is like the one on the shelf. And hang on —" I took my phone back and typed in a search term, then handed it back. "Here are the dragons." I watched him scroll through.

"Yes, I see. I recognize these from the room."

I looked back at the picture he had brought. "One of my favorites is — hey."

"What?"

"Hang on; let me get something." I jumped up and went into my room, where I had left Claire's Riverwood yearbook. I took it off the shelf and smiled at Cleopatra, who had left the mouse adventure and was curled up on my bed like a fluffy gray donut. I touched her velvet ear and brought the book back to the kitchen, paging to the

120

faculty section and finding the picture of Sandor Balog in his office.

Erik was almost finished eating. I sat down and said, "Go ahead and finish. This can wait."

He nodded and scooped up the last of his dumplings. Domo wandered in and said, "Antony is great. I think I have to convince Margie to get a cat."

"You should," I said. "Rescue one of them from the shelter on Sullivan. Maybe more than one. They always have bonded pairs, like my affectionate little siblings there."

"We'll see. I think Margie's pretty open. And Boris would be cool with it."

I nodded, smiling as I thought of Margie's placid wolfhound.

Erik stood up and took his plate and cup to the sink. "Thank you, Hana. I dreamed of your food all day. Now let's see what you have to show me."

He came back to the table and I set out the yearbook. "Obviously this picture was taken more than a year ago. Claire left Riverwood and went to culinary school. So this could mean nothing."

"Okay."

"But if you look behind him, you can see a gorgeous piece in a primary central location. See this woman, bent over and pulling up a fishnet? You can't tell in the black-and-white photo, but this is a gorgeous shimmering blue-green sculpture, with what's called an eosin finish. It's Zsolnay, not Herend. Here, I'll show you."

I pulled up another picture, this time of the Zsolnay Fisher Woman, a beautiful sculpted bowl with the bending woman on one end and tossing waves on the other. The net and the fish were blended into the overall veneer. "It's an antique, made around 1902. Look how lovely and luminous it is. No wonder he had it at the center of his shelving."

"Right."

"But on your picture, she's gone."

Erik reached for the folder he had given me and studied the color picture. "Ah."

"It wouldn't be unusual for anyone to switch a piece out, replace it with something else. Or maybe he wanted to display it at home. But wouldn't you think he would fill the hole? There's just a blank spot there now. That makes me think —"

"That the piece was removed recently," he said.

"Yeah."

We stared at each other; Domo was rooting around in my cabinets, most likely looking for dessert, but I was searching Erik

Wolf's green eyes for possible explanations.

He picked up his notebook. "What was this one worth, the Fisher Woman?"

"Not much more than the dragon. Somewhere between ten and fifteen thousand, I think."

"Geez. I never would have known. The price of art is so surprising."

"Yeah. Look at my original Kodaly on the wall in the living room there. I would never sell it now, but you wouldn't believe what his paintings are going for these days."

"I would," said Domo, butting in to the conversation with practiced ease. "Margie likes art, you know. She's always going on those auction sites to see what's affordable. The prices are crazy."

Erik seemed interested in all of these details. He started making notes in his distinctive handwriting.

Domo snorted, looking at Erik but pointing at me. "Hana watches you like you're a movie."

Erik looked up, surprised, then moved his gaze to me and offered his slow smile.

"Speaking of movies, who wants to watch one?" Domo said.

"You can start without me," Erik said. "I have to make a few phone calls. Hana, can I use your room?"

"Sure. Cleopatra is in there; she'll probably climb on your lap."

Erik seemed pleased at this prospect. He gathered his things, along with the envelope and the yearbook, and strode down the hall.

Domo found a package of cookies and opened them. "This will be a great second course."

"How about a holiday movie?" I said. "I've been trying to watch all the good ones in my spare time."

He shrugged. "I was thinking *The Godfather* or something."

"*It's a Wonderful Life*?"

"Blech," said my brother.

We finally agreed on *Elf* because Domo liked Will Ferrell. We settled on the couch, and Domo crunched cookies in my ear.

After half an hour, Erik appeared and sat next to me. I snuggled against him, and he slid an arm around me. Then I remembered something. "Domo, pause it for a second."

Domo picked up the remote and paused the TV.

"I forgot to tell you, there's an event tomorrow at the tea house. Sandor Balog was apparently going to have it for the language department, as a Christmas party. Now they're turning it into a sort of tribute event."

Erik sat up straight. "So — everyone he knew on campus will be there?"

"A lot of them, I guess."

"I want to be there," he said.

I frowned. "The thing is, they want to have a sort of — contemplative event. They don't want the police marching around asking questions. And Mom and Grandma don't want you guys — well, ruining everything."

Erik stared at me for a moment, then nodded. "Then we'll be there as staff. Okay? I'll tell Greg to wear black pants and a white shirt, similar to what you ladies wear. Maybe red ties for Christmas. We'll just walk around and bus tables and listen. Would that be all right?"

"Won't some of them know you already?"

He shook his head. "We haven't done many interviews yet beyond his family and his neighbors. And since most people have left campus for the holidays, we'll have to visit everyone at home or at the station and interview that way. This would give us a nice preliminary view of all the likely suspects in their shared culture. It would be invaluable, Hana."

I pursed my lips, thinking. "Let me call Mom."

Now it was my turn to go into my room,

where I spoke with my mother at some length about the pluses and minuses of having undercover police officers in our tea house.

She finally relented, with the final plea, "Tell him they have to be invisible, Hana! Absolutely invisible."

I returned to the living room and told this to Erik. Domo burst out laughing. "Invisible? You guys couldn't look more like cops if you had badges tattooed on your faces. Your partner, with his cop mustache and his gum? Everyone in the room will know he's five-oh."

"Maybe just Erik, then," I said.

Domo looked at my boyfriend with a dubious expression. "Sorry, man. If you walked into a bar where my friends and I were having beers, they would all start warning each other to be cool."

"What does that mean?" I asked, glaring at my brother.

"It means Erik looks like a cop. He's got that indefinable cop aura."

I would have protested, except I sort of agreed with him.

Erik shrugged. "Whether they think we're cops or not, they'll have no evidence of anything beyond some quiet busboys. And hopefully they won't notice because they'll be focused on their tribute."

"Yeah," I said uncertainly.

He leaned back on the couch and said, "And then I can focus on finding a murderer."

CHAPTER 7
THE MONKEY AND HIS TAIL

The next day Erik and Greg showed up in their black pants, white shirts, and red ties. My grandmother had been forewarned but appeared in front of the giant Christmas tree to glare at them anyway. "No more cops in this place," she said. I laughed, because I had never heard her say the word "cops" before.

Erik remained solemn. "Juliana, I promise that we will stay in the background."

"Interrogating is not background," she complained.

"We won't interrogate," Erik insisted. "We'll just — try to winnow down our list of subjects to talk to. By *listening.*"

She scowled some more, then turned to Greg Benton and pointed at his chest. "I have some goulash for you."

Benton looked so happy that I laughed. "I guess it will be a merry Christmas after all in Greg's house," I joked.

"You're not kidding. I am in love with your grandmother," he said.

My grandmother held up a hand to stop our jokes, but her flushed face told me she was pleased by the compliments about her food. My mother joined us at the tree, and Grandma murmured, *"Örül, mint majom a farkának,"* which made them both laugh.

Erik and Benton stood looking from them to me, awaiting translation, and I took pity on them. "She said that Greg is essentially jumping for joy. Except the Hungarian saying is different; it says he is as happy as a monkey about its tail."

"Not yet," Greg said, smoothing the mustache that my grandmother disliked. "But I will be as soon as I start eating."

"Meanwhile," my mother said, "I believe you two are bussing tables today, right? So if you'll go with me into the back room, I'll give you some basic training."

With a smile in my direction, Erik followed Greg Benton to the back of the hall, where they all entered the room that held our office space and François's workspace and kitchen. "François will be *thrilled* by the visitors," I said with a smirk.

My grandmother shrugged. "This place has become a train station. Is that what they say?"

"No, they say, 'It's like Grand Central Station in here.' You know, like the big one in New York."

"Ya." She waited until I met her eye, then pointed. "Look. Your mama hung the art. She pieced on some material, made it look good again."

"What?" My eyes flew to the back wall, where I could see the World Tree glimmering. "Oh wow, even from here I can tell it's perfect."

She nodded, then looked up. "Ah. Frank and his dad come to finish the job. When they are done, I'm bringing them in for tea, and to say sorry. You keep your wolf away from them."

She wasn't kidding, and I could see that she was mortified that young Frank had been accosted at the tea house, a place of welcome for all.

"Okay, I'll tell him." I put a comforting hand on her arm, but added, "It is important, Grandma. They are looking for a killer."

Grandma narrowed her eyes and her mouth. "No arrests. It is Christmastime."

I lunged forward and hugged her, inhaling her scent of cinnamon tea and Odyssey perfume. "No arrests. I'm sure Mom will make it clear right now. They should be invisible."

Since both Erik and Greg were over six feet tall and had a certain bulk to them, this was an ambitious statement, but I hoped it would be true.

The tea event had begun, and people milled about, greeting one another in subdued tones. There were still some holiday well-wishes in the exchanges, but it was clear that people understood the new focus of the day's gathering: to pay tribute to a man who had died. There were close to eighty people in the room, and we had been busy initially settling people at tables, pouring tea, and delivering sandwiches and pita bites made by François.

Wolf and Benton did look ridiculous, almost like overgrown boys, in their make-shift busboy costumes, but the amazing thing was that people really did not seem to notice them. Perhaps it was the fate of the bus-person to be viewed as inessential. At Grandma's instruction, they hunched over their carts as they moved back and forth, trying to look unobtrusive.

As she had promised, my grandmother had seized on Frank and his father when they finished the windows, pulling them into the back room for tea and conversation.

François had plied them with cakes, and we had all offered apologies. Mr. Dobos assured us that Frank would not be prosecuted and that their lawyer had "worked miracles" by convincing the police that Frank had been traumatized and in shock. My grandmother had nodded at this, pleased. She became even happier when she learned that Frank's mother had been questioned and dismissed as a suspect. The gun, Frank said, was not theirs. The Dobos men were still in the back room now, finishing their tea; they were relaxed and enjoying one of François's stories about his year living in Clichy when Wolf and Benton appeared. Frank stiffened.

I held up a hand. "They're not here for you, Frank. They're just observing."

Frank's father studied the two detectives; to my surprise, his expression held no resentment. "I hope you find the guy who did it. It was a terrible thing to happen, and a terrible thing for my son to have to see." He clapped a hand on Frank's shoulder, as he had done the other day.

Wolf nodded his agreement. Benton said, "Is your wife here today, Mr. Dobos?"

"Yes, she'll be out there somewhere."

Erik's green eyes were serious. "She's one of the few people out there who knows us, thanks to yesterday's interview. Can you go tell her not to identify us to anyone? For obvious reasons, we can't ask her ourselves. We are attempting to be incognito today."

"Sure. I'll do that now."

Mr. Dobos, made placid with tea and sweets, went out the door, and Erik looked pointedly at Frank. "I need a favor from you, too."

Frank gulped. "Okay."

"I'm guessing you know a lot of people out there, both as a student and as your mom's son. I'd like you to give us a quick heads-up so Greg and I can get a better context for what we're listening to. If we open this door, we can see the tables, but the people won't really see us. Can you do that for me?"

Now Frank looked interested, even a little pleased to be made important to the process. "Okay." He stood up and went to the door with Erik. Greg stood on the other side of Frank; my mother and grandmother were in the tearoom, tending to tables, and I was making a new "traveling pot" that I was supposed to be bringing back out, boiling hot and ready to replenish cups. I lingered behind the tall men, though, listening to Frank's information.

He pointed toward the table in front of

the Christmas tree. "That's Mom, as you know. Dad is whispering in her ear." Erik and Benton nodded. "That little Asian lady is Professor Lee. I think her first name is Wanda. She teaches Mandarin. My mom said she dated Professor Balog a couple times, while he and his wife were separated."

Oooh. Frank really did have the scoops on people. But of course his mother would probably come home from campus and tell things to her family, never thinking the information would leave their house.

He pointed to another woman at his mother's table. "That's Professor Yves. She teaches French. My mom calls her Yvonne. Mom said that Yvonne was one of the people who fought with Professor Balog." He glanced at Erik, his face panicked. "Not in a murderous way. Just — you know — a lot of people were mad about the decision to drop a language."

"Sure," Benton said. "Who else do you recognize?"

Frank scanned the room. "That table by the front window — that's Professor Weber. He teaches German. And that lady with all the brown hair — that's Professor Parravicini. She teaches Italian. All the guys on campus have a crush on her."

I looked at Frank, who had reddened

134

slightly. He scanned some more. "So — you know my mom . . . The only other people I know are Professor Balog's wife — she's the one there with the sort of blondish-gray hair, talking to your grandma," he said, throwing a glance back at me. "And then there's his friend that he was always playing chess with on those cool chess boards in the Union. I think his name is Tony. I always assumed he was another professor, but I don't know what he teaches."

Frank finished studying faces and turned to Erik. "That's everyone I know."

Erik had been jotting things down; he put his pen in his pocket, and now it was his turn to clap a hand on Frank's shoulder. "That's very helpful, Frank, thank you."

"Have another cake," I said, and Frank brightened.

"Thanks! Those are really good."

"*Oui,*" said François, who had been standing behind us at his workstation, not pleased about being ignored. "Here — this one has an icing mistake. You can eat it."

Frank lunged toward François. "That's a cool design you put on it. Just a few green swirls, but it totally looks like a Christmas tree."

"*Oui,*" said François again, softening slightly.

135

Frank looked uncertainly toward the door. "I would ask for one for my dad, but I think he might be sitting with my mom out there."

"He is," Benton said, peering out.

I tapped Erik on the shoulder. "I need to get out there, and you two giants are blocking the door."

"Sorry," Erik murmured, looking at his pad. He and Benton both stepped out of the way.

In the doorway I turned back. "And we could use some clearing of sandwich trays so we ladies can bring out the desserts."

I moved into the room and strode to the first table to pour tea. Most of the people ignored me because the woman who had been identified as Balog's wife had gone to the front podium, joining a man named Williamson, who identified himself as the president of Riverwood University. He looked at the people assembled and addressed them in a sonorous tone. "Sandor wanted today to be a celebration. He had wanted to offer you all a special treat in this beautiful tea house, and instead we are using the time to remember him. To acknowledge everything he was to us, everything he did for us, and to share a prayer for Sandor and his family. Nancy has selected a prayer that she'd like to read."

The room was silent. The blonde-and-gray-haired woman, who was tall and rather elegant, thanked everyone for coming and then read a simple prayer, in which she asked that God bless her husband's soul and bestow blessings, also, on everyone who loved him, so that they would be ever linked by those words of grace.

The audience members bowed their heads in remembrance — or in shame? Hadn't Frank suggested that many of these people had been furious with poor Sandor? Did they hate him? Or had the arguments just been temporary workplace squabbles that would have faded over time?

Mrs. Balog sat down, and another woman went to the podium. It was Wanda Lee. She smiled at those assembled. "Our department was not without controversy in the last few weeks. Sandor probably heard strong words from everyone in this room." Again, that guilty silence. "But everyone in this room also shared a friendship with him. Colleagues argue sometimes; perhaps they even argue passionately. But workplace drama doesn't ultimately change friendships. When we remember Sandor, it will be with love."

Now a heartfelt applause rose from the crowd. Wanda Lee nodded. "Let's focus on those good feelings today. I'm going to let you enjoy your delicious tea and sandwiches, but in a few minutes, we'll ask that if anyone would like to say a few words about Sandor, they come forward and share them with us."

She stepped down from the dais and returned to her seat, where the people sitting near her said words of congratulations.

I had finished replenishing teacups, and Erik and Greg had indeed come lumbering out to clear tables, after which my mother and grandmother had brought out extra sandwich trays to tables where supplies had been depleted. Erik and Greg now stood in the shadows by the back room; the World Tree glinted behind them. They exchanged some words and then went into the kitchen, returning moments later with their carts; they kept to the perimeter of the room, trying to look unobtrusive, but eventually moved in to take away empty cups or plates.

They both made a long process out of putting empty dishes onto their carts, giving them time to linger and eavesdrop on every table. I shook my head; what had we come to, our tea house? There had never been police in this building until a woman died unexpectedly, back in October. Now it seemed we had needed police on and off ever since, for one reason or another.

I took my empty teapot to the back and set it on the sideboard. François looked pleased. "The cakes are finished. They are magnificent."

They were; François was vain, but he had good reason to be so. The cakes, with delicate white frosting and artful touches of green, red, and gold, were like something from the cover of a culinary magazine. "Thank you, François! As always, you have outdone yourself."

He sighed, then stretched his arms above his head. "I will stay a bit later today to start on the dough for my St. Nicholas cookies."

"Oh, I'm so excited! You know it's my favorite day of our tea house year." St. Nicholas Day, or St. Mikulás Day, as the Hungarians called it, had already come and gone on December 6, but each year we celebrated this holiday with an event at the tea house, in which we invited children to come and have a special tea, receive a "shoe" filled with candy and a little plastic Hungarian dancer doll, and sing Christmas songs — some in Hungarian. Scheduling problems had caused us to postpone the children's party until December 12, but we were still anticipating about fifty children (with parents). We had a special tradition of creating a circle with all the children joining hands and walking around the Christmas tree, hands linked, while we sang our songs. It was quaint and beautiful, and last year a photographer from the Riverwood *Review* had come, and the picture had ended up in the Features section of the paper. Now, my mother was proud to note, it was a permanent fixture on the Village of Riverwood website.

François sighed. "Yes, it is nice. The children love my cookies."

"They do. Again, François, I must tell you: I don't know what we'd do without you."

He shrugged, pleased by the accolade. I looked at my watch. "I need to help with sandwich trays. I'll tell Erik and Greg to help bring out these cakes."

François looked uncertain. "They might — cast them on the floor, somehow."

I had generalized worries about this, too. "We'll keep an eye on them."

I went out into the hallway. The four people on the floor seemed to have things under control; I walked toward table ten, where my mother stood with her cart. "I'm going to do a bathroom check," I said.

We liked to keep an eye on the bathroom during events, making sure that there were enough paper towels, that the soap dispenser

140

was full, and that no one had tossed crumpled towels on the floor. I peeked inside and saw that things looked good, but that the door of the last stall was sticking shut again. I peeked underneath to make sure no feet were inside, then pushed hard on the door so that it opened. I stood in the stall, examining the door, wondering how to prevent sticking. Suddenly I heard voices outside the bathroom, and moments later two women entered. I instinctively stayed in the stall and shut the door.

"Wanda laid it on kind of thick," one voice said. I peered through a crack and saw that two women stood looking in the mirror: Yvonne Yves, the French professor, and Professor Parravicini, the Italian professor. Both women were examining their makeup. Yvonne was the one who was speaking. "You notice she didn't admit in front of Sandor's wife that she went out with the guy on numerous occasions."

Professor Parravicini stiffened. "They were separated. And you know perfectly well that I went out with him, too, Yvonne. The man presented himself as single, and he was dating. I assume his wife knows that, but since apparently they recently reunited, I'm sure Wanda didn't want to make waves. I actually think it was quite diplomatic of her.

She genuinely loved Sandor. She hoped for more from the relationship, I think."

Yvonne turned to her, brushing her dark, silky hair behind her ears. "And you, Livia?" she asked coolly.

Livia studied her for a moment, a look of mild disgust on her face. "I didn't love him, if that's what you mean. I'm not sure why you feel the need to be so judgmental."

Yvonne shrugged. "Not judgmental, just curious. I don't know what either of you saw in Sandor. He was a bore."

Livia said, "He was a good, kind man, and actually quite romantic. I think — I wish that I had not led him on. He thought there was more perhaps between us than there was."

"Not anymore, surely? If he had reconnected with his wife?" asked Yvonne.

Livia studied her hands. "There was still some interest, on his part."

Yvonne whistled softly. "Oh my. Sandor, you scoundrel. Who knew? Three women in his life. More, for all we know. How did he find the time, really?"

Livia shook her head. "As I said, he was sentimental. He liked falling in love. He said Hungarian men love romance; perhaps it was a fatal flaw."

Yvonne's look sharpened. "What does that mean?"

"Nothing. I'm being morbid. And I have to pee. Excuse me." She went into one of the stalls, and I came out of mine.

Yvonne gave me a cool look. I made a show of washing my hands. I looked at her with what I hoped was a blank expression. "Are you all enjoying the event today? It's some kind of Christmas party, right?"

Her brows furrowed in confusion or distaste. "No, we're actually paying tribute to a colleague who has died."

"Oh, I'm so sorry," I said. "I'd better get back to work."

I hurried out of the room without looking behind me.

I found Erik and Greg in the back room, murmuring together. Frank had disappeared; François said that he had put in his earbuds and murmured something about taking a Lyft home. Erik's voice distracted me. He told Benton, in a low whisper, "Weber, the German professor, was upset because Balog had toyed with cutting his study abroad program in Berlin. Apparently, he's run this program for fifteen years."

Greg nodded solemnly. "The man named

Tony is a doctor. He's not full-time — just teaches one course on campus for the premed undergrads. Something that blends basic biology with some medical knowledge."

"Mmm," Erik said.

I moved closer to them and told them what I'd heard in the bathroom. Erik's brows rose. "So he was not as committed to his wife as she might believe?"

I shook my head. "Livia Parravicini, the Italian teacher, suggested that she was not interested. Maybe Balog just liked the idea of having women available to him. Maybe he was still loyal to his wife. You'll probably want to ask Livia, though."

Erik made notes in his notebook. "Yes, I will. Thank you, Hana."

I went to the sideboard and began wiping it down. My phone buzzed in my pocket. I lifted it and saw a text from Runa: Surgery tomorrow 7 AM. Pray for me.

A chill ran through me. I lifted my eyes and met Erik's across the room. He murmured something to Greg and crossed to me. "What is it?"

I showed him the text and touched his arm, offering comfort. He nodded. "I'll be there. Can you be there, too?"

"Yes. Our event doesn't start until two. By

then — she'll be out, right? How long a surgery is this?"

"I have no idea. I just want to support Andy and Rue."

"Me, too. Mom and Grandma will be fine with it."

He kissed my hair. "Thanks. I'm going back out there."

"Take a tray of cakes, please."

Moments later we were all back beneath the big tree, dispensing François's artistic desserts, replenishing tea, and taking away empty plates. The people rustled with interest and murmured together. No one had come to the front since Wanda Lee had invited them, but now the German teacher, who introduced himself as Hans Weber, stood on the dais and gave a rather humble account of his affiliation with Sandor. "When I came to Riverwood," he said, "the enrollment was low, and the department was small. Sandor was brand-new back then, but he had a lot of great ideas for the expansion of our department, and I think he made just about all of them happen. We bonded over our shared love of Auslese Riesling." Those assembled laughed gently. "Anyway, I'll always have fond memories of Sandor in those days. So full of life and ideas. Our friendship was born one night in the Riverwood Pub, when we talked about the state of Europe and shared some wine and laughs. I'd like to think it lasted until his final day. Rest well, Sandor."

He descended the steps, and Livia Parravicini climbed them. She brushed some of her plentiful hair behind her shoulder absently and said, "Sandor was a good man, and a brilliant one. One of the reasons he made such a good leader of our department was that he was fluent in four languages, including Italian. I loved speaking Italian with him, because he knew it well, even many of our crazy idioms. Sandor loved language and learning. His death is a great loss to our university, and, like Hans, I feel I have lost a good friend." She hesitated, about to say more, and then shook her head. I wondered if she had been tempted to say how romantic Sandor had been. She left the platform, and people looked around, waiting to see who would go next.

The man named Tony rose and moved to the front. He slouched slightly, his hands plunged into his trouser pockets, but he was handsome, with graying temples that added distinction to his looks. He moved up to the microphone with confidence, like a lounge singer. "Sandor and I loved to play chess in the Union. Some of you probably even

watched one of our matches — they sometimes attracted an audience because they
tended to be exciting. That's what I liked
about Sandor: he was brilliant, and he challenged my intellect. Those chess games
weren't just a pleasant diversion for me.
They kept me sharp, and I often liked to
start or end my day by playing chess with
Sandor because, with him as an opponent
and a conversationalist, I was at my best."

People clapped quietly, and Tony stepped
down. I thought I saw him exchange a
glance with Sandor's wife as he walked past
her — just a quick glimmer, and I couldn't
tell if the expression was dislike or interest.
Then it was gone.

Yvonne Yves stepped gracefully onto the
platform, her short, silky bob swinging. I
took a tray of Christmas cakes to the final
table, where some unidentified people sat
— unknown, apparently, to Frank. Yvonne
spoke, with a slight French accent I had not
noticed in the bathroom, of her friendship
with Sandor, and how much she would miss
him.

Huh. Everyone was Sandor's friend; yet in
the bathroom, Yvonne had said he was a
bore. Were they all twofaced, or was it just
her? I bent to set a platter on the table, and
I heard someone murmur to her compan-

ion, "I don't think Yvonne was too thrilled with Sandor after he found out about her fourth-year French boy toy."

I tried to look entirely deaf and I grabbed two empty plates and headed for the back room.

François was cleaning; his coat and phone sat neatly on the table, which meant he was ready to leave.

"François," I said. "I need your help. Come to the door."

He joined me, looking intrigued. He smelled like frosting.

"See that woman talking? She's the French professor at Riverwood. Can you find a way to talk to her before you leave? Just connect with her as a French person? Just shoot the breeze, see if she reveals any interesting details."

His eyes lit up. "*Oui.* I can do that. *Un moment.*" He strode out into the tearoom, where Yvonne had just finished speaking and had stepped down; she was replaced by Frank's mother, Sarah Dobos. This I had to hear.

Sarah was so mild-looking I was shocked that Frank could have thought her guilty of even swatting a fly. She wore a plain gray knit dress with a red blazer and Christmas pin on the lapel. Her reddish-blonde hair was tied back with a red ribbon. She sighed and said, "You all had such positive relationships with Sandor. I'll be honest: mine was more problematic. And I fought with him, pretty intensely, the day before he died. I regret that now: regret that I didn't find some more diplomatic way of airing my grievances. It wasn't like me at all, to unload on him that way. But — Sandor was angry with me, too. It was hard. When I heard the news, it hit me like a bomb: I would never have a chance to apologize. So I guess my only chance is to apologize to all of you." She paused, looking around with an earnest expression.

"Sandor was a good man, just as you are all good people, and I need to treat you with respect and professionalism. I'm so sorry to his friends, and especially to his wife, for the fact that I added stress to his life in his last hours. I can tell you one thing that is more positive: Sandor was genuinely devoted to the people he loved, and that was evident, from the pictures in his office to the names he regularly dropped into conversation. One of those names of course was yours, Nancy. I'm so sorry for your loss. No matter how upset we were with Sandor, I hope he knew that we were still his friends." Nancy bowed her head in acknowledgment, and Sarah looked distressed. "Anyway, I've gone on too long. I will also merely add that my son, Frank, took Sandor's class, and he said it was routinely fascinating. Rest in peace, Sandor." She stepped down, her face grave.

I saw Erik Wolf in one corner of the tea house, hovering over a cart but focusing in on Sarah Dobos. He nodded once to himself, perhaps because she had proved a theory or suspicion, then walked into a far corner, where Greg Benton waited for him. Domo was right; they did look like cops.

A few more speakers paid homage to Sandor; then the president spoke again. Finally, someone asked my mother to put on soft music, so she put her Austrian Christmas album on once again, and the mood in the room shifted to something calm, contemplative, even happy.

François met me in the back room, where I had just brought some empty dessert platters. "Your cakes were *devoured,*" I said.

He nodded absently. "Your Frenchwoman is interesting, very. She is smart, *oui,* and sophisticated."

"Okay. So what's up?"

Something was obviously up; I could sense the excitement beneath his skin.

He leaned toward me. "She hit upon me."

"What? She hit you?"

"No — how do you say it? Proposition."

"What?" I repeated stupidly. "You mean she hit *on* you. What did she say?"

"We were speaking of France. How we miss it at the holiday, how we love the food, the music, this and that. She puts her hand on my arm, so." He put a hand on my arm, between my elbow and shoulder, and stroked it slightly. "Like *this,* Hana!"

"That's inappropriate," I murmured.

"She said if ever I want to reminisce, I could call her, or come to her house for a good French meal. She said something about how dinner could turn into breakfast."

"Wow. That is so — cliché."

"*Oui.* She gave me her card, as you see." He held it up; it identified her as a professor at Riverwood University.

"What did you say?"

"I flattered her. I said I had a girlfriend and I am a loyal man, but otherwise it would be tempting. Then I ran away!" He grinned at me, and I smiled back.

"Thank you, François."

"*Oui.* It was fun, being the detective like your wolf. But now I must go finish my Christmas shopping." He went to retrieve his coat and phone.

"Thanks again. This was helpful."

He waved and disappeared out the door. Erik and Greg came slouching into the room, trying and failing to be as invisible as my mother had demanded.

Erik pointed at me. "You know something."

I kept my voice low. "Yvonne Yves just hit on François. Like — openly propositioned him. And someone at a back table said that Sandor had confronted her about a 'fourth-year boy toy.' "

Erik practically dove into a chair, took out his notebook, and jotted something down. Greg Benton let out a low whistle. "That's good stuff, Hana."

"I assume you two are hearing helpful things, as well?"

Erik looked up. "A literal gold mine," he said. "Thank you, to all my Hungarian ladies, for letting us in."

"Okay. They'll be leaving within the next half hour, so get whatever you still need."

"Right." He made a few more notes, my boyfriend, surrounded by a gentle halo of light that I saw around no other person. He looked up at me and smiled, and something ticklish fluttered in my stomach.

"I have to go clean. See you out there," I said. Despite the presence of Greg Benton,

I leaned over and planted a warm kiss on Erik's cheek.

Greg grinned at me as I sailed past him and joked, "I've heard about you Hungarians and your romantic souls."

I laughed, but out in the hall, amid the slightly more festive conversation and the gentle clinking of spoons, I thought of Sandor — clutching Inspektor and strolling through Falken's store; posing in front of his shelf full of Hungarian porcelain, with treasures of great monetary value; telling Livia Parravicini that he still had feelings for her . . .

My eyes moved to Livia, who moved gracefully toward the door, a coat slung over her arm. Had she been telling the truth about not reciprocating Sandor's feelings? I managed to make it look natural to run into her near the exit. "Hello," I said. "I heard what you said about your colleague — your words were so beautiful."

"Thank you," she said, her expression warm. I sensed in that instant that she was a friendly person. An open person.

On a sudden whim, I said, "I took Italian in high school, and I've forgotten almost all of it. I wish I could learn it again. I'd love to visit Rome, or Florence, and be able to speak the language."

This animated her even more. "It's not too late! Italian is not difficult to learn."

"I don't suppose you tutor people?" I said, making it sound like a joke.

She shook her head with a small laugh. "No, but I'll tell you what. I'm still on campus for a couple more days. You could stop by my office and I can give you some beginner's materials. I have a good CD, too. You could listen to it here in the tea house while you work."

That actually sounded quite appealing. "I would love that."

She reached into a pretty little purse, pulled out a business card, and handed it to me. "Call me and we'll set up a meeting time. But I have a favor to ask in return."

"Oh?"

"Do you speak Hungarian?"

"Not fluently, no. Only my mother and grandmother do — they were both born there."

She nodded. "Maybe enough to get me started? It's a language I'd like to learn. Sandor was going to teach me." Her face clouded over with sadness.

"So, you're proposing a language exchange?"

"I am!" she said. She stuck out her hand. "I'm Livia, by the way."

I shook it. "I'm Hana. I would love to do it, yes."

"Wonderful! Talk to you soon, Hana."

She left the tea house, and my eyes landed on Nancy Balog, Sandor's dignified-looking wife. She was an attractive woman, but not sexy in the way Livia was, and probably twenty years older. Was Sandor trying to maintain two relationships?

The man named Tony walked past me, wearing a coat and texting on a large phone. "Did you enjoy everything?" I asked.

He looked up; he really was quite handsome. "Hmm? Oh yes. It's a cute little place you have here."

"I'm sorry for the loss of your friend. And of your intellectual challenges."

Something flickered in his eyes before his smile reached them. "Oh — you heard my speech, huh? Yes, Sandor was one of a kind. We enjoyed each other's company." He made a show of looking at his watch. "Well, I have to be going. You have a merry Christmas."

"You, too, sir."

He grinned. "You can call me Tony."

I couldn't imagine why I would ever need to call him something again, but I nodded, and he made his way out. Yvonne Yves appeared beside me, also holding a coat. She wore the slightly sneering expression she had worn in the bathroom. "Ah, Tony can't resist flirting, can he? Maybe to distract you from the topic at hand."

I looked confused. "I'm sorry?"

A thin smile. "Oh, I'm just thinking aloud. Sandor and his friend Tony played for money. And I think Tony owed a great deal . . . Sandor's death was probably a relief, in all honesty." She shrugged and swept a hand across her hair. "In any case. Thank you for an enjoyable event."

She strolled out into our parking lot, and immediately I could breathe better; the poison of her gossip had stayed with her like a cloud. Still, I would be sharing that gossip with Erik Wolf, since it seemed to give Tony a possible motive for Sandor's murder. How much money, I wondered, were we talking about? A hundred dollars would be nothing, maybe a thousand would be nothing, for a doctor. But more than that? Many thousands? Did people really play for that kind of money? If so, the debt might become problematic.

I turned back toward the room; people were rapidly departing now that the first of them had left. My eyes drifted toward the hallway, and I gasped.

The World Tree was on fire.

CHAPTER 8
THE CHRISTMAS CHILD

I raced to the back of the tea house, wondering desperately if I could grab the fire extinguisher before the material was totally destroyed. I noticed, in the blur of my rapid journey, some surprised faces turned my way. Why had no one else seen it?

Then I reached the back wall and saw why: the tapestry was fine, untouched, beautiful, and glimmering with its various beads and sequins. It had been a trick of the light, just as now the light seemed to shine only on the evil smile of Ördög as he stirred his souls in the world beneath our own. Even the snake at his feet seemed to be smiling.

"Hana?" Erik said, appearing next to me. "Are you okay?"

"Oh — yes. It's so weird. From across the hall, it looked like this thing was on fire. The light was hitting it in such a way . . . just an optical illusion."

157

Erik frowned. "There is no light here. This hall is pretty dim. Are you — sensing something?"

I was. I felt it, deep inside, but I had no idea what it was, or how to make it rise to the surface. "I guess. Just sort of general."

"A general feeling of what?"

I sighed. "Evil." My hand rested now on the roots of the World Tree, where darkness surrounded both the unrepentant and the remorseful souls who had to pay the price for their sins.

The next morning, I sat in a small lobby on the eighth floor of St. Francis of Assisi Hospital in Chicago. Runa had been in surgery for one hour, and I joined a tense group who waited for word: Erik, Thyra, and Andy, who got up to look down the hall every five minutes or so.

I had brought a bag full of *kiflis* in case people wanted comfort food, but it was a bit early to be indulging in cookie crescents filled with rich jam.

Erik had been texting, but now he looked up at Andy, who had just returned from one of his jaunts to the hall. "No one's coming," Andy said dispiritedly.

"Did the doctor indicate how long it might take?" Erik asked.

158

Andy folded his arms. "She said anywhere from one to three hours if there are no complications. I mean, there is a complication, but barring any *other* complications . . ."

In a moment of extreme empathy, I absorbed Andy's emotions and understood. This was not just his lover having surgery: this was a tiny daughter he hadn't met, a baby he'd only known about for a couple of months. He was the strong, practical one in their relationship, and he'd been the firm counselor that Runa needed. But he was afraid.

I stood up, went to him, and put my arms around him. He immediately wrapped his around me and said, "God, I just want this to be over."

I willed myself to be calm, and to send some of that calm into Andy. I felt him relax against me. "Thanks, Hana."

I let go of him; he looked better. "Of course. I know how scary this must be." I paused. "You've never met my grandma, have you?"

Andy managed a smile. "No, but I've heard all about her. At length. I know she told Runa about our baby before Runa even knew."

"Yeah, she's impressive that way. She also

told Runa that your little girl is funny and fierce and strong. Someday she'll be hassling you with her strong personality, and you'll remember this."

He laughed. "I hope so. I want that. I want her to have a chance to sass me in the future."

I picked up my bag of *kiflis*. "Take one of these. Dr. Hana diagnoses that you will want one with raspberry filling."

"Okay." He pulled out a *kifli* and took a bite. His eyes widened. "Oh, wow. This is really good."

"Help yourself. Food can be comforting."

He sat down again between Thyra and Erik, and near a small artificial Christmas tree that sat on a side table. It was not a very compelling holiday scene, but I took some cheer from the fact that his face looked less pale than it had moments earlier. Erik gave me a thumbs-up, and Thyra sent a wan smile. She hadn't talked much this morning, and it made me wonder about that mysterious connection between twins. Was she somehow feeling Runa's pain, or even her sedation?

Suddenly, Erik straightened in his seat. "Mom, Dad! We're in here," he said.

I froze. I had been dating Erik since October, but because of our busy schedules,

I had never met his parents. Now here they were, a tall silver-haired man and a tall woman with highlighted gray hair. Both of them wore jeans and sweatshirts with the Trekker logo on them. Trekker was an outdoor enthusiast's supply company owned by Erik's parents. His family was full of entrepreneurs.

Now the two of them were in the little lobby with us, hugging their children and Andy hello. Erik smiled, grabbed my arm, and pulled me closer to the group. "Mom, Dad, this is Hana."

I had expected his parents to be relatively cold, not only because Erik himself was quite introverted and because Runa and Thyra, in their beautiful oddity, had taken some getting used to, but because Erik had implied early in our relationship that he wanted to hold off on introducing me to them. This had made me fear the worst. Would they be mean? Judgmental? Aloof? Annoying?

I faced them with a brave smile, and Erik said, "Hana, these are my parents, Martha and Magnus."

I held out my hand; Magnus Wolf bellowed out a laugh and engulfed me with an unexpected hug. "So this is our little Hungarian girl, eh? We've heard a lot about you." He leaned back, smiled down into my face, then pulled me back for another hug. It was like being embraced by some medieval king.

He let go of me, and Erik's mother darted in, hugging me, too. "Oh, Hana. What a pretty name. Runa and Thyra are right, you do look like a little doll."

I was confident that I did not, but I smiled. "It's nice to meet you both. Erik has told me so much . . ." He really hadn't told me anything, but that was Erik in a nutshell.

Martha had already moved away from me. She sat down next to Thyra and gazed into her face. "How are you holding up, my baby? Are you missing your sister?"

Thyra nodded. "It's weird. She's never been sick a day in her life. And now this unexpected surgery. For an unexpected child." She brooded for a while, then said, "I hate the smell of hospitals."

Martha put an arm around her. "I know, *elskling.* I'm sorry we weren't here sooner, but Dad and I had some things to do in the warehouse before we could take time off. We weren't sure how long you and Andy and Runa would need us."

Magnus sat down next to Andy and thumped a hand on his shoulder. "You're good for her, son. We were so happy to hear about the engagement."

"Me, too," said Andy weakly. "I'd wanted to ask her for a year, but I was afraid of what her answer might be. All this has brought us closer, actually."

"Of course it has," Magnus agreed. Then he lifted his head. "What is that delightful smell? Is there a cafeteria near here?"

Andy pointed. "Hana made some of her Hungarian cookies. I ate one and it was delicious. Try them."

Erik's parents, fit as they were, still did not seem to mind eating a *kifli* for breakfast. They both selected one and bit into it. Martha said, "Oh, Hana! I will need you to make these at Christmas. I assume you will be at our family celebration, right?"

"Uh — I —" I said before Magnus boomed in my ear, "This is delicious! Marth, this has some kind of cheese — oh, take a bite of mine!" The two of them twined arms past Andy's face so that they could taste each other's food.

My eyes slid over to Erik, who smiled sarcastically, as if to say, *You see why I didn't bring you home?*

Magnus eyed me with a royal expression. "Hana, we've heard great things about your tea house. We plan to have a Trekker employee retreat in January, and we thought we might hold it there."

"That would be terrific. We might have a couple of openings. We're generally booked up until spring," I said.

"Oh, so business is going well? Good, good," he said, nodding his approval. His knee jostled up and down, and Martha's fingers played automatically in Thyra's hair, and I realized that they were nervous, too.

I sat down on a chair facing the group and took out my phone. I found Spotify and selected a list with some soothing, instrumental Christmas songs. I turned it on as background music, but soon the room went quiet as tension mounted, and the music dominated.

We listened to a rather mournful "It Came upon a Midnight Clear," played primarily on strings. My eyes went to the Christmas tree. I thought of "angels bending near the earth to touch their harps of gold." What did that mean? Could they not play the harps unless they were near the earth? Or was it just that they had to be near the earth in order for humans to hear heavenly music?

If only we could bring some angels here, to help every suffering person in this hospital. Perhaps the angels were already doing so. To hear my grandmother tell it, Runa's child was like a little angel, trying to come to earth but requiring some intervention.

I tried to imagine how tiny her heart was, Runa's little daughter. How they could possibly operate on something so small, and how invasive it was to delve into her cocooned existence.

My eyes moved to the nativity scene under the tree — a ten-piece affair with Holy Family, two shepherds, two sheep, one donkey, one cow, and one suspended angel, looking down. *Angels bending near the earth . . .*

I closed my eyes. The music had changed now to "O Tannenbaum," played on strings and what sounded like a glockenspiel. I tried to see with what my grandmother called my "inner eye," a reality she assured me would give me more presence of mind and confidence in my understanding of the truth. I pictured Runa's daughter, not as a baby, but as a little girl, blonde like her mother and playing in a field of swaying grasses. She was smiling, free of care, brushing away strands of golden hair that the wind blew in her eyes.

Baby, I said in this daydream.

She looked up at me with bright eyes. She held out her hand, and I clasped it in both of mine. I wanted to warm her, to hold on to her and bring her to her mother.

Stay, I said.

She laughed up at me — a sweet, childlike sound — and nodded.

My eyes flew open. Had I been sleeping? The feeling of the dream was still so strongly with me that I couldn't stop smiling, and I sat up straight, wanting to share my vision with everyone in the room.

Andy looked at me, and whatever he saw in my face made his own expression change from tense to calm. He smiled, too.

The rest were looking at me, their faces uncertain, when the doctor walked in, pumping her fist in the air in a sign of victory.

Andy walked Erik and me to our cars. "It's of course a triumph that the baby survived. That's what the doctor made clear. That surviving the surgery is the strongest indicator of overall survival. But each day that the baby lives is a bigger sign that she will be all right. Runa will have to stay here for several days; they cannot risk premature labor when the child is this small."

Erik nodded, his face solemn. "Can we visit her?"

"Imagine what she would say if we didn't. She'll be so bored, I know. I'll need you guys to help me out; we'll visit her in shifts."

"Of course we will," I assured him.

Andy bent to study my face with his brown eyes — happy eyes now. "Hana. You knew something, didn't you? You had some sort of feeling, right before the doctor came."

Erik turned to me, surprised.

I hesitated. "Not exactly. I was trying to do what my grandmother does — use my inner eye. I pictured a little girl; I could see her face very well. She looked at me. She didn't have blue eyes; they were brown eyes, like yours. I — just got a sense from her that everything was all right, and I opened my eyes and you saw me, and then the doctor came in."

He took my hand and squeezed it. Then he laughed. "God, I'm so relieved. I have to get back inside; I want to be in the room when Runa wakes up."

"Keep in touch," Erik said. "And take breaks. Make sure you eat. She needs you to stay healthy."

Andy gave us a thumbs-up and went back into the building.

Erik looked at me. "Well, thank God." He took a deep breath, then said, "I need to get back on the case. We've got a lot of interviews to do, and Greg is handling everything alone right now."

"Yeah. And we have more than fifty children coming to the tea house in a couple hours, so I have to run, too. I have time for one kiss."

He bent down, smiling, and pressed his lips to mine. "Haniska," he said.

"Detective Wolf."

"See you tonight. I'll text you."

I waved and watched him lope off on his long legs. How strange, really, to have to search for murderers as a full-time job. And how sad. I wondered what had drawn Erik to his career at the beginning, before he knew the disturbing truths he knew today.

I shrugged and returned to my car.

That afternoon I stood in a full tearoom, surveying the sweet faces of our visitors and their doting parents as my grandmother swept grandly onto our stage, wearing her "Christmas cape" of Hungarian red, green, and white. My mother had made it years ago; it was heavy silk, and it was rather breathtaking — certainly a sight to impress children, especially when Grandma flung it out to the sides and let it fall back into place over her tea house uniform.

"Good afternoon, children!"

"Good afternoon!" the children called back.

"Jó napot!" she cried.

"Yo nah pote!" the children managed. Pretty good.

"Who was here last year?" Grandma asked.

Several tiny hands went into the air.

She homed in on those children. "What are we celebrating today?"

"St. Nicholas!" said a few tiny voices.

"Yes, Nicholas! In Hungary, we call him Mikulás, or Szent Miklós, but the same guy! He is a famous saint who loves all people, especially children. He is like a cousin to your Santa Claus."

The children beamed. I had to hand it to my grandmother; she was always able to find a simple way of presenting the complex. St. Nicholas was often equated with Santa Claus, but it depended on the country, the tradition, the belief. There was a real saint, Nicholas of Myra, on whom the legend was based. But the Mikulás who had evolved into a Christmas tradition held the complexities of the passage of years.

"Today, we asked Mikulás to come to us with his assistants, his Krampus. Can you say that?"

"Krompoosh," the children said.

Some of the children screamed, and my grandmother nodded. "Yes, yes, some of you remember that one Krampus is good, but the other is bad. One is an angel, with a good heart like Mikulás, but the evil Krampus wants to chase you and give you coal and tell Santa bad things about you."

As she said this, Domo and Margie crept into the room. Domo had been forced to wear the bad Krampus outfit since high school, and he had once hated it. Now he loved the role, took the day off work to play it, and acted like a total ham. It was Margie's first year as the good Krampus. My mother had made her an angel costume, with a halo that glittered with gold sequins. Her blonde hair was held up in a bun, and she looked beautiful, gliding along in her white dress.

Domo, on the other hand, had been given the bottom of a Bigfoot costume and the weird elk-like horns of the traditional devil beast. He had painted his face in an appropriately ugly way, and he crept around the tables, making the children laugh and scream. Margie then glided up behind him and touched him with a wand that sent him scurrying away to the next table. Then she, as the angel, handed each child a gold star (which we had painstakingly cut out a few days earlier).

Finally, my grandma called, "Mikulás!

Can you come to see the children, and save them from this bad devil?"

My father, resplendent in the pope-like robes of Mikulás, complete with a tall red-and-white hat, came gliding into the room, pushing a cart filled with little plastic shoes. Each one contained chocolates, marbles, a Hungarian dancing doll, and a tiny scroll with the history of Mikulás printed upon it. "Good Krampus, do these children have pure hearts in this Advent?"

Margie glided forward, holding her wand. The children watched her. She turned to look at Domo, who capered around like an idiot, and then she looked back and nodded. "Yes. All of them, Mikulás."

My father sent a benevolent glance around the room. "Children, help me send away this devil. We do not want evil in our hearts at Christmastime. We want to love everyone and do good for all."

He instructed them to yell "Go away!" to Domo. My brother proceeded to act like a dog who had been sent away from his family, dragging his feet and looking over his shoulder. Some of the parents said "Awwww" in sympathy, and then Domo ran back into the room, making monster faces.

Laughing, the children cried, "Go away!" again and again until Domo finally dragged himself into the back room; Margie went to hug Szent Miklós, and everyone clapped. Then my father and his pretty angel companion, with help from my mother and me, passed shoes to all the children.

While the tiny visitors investigated their treasure, my grandmother returned to the edge of the stage. "Who remembers what else good children get in Hungary at Christmastime? Because we ladies are all Hungarian here, ya? So you get the same treats that the children in Hungary receive. Who remembers?"

A tiny hand went up. "The pretty cookies."

My grandmother clapped. "Yes! Can you say *mézeskalács*?"

"May-zesh-koh-lotch," the tiny voices repeated. *Perfectly.* I exchanged a surprised glance with my mother.

My father, almost as big a ham as Domo, looked around the room, making eye contact with the rapt children. "We know you have been good. But have your parents? Do they also deserve *mézeskalács*?"

"No!" yelled some tiny voices, and much hilarity ensued. The parents exchanged some eye rolls from table to table, but I found myself thinking, *No, some of you have not been good. We have dark sides, or my*

*boyfriend wouldn't have to investigate mur-
ders.*

Eventually, the Hungarian St. Nicholas asked everyone who had been good to raise their hands. Everyone raised a hand, but some children jokingly tried to pull their parents' hands down again.

Then François appeared, looking perfect in a white silk jacket my mother had made him when he was first hired, a blazer re-splendent with red and green beads at the collar. On his tray he bore the handmade *mézeskalács,* a recipe my grandmother had taught him but which he now knew by heart, a variation on traditional gingerbread that incorporated a touch of honey and a thinner dough, which resulted in a lighter cookie. These cookies were famous for their art: each one was hand-painted with piped-on traditional floral and lace patterns. François had taken to this Hungarian specialty like a duck to water, and the cook-ies were literally works of art.

He set them down on a side table with a flourish, and my mother and I, along with Mikulás and his angel, grabbed platters of them and began delivering them to tables.

This brought a communal "Ah!" as people got a look at their treats.

Meanwhile, my grandmother was getting

ready to sing. "Who remembers our Mikulás songs?" she asked the crowd. Some children raised their hands.

"Good. You help me teach the others, and then we make a circle around the tree."

She began to clap. "You sing like this: *Mikulás, Mikulás, kedves Mikulás . . .*"

The children sang after her in sweet little voices. Suddenly, I imagined that in three or four years, Runa's girl could be sitting among them, warbling Mikulás songs.

"Come, now! Szent Miklós and the beautiful angel will help us make a circle around the beautiful tree. We have sent away the bad Krampus, and now we sing songs to Nicholas about how we wait for him, and for Santa later on."

Grandma marched down the steps of the dais and headed for the tree. Children left their seats and flowed toward it, as well, ready to be diverted and probably hoping for more surprises.

As I watched them, my eye was caught by something in the doorway. *Someone* in the doorway. "Oh God," I murmured. It was my mother's friend with three annoying names. What had they been? Oh yes. *Alessandra Spencer-Malandro.*

She glided past the circle of children, who were now moving clockwise at a slow pace under my grandmother's ministrations, and stared at them as though she wasn't sure what children were for.

I hid my smirk because she reached me first. "Hello, Lana."

"Hana," I corrected. I suspected that she knew my name and mispronounced it just because that's the kind of thing she liked to do.

"Oh yes, forgive me. I wonder if I left my gloves behind? They're pale pink cashmere."

She had been wearing the gloves when she left; I remembered that. Suddenly, my radar switched on. The gloves weren't the reason she was back. She wanted something.

"Gee, no. We have a lost-and-found box, but there's nothing in it today. If you'd like, you can try later in the week; maybe people will bring something back. If someone accidentally walked off with them . . ."

"Oh yes — well — maybe I can hunt under a few tables," she said.

We spoke in our regular voices because the room was currently loud. I shook my head at her. "Not during an event, if you please. There are people at the tables right now."

"Oh, of course I can wait. I'll just go in your back room there, if that's okay?"

No, of course it wasn't okay. What did this

woman want? "Um, Ms. Spencer-Ma—"

"Call me Alex, dear." She was close to me now, so close that I was overwhelmed by her perfume.

"Alex, our chef works in the back room, and he does not like to be disturbed." François, finished with the distribution of his beautiful cookies, sailed past us in his resplendent silk, the large tray dangling from his hand, and disappeared behind the door.

Out of excuses, she nodded. "All right, then, I can come another time." Then, with an attempt at bonding, she said, "So, I heard you had police here yesterday."

My body stiffened. I kept my voice low, although the singing had reached a high volume and there was no danger of us being heard. "I'm sorry? Where might you have heard that?"

She shook her head, trying to appear playful but looking oddly miserable. "I'll never tell. I wonder why they were here, though?"

I put my hands on my hips, trying to summon the proper words to tell her how incredibly inappropriate just about everything she had said was, and how much I wanted her to leave and never come back.

Apparently, she saw all this in my face, because she dropped the act and allowed me to see the worry on her face. It made her look ten years older. She touched my arm. "Hana, I know I'm intruding. But I — have reason to want to know this."

"Alex, listen. We have this event right now —" Something in her eyes made me relent. "All right, fine. Come in the back room."

I led her into François's workspace, where he was chatting with Domo. My brother's monstrous attire contrasted comically with the delicate way he was eating his holiday cookie.

I took shameful pleasure in Alex's response to Domo, with his fur and antlers; she stiffened, and her eyes widened with something like fear.

"My brother is part of the event," I told her. "He is Krampus, the bad companion of St. Nicholas. An old tradition."

"Ah," she said.

Luckily, François seemed just about finished, so he didn't scowl at our interruption.

"Hana, I will leave soon," he said. "Did you need anything else?"

"No, you're good to go. Thanks, François. Those cookies looked amazing. There was an extra one on my tray, and I ate it. Sublime. It's such a shame we have to eat your creations."

For that, I got his Gallic shrug. "Food is to be consumed, as is art."

Alex horned in on the conversation, because — of course she would. "You have a real philosopher here," she said. "Hold on to this one."

François sent her a blank glance, then nodded and went to the corner for his coat. "Hana, I hung the Christmas jacket near the cupboard," he said, pointing to the corner of the room.

"Thank you. Are you sure you don't want to take it home to help you seduce Claire?"

François laughed right out loud, and Domo joined him, his antlers wobbling. This was a rare butterfly of a moment; I had not seen François really laugh since October, when our groundskeeper was tackled by someone who thought he was an intruder. François's sense of humor was generally well hidden, and I felt proud that I had elicited his laughter.

"I can think of better ways to seduce Claire," François said. "But thank you. Domo, it was good to see you! Good-bye to all." He waved to me and sent one more confused look to Alex before he swept out of the room.

Domo's phone buzzed on the table. He looked at his text and said, "Ah! Picture time! Krampus is needed in the main hall." He stood up, looking suddenly huge with his high antlers, and nodded to me and Alex. He didn't seem particularly interested in an introduction, and since Alex had intruded on our event, I didn't feel she deserved one. Domo swept out in his hairy costume, and Alex seated herself at the large table; I turned to her, not certain what to say, and my mother hurried in. She stopped abruptly in the doorway and said, "Alex? What — who — ?"

Alex held up a hand. "I'm so sorry, Maggie. I told Hana I didn't mean to intrude. I was just looking for my gloves —"

"Let's not start with that again," I said sternly.

She looked as chastened as a child. "No, all right. That was my excuse for coming here. I'm concerned. I heard the police were here yesterday."

My mother's blue eyes flew to my face, and I shook my head. "Not from me, she didn't."

She looked back at Alex. "From whom, Alex? We did not broadcast that fact to the public."

"Well, from my husband, actually. He was here, and he felt that some of the serving men looked — official."

Her husband? I tried to recall how many men had been at the event for Balog. Upon reflection, there had been quite a few: perhaps a dozen or more. I wondered which one of them had been Mr. Malandro. But something wasn't making sense. I said, "Why would that send you here today? You must be very busy with your job."

Her face reddened slightly. "Yes. Good question. The thing is — I want to make sure — I mean, if they suspect anyone. I just want to clarify —" She paused, at a loss for words.

My mother relaxed slightly and sat down across from her. "Is there something you want to tell me, Alex?"

Her old friend softened, and for a moment I saw a trace of the girls they had once been. Perhaps my mother had always been the strong one; perhaps Alex had always needed that strength.

"I'll go clear up," I said. "Things are winding down?"

My mother nodded. "Yes — some families have already left. Dad and Grandma are wiping tables and saying good-bye. Margie is having lots of fun, I think. Such a good way to get her interacting with people, Domo's shy flower."

"Yeah. Okay, I'll be right back."

I returned to the room and joined my family members in clearing tables and saying farewells, finding coats and shaking tiny hands. Several people wanted pictures taken with Margie the angel and with Mikulás, and even more wanted photos with Domo's evil Krampus. Domo was nothing but friendly now, and the children sensed his goodness. They wanted to climb right into his lap, despite his ugly attire, and I took picture after picture on people's cell phones as their children, and sometimes their whole family, posed with my hairy, antlered brother.

"This is going to be my Christmas card," said one woman when she viewed the results on her phone. "That gorgeous tree, and these wonderful costumes. Thank you so much. There is nothing else like this at Christmastime, even in Chicago. I wouldn't miss it!"

Pleased, I smiled and thanked her and turned to take a picture of a tiny girl in a red dress who was intent on pulling hairs out of Domo's Bigfoot costume. He said, "Ow," each time she tugged on them, and giggles bubbled out of her while her grinning mother took a video.

Yes, this really was my favorite event of the year. But by the time we had ushered all the happy children out the door, I was exhausted, and I could tell that my costumed family members were, as well. Domo lifted Margie in the air and her laugh was like the tinkling of a Christmas bell. He swung toward me, antlers wobbling. "Margie and I have a date with our couch, some Chinese food, and some Netflix."

"See you later!" I called, and they left.

My father loomed up with his pope's hat. "Good job, all of you tea ladies."

"Thanks, Dad. You helped to make it such a special day," I said. He bowed, then took off the hat. "Grandma gave me some janitorial tasks, so I think I'll remove my holy garb."

We grinned at each other, and he went into the back room.

My grandmother finished talking to the final group, which contained a person who spoke Hungarian. She had chatted animatedly for a long time, and now her voice was almost hoarse.

She walked to me and patted my head. "Another fine St. Nicholas Day, Haniska."

"The best yet, Grandma. Really."

She sighed. "Ya. Now Grandpa and I will warm up some chicken soup and start planning for Christmas. Will you bring your wolf, Christmas Day?"

"Uh —" We hadn't talked about it. And Erik's mother had said something about expecting me at their house, which could be awkward. I didn't intend to miss my own family's Christmas celebration. "He might be working. You never know, with his job. I'll be there for sure, Grandma."

"Good." She patted my arm and walked toward the back room. She returned soon afterward with her coat. "Your dad is finishing the sweeping; François's kitchen is already clean. Grandpa is outside."

I leaned in to give her a kiss on the cheek. "You did a great job today."

She nodded, pleased. "And tomorrow we rest," she said. We had a rare day off in an otherwise jam-packed month. She put on her coat and smiled at me, then moved toward the front entrance. Domo and Margie were close behind her, and they all disappeared with a final wave.

I spent a few minutes studying my phone and answering texts I hadn't had time to read.

Suddenly, Alex Spencer-Malandro appeared, looking pale but composed. "Thank you for allowing me to crash your party, Hana." She smiled. "Your mother is a good person. You should treasure her."

"I do," I said.

"Merry Christmas," she murmured, and whisked past me to the exit.

My father had removed the rest of his Mikulás costume, and he appeared beside me in jeans and a T-shirt, jingling a set of keys in his hand. "Is your mom ready?" he asked.

"She just finished talking to that Malandro woman. Do you know her?"

"Alessandra? I *thought* that was her! Wow, I haven't seen her for years. We got together a few times when your mom and I were first married. She's kind of —" He stopped, clearly not wanting to be rude.

"Annoying? Obnoxious? Self-centered?"

"Sometimes," he said. "But she means well, overall."

"Huh. Okay, here comes Mom."

My mother approached, coat in hand.

"What was that all about?" I asked her.

She studied me with troubled blue eyes. "You should probably mention this to Erik. Alex's husband, Tony, is a bit of a gambler. He and Sandor had started to place wagers on their chess games —"

I held up a hand. "Wait — that guy with the gray temples, the handsome doctor who said he played chess with Sandor? *That's* Alex's husband?"

"Yes, Tony Malandro. He's always had this gambling urge, apparently, much to Alessandra's dismay. The stakes were getting higher and higher, and when Sandor died, Tony owed him more than one hundred thousand dollars."

"What!"

"He needs to get in a program," my father said. "That's an addiction."

My mother shrugged. "Alex and Tony are wealthy, but his gambling has put a dent in their finances and a rift in their marriage. Apparently, Tony was talking rather wildly before Sandor died, suggesting that the debt was Sandor's fault, and that as Tony's friend he never should have let him bet that kind of money."

I thought of Sandor's wall full of Herend treasures. "Sandor had an expensive hobby. He probably welcomed the gambling windfalls as a way to fund his Herend purchases."

"I don't know. But Alex is worried. She doesn't really think her husband is capable of murder, but the timing of his erratic behavior and Sandor's death has her upset."

"But what does that have to do with you?"

"Well, Tony told her it looked as though police were here yesterday. Apparently, he felt a bit uncomfortable about it. She wanted to know if I'd heard anything."

"Maybe he's guilty," I said.

My mother nodded. "They were all guilty,

right? Of treating him badly in his last few days."

"But only one person killed him. That's the only one the police want. Everyone else can stop worrying. And if he is the guilty one, his wife's chat with you isn't going to help him."

My parents looked at me with surprise. Perhaps I sounded grim.

"I never knew you were such a realist," my father said. "My dreamy Hana has been influenced by her police connection."

"The law is the law," I said, and my eyes lighted on the World Tree across the room. "And anyone who would kill another person belongs in the realm of suffering, in Ördög's cauldron of souls."

My mother was more compassionate. "Or perhaps they were already there," she said.

CHAPTER 9
THREE SPARKLING STARS

The next morning, I met Livia Parravicini on the campus of Riverwood University. The campus was small but attractive, located in front of a forest preserve and tucked beneath a number of ancient elms that gave it a fairy-tale quality. Livia had texted me and suggested we meet in a place less small and stuffy than her office. I made my way past two giant lecture halls and an ivy-covered library, then spied a sign that said "Student Union." There was ample parking in front of this handsome building; in fact, as Livia had promised, the campus was essentially deserted. The next building, a grand brick five-story affair, had police tape around the perimeter. Some of the gray feeling returned, but I consciously turned away and focused on the pretty Christmas tree in front of the Union.

I climbed out of my car and made my way to the front staircase with its side ramp. The

Union was made up of one giant main hall, filled with conversational groupings and study nooks. A central fireplace, complete now with dancing flames and a cozy crackling sound, was surrounded by comfy chairs and tiny tables where students could sit and talk, or study, or share coffee or some other hot beverage on this cold day. I saw Livia at one of the tables, drinking out of a big red teacup. She waved at me. There were a few young people scattered around, along with a lonely-looking person at the information desk, a girl whose name tag said "Brady."

"Can I help you?" she asked, seemingly with little hope that she could.

"I'm meeting Dr. Parravicini; I see her over there by the fireplace."

"Okay, great," Brady said.

I lingered for a moment. "Do you get to go on Christmas break soon?"

She shrugged. "I'm not actually going home for Christmas, so I volunteered to work. There are some students who need the Rivulet to be open so they have a place to hang out."

"The Rivulet? That's the name of the Union?"

"Yeah. Because we're Riverwood."

I had figured that out. "Not going home for Christmas, huh? Where do you live?"

Brady stroked a piece of her pretty brown hair. "Utah," she said. "It's too far to go, really, and very expensive to fly at this time of year. My parents are going to come see me in the New Year, and we'll Skype and stuff."

"So — what will you do?"

"There are some professors who throw a big Christmas dinner. I'll go to that with the other kids who stay on campus. We have kind of a party, and then some of us take a bus up to Chicago to look at the Christmas windows. It's actually pretty fun."

"Well, that's good." It did sound appealing, although I could not imagine spending a Christmas Day without my family. "Thanks, Brady. Merry Christmas." I waved and moved toward Livia, who was sipping again from her cup.

She pointed at it as I approached. "Hot chocolate with whipped cream. They're selling it at that little window there. Do you want some?"

I did. I wandered to the window and asked for hot chocolate with the works. Moments later I had my own big red teacup filled with cocoa, plenteous whipped cream, and chocolate shavings on top of that. "Oooh. Thank you," I said to the woman behind the counter. "Happy holidays to you."

"You, too," she said, offering a brief thumbs-up.

I returned to Livia, feeling suddenly festive and nostalgic for my own college experience. She waved to the seat across from her with a graceful gesture. I had wondered briefly when I woke up why on my day off I had agreed to meet with a woman whom I barely knew, but now I remembered: Livia was extremely likable. She projected friendliness and fun.

"Ciao, come stai!" Livia said with a bright smile.

I set my cup down and settled into my comfy chair across from her. "Okay. Starting with the basics. That's 'Hello, how are you,' right? Oh, this fireplace is wonderful."

"*Sì,* 'Hello, how are you.' Or you could say, *Come stai oggi?* which is 'How are you today?' "

"Come stai oggi," I repeated.

"Nice accent. You said you spoke Italian in school?"

"Yes — I took it for two years in high school. But I didn't go abroad or anything, and you know how quickly you can forget. And high school was a long time ago."

"*Sì.* This is *deplorevole.* Regrettable." She took another sip, obviously savoring the flavor of her chocolate. "So, what makes you want to learn Italian?"

I put a finger into my whipped cream and tasted it. "Mmm. I have this fantasy of taking my boyfriend to Italy. It just seems like the perfect place to bring him for our first vacation together. And I thought someday I might just give him a gift certificate that says, 'We are going to Florence, or the Amalfi Coast, or Rome.' I guess I'm chasing a fantasy."

She shrugged. "Not hard to make that fantasy come true. Just buy tickets. I can give you advice — times of year to go, where to stay, things like this." She touched the bright red handle of her cup. "This is a new boyfriend? A new lover?"

"Yes, fairly new. Since October."

Her wide brown eyes lit up. "Ah, *L'Italia è per gli in-namorati!*"

I sipped my drink and smiled at her. "I know that one. Italy is for lovers."

"Yes. We can have you ready to go in no time. Focus on conversational Italian. When are you looking to travel?"

"Oh, nothing's set. He has a very unpredictable schedule; he's a police detective."

"Police?" Her smile wavered. "A homicide detective? Named Wolf, perhaps?"

"Yes! How did you —"

"I have an appointment to meet with him

191

today. He wants to interview me about my relationship with Sandor Balog."

"Oh — yes."

"I told him that I preferred to meet here, in the open, rather than in my home. Some other professors feel the same. I know he has contacted several, and many are coming back to campus for the uh — chat."

"It's important," I said. "He needs the information. It's a very big puzzle, and he's working with very tiny pieces."

She nodded. "Yes, I understand that." She sighed. Then she sent me a naughty smile. "So, a policeman. They seem so cold and unfeeling always. Yes?"

"No. They have to wear that mask for their jobs. Objectivity is a process, not a personality."

She shrugged. "Yes, I suppose. So what is my lesson? Will you also tell me how to greet someone in Hungarian?"

"Yes — well, it depends on the time of day. There is a different greeting for morning, afternoon, evening, night."

"My goodness. Well, it is morning. So I would say?"

"*Jó reggelt,* or *Jó reggelt kívánok.* That is a good morning, until about nine or ten, at which point you would say *Jó napot kívánok.*"

"I think the pronunciation is not so hard, but the alphabet! *Oi.* Sandor lost patience with me over that."

"It is difficult to go from English to Hungarian." I reached into my purse. "My grandma gave me these books to lend you. Years ago, she tutored for some extra money. She used these with her students." I handed her two basic primers in Hungarian vocabulary.

Livia brightened. "Oh, wonderful! Thank her for me. It will help to look at the words while you tell me the pronunciations. I tried to do this with a lesson online, but the instructor spoke much too quickly. I need to start simply, I am afraid. But I love the sound of the language. I want to learn, and I want to visit Budapest." She pointed to a bag on the floor. "I have materials for you, too."

"Good. Both to Budapest and the materials."

"*Bene,*" she corrected.

"*Bene,*" I amended. "And also, *jó.*"

"*Yo,*" she repeated, grinning. "This is fun, Hana!"

"Yes, it is." I studied her pretty face, her long chestnut hair. "I'm going to invite you to my next tea party."

"Tea party? At the tea house?"

"No — I just had one with my women friends." I told her about my uncle and the birthday gift, and the lovely evening where we talked and dreamed and drank tea together.

Livia's eyes were shining. "Oh, *please* do include me next time. I am afraid to say — to admit — I don't have many female friends. On campus, we academics tend to be rather competitive. And outside of campus, I focus on my love life. I am a passionate Italian woman, after all," she joked. "Beyond that, and preparing for my classes, there is no time left."

"You have to make time for your friends. If I ever forget that, my friend Katie calls and reminds me."

"Yes. I need a friend Katie." She smiled again and played with a necklace that glittered against her black turtleneck sweater.

"That's a pretty piece," I said. "Are those diamonds?"

She nodded thoughtfully. "Yes, the middle one is. I think the outer ones are zirconia. It's a star, see? It shines very bright." It was a beautiful pendant, perhaps an inch wide, and it caught the lights of the Union and sparkled each time Livia moved. She sighed. "It was a gift from Sandor, actually. Last

Christmas. We had been dating a month or so."

My inner antennae rose. "Sandor? How long did you keep dating after that?"

She shrugged. "Perhaps another month or two. I knew from the start it wouldn't last, but he was an enjoyable distraction. Attentive, romantic, fun. He never claimed that he wanted something permanent. We enjoyed each other's company, that's all — or so I thought. When I decided to end things — I wanted to start dating someone else, actually — he acted quite upset for a while. I finally had it out with him and made him admit he didn't really want anything permanent with me. He agreed. But you know what? He had hoped to keep me as an option forever. An ever-available dalliance. I don't even think he was exclusive with me."

I thought of Sandor's shelf full of beautiful things. "So he was a hypocrite."

She shrugged. "Yes, I suppose. There was something about Sandor, though. You couldn't stay angry with him."

I nodded. "I can see that. I knew him, too. He and I loved the same store, an antiques store —"

She pointed at me. "Timeless Treasures?"

"Yes. I'm friends with the proprietor, Falken. I'm there all the time, and I would

195

encounter Sandor there quite often."

"Oh yes, he scoured the shelves! He dragged me with him on at least two occasions. It's a delightful store. That Falken has an antique-jewelry display up at the front counter that just makes me drool."

I remembered what she had said to Yvonne Yves in the tea house ladies' room. "So — even recently, Sandor wasn't entirely willing to give you up, was he?"

She shrugged. "I suppose he kept hoping that I would at least keep him as one of my — men friends. But believe it or not, I am a one-man woman." She held up her hand, on which an emerald ring glittered and distracted her briefly. "I bought this at Falken's jewelry counter, by the way."

I didn't miss this adept subject change, but I went with it. "Yes, it's a magical store. I'm going Christmas shopping today, and that will be one of my stops. I have such a long list, I really need to get started."

Livia looked into her cup. "It's a blessing to have a long list, really."

Her loneliness hit me like a wave, surprising me. "Livia, listen —"

A shadow appeared next to us. I looked up to see another of the professors from the funeral — what was the German professor's name? Weber. He held out a hand. "Hello,

I'm Hans Weber. Are you a friend of Livia's?"

I shook his hand. It seemed presumptuous of him to simply walk up to our table, and I turned to Livia, who shrugged. "We're having a language session, Hans. Did you need something?" It wasn't unfriendly, but it was encouraging him to go away.

Hans Weber grinned and pulled up a chair. "I can take a hint, but first I must know where I recognize this young lady from. Do I know you?"

He smiled at me in what seemed a genuinely friendly way. He had a full head of reddish-brown hair; he wore a Riverwood tracksuit that didn't seem very warm, but then again it was almost hot in front of the fireplace. He had straight teeth and an appealing smile. Hans had charisma.

"You probably remember me from Maggie's Tea House, where I was waiting on tables when your group met to pay tribute to Sandor Balog," I said.

Weber's brows rose. "That was concise. And did you and Livia know each other before — ?"

"No," Livia said. "We are brand-new friends, doing a language exchange. Hana is teaching me some Hungarian. As Sandor had said he would do."

"Ah," Weber said. A small scowl appeared on his face before he smiled again at me.

I said, "My name is Hana Keller. My family owns the tea shop."

"Well, good to meet you, Hana. It was such a treat to see you pretty ladies in front of the fireplace, like an advertisement for a ski lodge."

Livia and I laughed, and she touched the top of his hand. A small gesture, but somehow an intimate one. Ah. Weber was her new lover.

Still processing this, I looked up to see Wanda Lee approaching our table. She pulled up a chair and slumped down next to Weber. "Is this where we're all awaiting interrogation?" she said. "I swear, these policemen are so rude! I have a million things to do today."

Livia looked uncomfortable and shot a look at me. "The gentleman doing our interviews has an impossible task ahead of him. Hana has made me see that."

Wanda Lee turned to me. "Hana? I'm sorry, I don't —"

"She's from the tea house," Weber said. "She and Livia are new friends."

I could tell that Livia was trying to hold back, but it seemed to burst out of her: "She's also dating the man who will question us today."

This surprised both Weber and Lee. Wanda's eyes widened and grew rather distressed. Weber looked shocked, then amused. "Well, a small world," he said. "And how did you come to be dating a homicide detective?"

"I reported a murder."

They all laughed until they realized I was not kidding. Finally, Hans Weber snapped his fingers. "Ah yes! I remember the story in the paper. A woman was poisoned."

"Yes." I still hated to think of it.

Livia's eyes sparkled above her sparkling star pendant. "And you fell in love with the man who came to investigate? Oh, *romantica*!"

Wanda Lee still looked uncomfortable. "Listen, these guys coming today are going to be reasonable, right?" She directed the question at me.

"I'm not sure what you mean."

"I mean, they don't jump to conclusions?"

"I'm sure they won't."

Hans poked Wanda in the arm. "Need to unburden your soul?"

She frowned. "I have no problem admitting that I was dating Sandor before he decided to go back to his wife. We were —" She shook her head, blushing slightly.

"Anyway, I used to hang around in his office while he finished his work. He had all those china pieces, and sometimes they would get dusty, which I can't abide. I'm too neat. So I would polish each one; it took me forever." She looked at me, wide-eyed. "But the reality is my fingerprints are probably on every surface in that office. And I heard they're taking fingerprints today."

I sipped my chocolate. "I would think you just have to tell them what you told me. They're not monsters. They're very nice men, Greg and Erik both."

The three academics exchanged a glance that suggested that they would prefer not to be interrogated.

Then Hans Weber laughed. "Oh, look who we have here. The new head of the World Languages Department."

I turned to look at the doorway, where Yvonne Yves had entered with a swirl of her pleated coat. She looked like a model on a Paris runway: thin, well dressed, and utterly humorless. She spotted the table of her colleagues and lifted a hand.

Hans sighed. "If you'll excuse us, we have a meeting with our new leader."

Livia shrugged. "Fill me in later, Hans." Again, a subtle but intimate connection between them, this time with a quick, intense glance.

Hans and Wanda left to join Yvonne at a table near the entrance.

I smiled at Livia. "How long have you and Hans Weber been an item?"

She looked surprised, then amused. "Clever girl. And about ten months. He's the one who persuaded me to break up with Sandor."

"And is he more devoted than Sandor was?"

"Yes." It pleased her, clearly. "He's proposed to me several times, actually. He'll probably do it again on Christmas."

"Why does he have to keep proposing?"

She smiled and stretched. "I put him off. I like my drama; I also like my space. I want to get married — and I'm pretty sure I want to marry him. But I'm going to make sure he really wants it, too."

"Fair enough. Should we get down to business?"

"We absolutely should, Hana *mia.*"

I spent the next half hour bent over a notebook, jotting things while Livia pronounced words with her alluring accent. Then I taught her the basics that I had known since childhood. "This is just nursery school Hungarian," I told her when we finished. "For the sophisticated stuff, we have to bring in the big guns, who are Maggie and Juliana. Or my grandfather."

"Wonderful. How good to have your whole family as a connection. Your tea house is lovely, by the way."

"Thank you! It's especially nice at Christmastime, I think."

Livia leaned back in her chair; the fire behind her created a halo around her dark hair. "We can have our next session there, *sì*?"

My next two stops were Christmas shopping related. I had wanted to investigate Stones by Sparkle, and when I drove past, I saw an open parking spot on the street that was impossible to resist. The spot was not far from where I had parked when I saw the boy in the snow — the boy who had ended up being Frank. Today there were no snowflakes, but it was still cold when I darted out of the car, paid the meter, and crossed the road to the stairs in front of Stones by Sparkle. Pine swags wound around the metal banisters, and bright holly berries appeared at intervals in the green. The branches were real, and a fragrant treat for my senses as I climbed the stairs.

The moment I entered, I felt a strong wave of something relaxing. The store felt inexplicably comforting. The walls were lined with alluring Christmas-themed wares, from candles to decorative glass paperweights to light-up Christmas villages. In the center of the space were displays of jewelry, glinting in lighted boxes, and providing justification for the store's name. Necklaces, bracelets, and rings clustered artfully around patches of faux snow against a black velvet background. In one box were simply stones, divided into categories of "precious" and "semiprecious."

A woman approached me as I gazed into the box. She had shoulder-length blonde hair and warm brown eyes, and she peered at me over turquoise reading glasses. "Hello, dear. Can I help you with anything today?"

"I'm not sure yet. I am Christmas shopping, but I've also just been dying to get in here since the store appeared. You've been here at least a couple of months now, right?"

"Oh, more than that. Grand opening was August fifteenth."

"Time flies." I grinned at her. "And I work weird hours."

"Yeah? Where do you work?"

"At Maggie's Tea House, over on —"

"Oh, I know Maggie's Tea House! It's terrific. I went to a wedding shower there last year."

"My mother is Maggie. So I'm part of the family business."

"How nice." Her smile was warm and genuine. "You know what? I met your mother when I was there. She has that china-doll look, and those big blue eyes."

"That's her."

"If you don't mind, I would suggest a gift for her. I don't know what your budget is, but this isn't too expensive."

"Lead on," I said, intrigued.

She walked me over to the next aisle of lighted jewelry tables and pointed at a delicate necklace with a silver star pendant of about two inches. Inside the star were three sapphires, the first seeming to cling to the star itself, and the others seeming to hold on to each other. It looked like a trail of blue fire inside a heavenly body.

"Wow! Are those real sapphires?"

"Swarovski crystals. But a quality necklace. I only work with two artisans right now, and both of them do great work."

"It's beautiful. And perfect, I think. She doesn't wear a lot of necklaces, but you're right — this would go so well with her coloring." I turned to her, feeling skeptical. "You really remember her eyes from a meeting a year ago?"

She shrugged. "My brain is like that. I'm

a sensory person. Sights and smells especially stay with me."

"Your store certainly looks and smells great. I'm sure I won't leave without buying a candle or two."

"Great!"

I peered at the price tag for the pendant. She was right: it was affordable. "And I'll take the necklace."

"Excellent. I'll wrap it up, and you keep looking around if you want."

"I'll do that. Are you — Sparkle?"

She laughed. "I am Sparkle, and, yes, that is my real name. Sparkle Bascomb. My parents were poetic souls who said that the world shone more brightly the moment I was born. Isn't that sweet?"

"It is," I said, studying a ceramic Christmas house with gingerbread-looking trim. On an impulse, I said, "I was near here the other day, and I saw a guy right next to your store. Long story, but the police ended up searching your alley."

She had opened the glass case to take out the necklace, but her eyes, suddenly sharp, studied me in more detail. "During the snowstorm? You saw that kid with no coat on?"

"Yes! That's why I noticed him. He was

making me cold, wandering around without a coat."

"Me, too. I hadn't opened yet, but I was making a display, and I saw him out the window. And, yes, the police showed up that afternoon and sealed off the whole alley. Huge crime scene, with big lights and stuff. And they questioned me, of course."

"Wow. Right in the center of the action, huh?"

"Even more than you'd think. I told them I saw him throw something into the tree."

The pine tree. I had laughed because it looked as though he were about to walk into it. His hands had been in his pockets, but when he turned they were visible again, pale and gloveless . . . "Do you know what it was?"

"They insisted that I go out with them and show them where he stood and what he threw. I wasn't sure. But I showed them, and all they found was a lipstick and a discarded beer can."

"Huh." I had moved on to a display of pillar candles, all of them scented. I lifted one and breathed in the aroma of cedar.

"What made you call the police in the first place?" she asked. "I got a weird feeling at the time, but not enough to call the authorities."

"Uh — it's hard to explain. But I had a bad vibe."

"Really?" Her eyes brightened significantly, and she moved toward me, pendant in hand. She leaned in and studied my face, then nodded. "Ah. You have a psychic ability."

"Uh —"

"I do, too, a little bit. I don't make a big deal of it, but it's why I'm so good at this job. I know what's right for people. Not just what looks good on them, but what will make them happy. I learned I had that ability way back in high school, and it's helped me in my career. It's why I was able to open my own shop. I had started out just selling stuff out of my home, but I'm really good at matching people to their desires. Huge client base now." She wasn't bragging, but she was confident.

"The store is so glittery, it's — enchanting."

She nodded with a pleased expression, looking around appreciatively at her own space. Then she turned back to me with those sharp brown eyes. "So what happened to that boy? I felt sorry for him; his face was so vulnerable. Did he do something bad?"

"No. I know him, actually. They questioned him and released him. But — he provided information for them. A man was murdered."

Her eyes grew round. "Oh no! That professor who was killed? That was somehow related to — well, you probably don't know much more than I do, huh? The police are so closemouthed when something like that happens."

The door opened, and a group of women entered, their eyes bright with the love of shopping. "Welcome, ladies," Sparkle said. "Let me know if I can help you find anything."

Then she leaned toward me, her voice soft and confidential. "I saw that professor's picture in the paper. He was here once; he commissioned a ring with one of my artisans. A beautiful thing with an amber stone."

My brain jumped to the obvious question: for whom had he made the ring? His wife? One of his many girlfriends? And yet how many men were thoughtful enough to have a special ring made for *any* woman?

Sparkle nodded, as though I had said my thoughts out loud. "Anyway. Back to shopping. I can prove to you that I know what gifts people will like best. You haven't even seen the table that will be your favorite. I call it the snow table. Come and see."

Intrigued, I followed her to the back of the store, where a table sat under a window, across from the checkout counter. She had created a whimsical display of all things snow and surrounded it with real pine branches and straw stars. My eyes scanned the treasures scattered along the black velvet cloth: crystal snowflakes and silvery icicle tree ornaments; snowflake stationery on pretty torn-edge paper; a book of snow poems; snowflake earrings and necklaces; snowman pins and whimsical snowman statues; Christmas trees made of Styrofoam snowballs; snow globes with charming scenes inside. I moved to this last part of the table and bent to study the globes. I spied one and gasped. The tiny village inside could have been anywhere in Europe, perhaps, but to me it cried Békéscsaba, the land of surreal snows, the childhood world of my grandmother's memory. I could evoke those memories for her with this delicate glass ball. I lifted it and shook it. "Ah," I said. It was not cheap dime-store snow, but a delicate, silvery snow that hung suspended around the town and only gradually drifted down again. "It's so —" I paused, at a loss for words.

"You love it," said Sparkle. I had forgotten she was standing beside me.

"I do love it. I have to have it, for my grandmother."

"Perfect! I have a pretty red box for it."

"I think it's the best gift I've ever found."

She patted my shoulder. "You're a snow person." She studied me again. "You were born in winter, huh?"

In the fluorescent store lighting, her brown eyes were luminous, like my grandmother's. "I think it's officially in fall, but it's just before the switch to winter. December eighteenth. It does tend to snow on my birthday, though." I remembered again the snowball fight with Zoltan. Had that been on my birthday? I had a vague memory that my mother had wanted him to distract us so that she could prepare a birthday party . . .

"Yes. I saw you and thought of snow. But there might be other reasons for that. It was snowing, the day we both saw the boy. It bothered us both, stayed in our minds."

I nodded. My hands traveled to some star-shaped paperweights, glittering with some inner crystals, the star points dipped in pale blue. They were meant to be snowflakes, I suppose, but to me they were starlike, continuing a theme that had begun when I stared at Livia's necklace. This snowflake had Margie written all over it.

"This, too," I said. "The necklace, the snow globe, and the crystal star."

"You have wonderful taste. Your loved ones will be pleased." She took my choices and carried them to the counter, where she began to wrap them.

I looked over at the group of women, who were staring into the jewelry cases with enraptured expressions. Then I looked back at Sparkle, placid behind her counter and happy amid her white tissue paper speckled with gold, tucked into alluring red gift boxes.

"Perfect gifts and perfect boxes," I said. "I think I might ask my boyfriend to come here."

"You definitely should," she said. Her eyes were warm, maternal. "Because I know exactly what to show him."

Sparkle's store was so peaceful, fragrant, and beautiful that it was rather sad to have to leave, and I would have felt downright dejected if I hadn't glanced at the bag in my hand and remembered what a perfect half an hour of shopping I had just experienced. I was starting to get excited about seeing people open my presents.

Shopping was rewarding, but tiring, and a part of me wanted to go home and lie on my couch. I had told Falken I would stop by, though, and his store was on my way home. I climbed into my car, flipped on the radio, and turned to the Christmas station, which prided itself on playing Christmas songs from every era. For this reason, I kept it on for the whole season. They were playing something by James Taylor — I recognized his voice because I liked the song "You've Got a Friend." I waited until the end so that I could hear the title, which the DJ told me moments later: "New Star Shining."

As I pulled away from the curb, my eyes went to the pine tree that stood in front of Stones by Sparkle, and I thought once again of Frank. Had he thrown something into the tree? If so, had he returned and removed whatever it had been before Erik and his team searched the area? But that would mean he hadn't been honest with Erik, and it was hard to believe that young Frank wouldn't have told the truth, especially after his frightening interrogation. Besides, the whole crisis about his mother had been a misunderstanding.

Now the Christmas station was playing an instrumental "God Rest Ye Merry, Gentlemen," and a delicate, fairy snow drifted down from a mysterious gray sky. I drove down the street and smiled at the bag on the seat beside me: navy blue with silver glitter with lettering that read: "Stones by Sparkle."

I thought of Sparkle's brown eyes, warm and kind. What a nice woman.

But then the gray feeling was back, and with a sudden frisson of alarm I realized, in retrospect, that I had seen something else in her eyes. Something like concern — or warning.

CHAPTER 10
INSPEKTOR

Falken's store, like Stones by Sparkle, was decked in holiday finery, including white lights in the spruce trees on either side of his porch, and swags of red ribbons looped around the deck where some of his weather-proof wares sat gathering snow.

Inside Timeless Treasures it was warm and bright, and the beautiful wall of china and porcelain called to me in a visceral way. I moved toward it, but Falken appeared from his back room and called, "Hana! Did you just get here?"

"Yes, just this second."

"Come on back for a minute. I want to introduce you to my friend Nancy."

"Be right there," I said. I had spied Inspektor, the stately store cat, and I wanted to pet him. He was keeping his distance, but he was watching me. He sat near Falken's New Arrivals table — always a treat — and lifted a gray paw, but he kept his eyes on me while he licked it.

I got within a foot of him and squatted down. "Hey, Inspektor. I'm sorry about your friend." Again, I pictured Sandor, Inspektor tucked snugly against his chest, strolling through the store and eyeing Falken's wares.

Inspektor squinted at me and deigned to let me pet his large head. His purr was a bit rusty and uneven, but still heartfelt. "You're a great guy. I love visiting you here," I said. He crackled out some more purrs, then strolled under the table and out of my reach.

I laughed. "Okay, buddy. No more socializing, huh?"

Halfway back to a standing position I met the gaze of the Fisher Woman. I gasped. The Zsolnay piece, more than one hundred years old and at least a foot long, eclipsed whatever else might have been on the table. "Gorgeous," I whispered. "Oh, you are gorgeous." I ran a reverent finger across the eosin surface, admiring the unique shade of green that suggested ocean water. After a moment of admiration, rationality returned. "What are you doing here?" I whispered.

Indeed: where had Falken gotten this extremely expensive piece? I lifted my phone and took a quick picture, then sent it to Erik with the words, In Falken's store right now!!

Are you doing campus interviews?

Ten seconds later I had a text from him. Keep it there. Coming over now. Greg can run the show while I'm gone.

I looked around the store; there were only two people that I could see. One was a woman who seemed determined to find a whole set of matching teacups; the second was a man who was looking through some old stereo equipment. Neither seemed likely to come near the Fisher Woman.

Reluctantly I left the beautiful antique and the still-hiding Inspektor. I walked behind Falken's counter and into his stockroom, where he and a familiar-looking woman sat in two folding chairs. "Hello," I said.

Falken lifted a hand. "Hana, come have a seat. This is Nancy — she's Sandor's wife."

"Oh yes. I saw you the other day, at the tribute."

She blinked at me. "I'm sorry?"

"I work at the tea house," I said.

Nancy Balog inclined her gray-blonde head. "Oh, I see. Yes, that was a nice tribute they put together. Nice to meet you." She held out her hand, and I saw that she wore a ring that glimmered with an arresting topaz stone. So it had been his wife for whom Falken had special-ordered a ring at Stones by Sparkle. Perhaps he had given it to her when they reunited.

Nancy sighed and scratched absently at her arm. "I can't help but feel that Falken's tribute was a a bit odd, as well."

"Odd?" Falken asked.

She nodded. "They all admitted they were angry with poor Sandor before he died. Some departmental changes were happening, and he was suddenly unpopular. The price of leadership, I guess." She sighed and sipped her coffee.

"Yes, but it still seemed there was a room full of real friends there," I offered.

Nancy shrugged and nodded. She looked tired; I wondered if it was overwhelming to deal with the papers and possessions of a dead person.

Falken pointed at his coffeepot, sitting on a counter against the wall, but I shook my head. "Listen, this is kind of weird, but I had to call Erik. He's coming over."

Falken's brows rose. "The cops?" he joked. "Did you find some smuggled diamonds in one of the vases?"

"No — but I saw your Zsolnay piece. The Fisher Woman."

His eyes glowed. "Isn't it amazing! I was going to surprise you with it. I couldn't believe it when I found it."

"Yeah — hold your story until Erik gets here."

Nancy Balog was trying and failing to smile about what she probably thought was a rude private joke. "What is it that you found?"

I turned to her. "I think it belonged to your husband, actually. He had it on the shelf in his office . . ."

"What?" Falken's mouth was a giant *O* of surprise. "This must be a different piece."

"They're not common, Falken. And this finish looks exactly like the one I saw in the picture."

"What picture?" asked Nancy, her expression blank.

"A yearbook picture of the Riverwood World Languages Department. There's one of — Professor Balog — sitting at his desk, and his Hungarian porcelain is visible behind him."

She stared at me, still confused. "I don't understand how *you* know all this."

"Oh, because — I'm Hungarian, and Sandor and I used to enjoy the same pieces at the store here. And because my boyfriend is the homicide detective investigating his murder."

She sat up straighter. "The man named Wolf? Or the one named Benton?"

"Wolf," I said.

She frowned. "So many coincidences, these last few days . . ." She turned to Falken. "This Fisher Woman piece — can I see it?"

He jumped up. "Of course! I had no idea, Nancy." He set his coffee down, as did she, and Falken led the way out of the back room. I followed them, and we all stood in front of the New Arrivals table. The tip of Inspektor's tail was just visible underneath the curtained lower portion.

"This one!" Nancy cried. "Oh my, yes! Sandor has had this for years. God, it's so weird seeing it here, instead of in his office. It was there so recently!"

"When was the last time you saw it on his shelf?" I asked.

She shook her head, her expression uncertain. "Oh, I'm not sure. I guess the last time I was there. Maybe early December. Yes, December second, I think. But wait a minute — no! I think it was gone even then, because he had been sorting some files while I was chatting with him and he set them on the shelf behind him, and I said they looked out of place with all his treasures. He took them away eventually, but it struck me that he had found that empty space on his pretty shelf."

"And the files were right in the center, on the third shelf?" I asked.

She squinted at her memory, then nodded. "Yes — yes! That's where they were." She looked at the Fisher Woman. "But Sandor didn't bring this piece home. How in the world did it end up in a pawnshop?"

Falken looked nonplussed; he opened his mouth to speak, but the bell on the door jangled, and Erik Wolf marched in, his expression grim.

He sent me a brief glance before nodding at Falken and Nancy Balog. "Mr. Trisch, Mrs. Balog. I understand that one of Sandor's pieces has ended up here."

We all pointed at the Fisher Woman, whose gaze remained on the net she cast into the sea. Erik took out his phone and snapped a couple of pictures of the table. "Anyone touched it?"

Falken sighed. "Well, I did, unfortunately. I handled it quite a bit."

"Where did you get it, Mr. Trisch?"

He shrugged. "I make the rounds of the local pawnshops once a month. I found this at one on the border of Riverwood and Carrolton. The one on Sunday Road."

"Ah. I know it," Erik said. "When was this?"

Falken scratched his head. "I went early

this morning. The guy opens at eight. I saw this right away, and I couldn't believe it. I asked where he got it, and he said some young kid came in, told him his grandmother had died and he was going to be selling off some of her porcelain. I don't know what the pawn guy paid the kid, but he was asking three thousand for it. That was a steal."

Nancy Balog frowned. "How do we determine if this is my husband's piece and not someone else's? If it's Sandor's, then I assume it was stolen, correct? I think this was perhaps his most valuable piece. I remember he had to — move some money around to pay for it, at the time."

"The curse of the collector," Falken said.

"What's that?" Nancy asked.

"Everything seems urgent in the moment," I said. "I've felt that way myself. Reluctant to leave this store unless I have obtained the treasure I found on the shelf."

"Ah," she said, studying me.

Then she turned to Erik. "And what about poor Falken, who just paid three thousand dollars for a potentially stolen piece of art?"

The four of us stood contemplating the Fisher Woman; the moment had become fraught with embarrassment, and I felt a wave of discomfort so strongly that I squatted down and began to play with Inspektor's tail. He came out of hiding and crackled out some more purrs at me.

Erik said, "Well, for the time being it has to go with me. It's potential evidence, and we'll need to dust it for prints, talk to the proprietor of the pawnshop. If need be, I'll have him refund Falken's money."

Falken shook his head. "Such a shame."

Someone official-looking appeared in the doorway and Erik said, "Here's my tech guy. He'll wrap this up."

I sighed into Inspektor's noble face. It seemed that the police were always taking away beautiful porcelain treasures. How often, in this town, those works of art had been associated with cruelty!

Erik touched my shoulder, murmured a good-bye, and turned to go. Nancy Balog straightened and said, "Excuse me, sir. Uh — Detective."

Erik turned, surprised. "Yes?"

"I . . . the fact is . . . I've learned that when Sandor died, someone owed him a great deal of money. So, I'm wondering. Is that something the police can enforce? I mean, making sure he pays?"

A little gleam of interest appeared in Erik's eye. "Do you mean someone owed him money in an official way — some sort of tuition, or school-related —"

"No, not like that." Her face reddened. "My husband was a gambler. He made bets. It sometimes put us in a precarious financial position. And as we just discussed, he had expensive tastes." Her eyes wandered to the Fisher Woman, whose sad eyes now contemplated us through the Bubble Wrap being applied by a gloved technician.

Erik cleared his throat. "I'm afraid we can't enforce private promises, monetary or otherwise. So whoever you are referring to has essentially been freed of obligation by your husband's death. And I'm going to need to know who that person was, Mrs. Balog."

She reddened even more and said, "Oh — uh — the thing is, I can't be sure. I just heard a rumor. So if there's no point in pursuing it, I'd rather not say."

"Mrs. Balog," Erik began, but she made a show of looking at her watch.

"Oh my goodness, I have a meeting with the executor of Sandor's will. He assigned the role to his brother while the two of us were separated. I'll speak to you later, Falken." She forced a smile at Erik and me and moved swiftly across the room, grabbing her coat off a chair by the door and not even bothering to put it on.

"Interesting," Erik murmured.

Falken looked scandalized, perhaps by the technician, or Nancy's behavior, or Erik's. I wasn't sure. When Erik moved to the door, I followed him.

"You know who owed Sandor money," I said in a low voice.

He nodded. "Yes. Thanks to your friend Ms. Malandro."

"So why did you —"

"I wanted to see if she would implicate him. She seems to be more interested in getting the money than in naming a suspect."

"Alex Spencer-Malandro and Nancy Balog actually have some things in common, starting with husbands who have squandered their money. Husbands who happen to be respected professionals."

"Yes. Isn't that interesting?" he said.

His face told me that Alessandra Spencer-Malandro might in fact have been right to be concerned about a police focus on her husband. I mulled this over as I walked Erik to the door, but he turned and said goodbye before we got outside.

"See you tonight," Erik said. He kissed the top of my head and moved swiftly out, a December Hamlet with a gold cap of hair above his black coat.

I turned to see that Falken had picked up Inspektor, and they were both regarding me with somber expressions from across the room. I no longer felt like Christmas shopping; I waved to Falken and said, "Sorry about all this. I'll be back soon."

And I, too, escaped into the wintry, snow-flecked air.

CHAPTER 11
DUALITIES

Back at my apartment I had a joyful reunion with my cats and fed them some late lunch. They followed their repast with a leisurely bath, which they took on the mat in front of my fridge while I dug out some wrapping paper and began to unpack my wares. I was a wrap-as-you-go person because I didn't like to have a huge task right before Christmas. My mother called it "wrap and stow" because she'd witnessed my habit of creating artistic packages and then hiding them in my room. Often, by the time the twenty-fifth had rolled around, I would forget what was in some of the boxes, and then I would be surprised, too, when my loved one tore off the decorative paper.

Now I sipped tea out of one of my twin lizard cups and laid out a smooth sheet, embossed with gold reindeer, on my kitchen table. First, I would wrap my grandmother's beautiful snow globe, tucked safely into a

226

well-padded box. As I folded and smoothed, taped and flipped, I appreciated the Zen-like quality of wrapping a present.

I finished taping the bottom and flipped over the box to see the finished product. Perfect. Two gold reindeer held pride of place in the center of the present. I studied their gold antlers. They reminded me of Iris's Ulveflokk sweater, but of something else, something that happened in twos . . . Suddenly it felt very important that I should recall what was in the back of my mind.

I had been standing over my workspace, but now I sat down and took a calming sip of tea. The twin lizards looked at me with their tiny eyes, black dots painted on by an artisan long ago. Twins. Doubles. Dualities. What was bothering me?

Perhaps if I made a list . . .

My phone rang and I answered it, glad for the distraction. "Hello?"

"Hana? It's Livia."

"Oh, hello." I had genuinely felt that the bud of a new friendship had emerged after my meeting with Livia at the Union, and her call warmed my heart for that reason. "How did your interview go?"

I could almost hear her shrugging. "Oh, it was nothing. Not as bad as I feared. Your boyfriend is actually quite charming, but absolutely immune to distraction."

I laughed. "Why were you trying to distract him?"

"You have seen me now. I love to talk, to engage people in dialogue. He was not having that."

"Just doing his job."

"So sweet, the way you defend him. I told him I knew about you, and I said that I could see why he fell for you so quickly. He turned very red." This time she laughed, and I felt a spurt of pity for Erik.

"What are you up to today?" I asked.

She sighed luxuriously. "This is why I'm calling. Have you already done your Christmas shopping?"

"I started today and found some amazing things. I tried to make the most of my day off. How about you?"

"No, and I hate to go alone. I wondered if you would join me?"

"It depends. I have events at the tea house for the rest of the week, but we could plan around them."

"I would like that, Hana! Let me get my calendar."

I took a sip of tea, and then she was back, breathless and excited. "Okay, tomorrow is the fourteenth. You are busy?"

"For the first part of the day, yes. An event

for a Brownie troop. Between setup, event, and cleanup, we're looking at six hours, at least. So I wouldn't be free until after three."

"Hmm. A possibility. And on the fifteenth I have a date with Hans, some event in the city."

"The sixteenth is pretty busy for me," I said, glancing at my own wall calendar.

"We should seize the one possibility we've come up with. I'll pencil you in for tomorrow at four. I'll wear my comfy boots and bring my big wallet. Where shall we meet?"

"How about the big parking lot on Andrews Street? Then we can just walk to all the shops."

"Perfect. I'll text you when I arrive so we can find each other."

"Great, Livia. See you then."

I ended the call and smiled at my cats, who sat on the mat now with their heads together, their arms around each other in a feline embrace. I took a picture of them and sent it to Erik. A moment later he texted back, I love those guys.

"And I love you," I murmured. But I simply sent a smiley face.

I stood up and finished my wrapping: my mother's necklace, Margie's star, a book about carpentry I had ordered for my grandfather, and a scarf for Erik.

I stowed the wrapped presents in a cabinet in my living room. I finished my tea and rinsed out the cup, then dried it and put it back in its display case. I realized I hadn't yet called my uncle Zoltan to thank him for the gift, although I'd sent him a brief e-mail. I didn't want to call now, either, because when I did we would both want to catch up, and I still had a task to do. I texted him: Dear Uncle Z, I'll call soon to thank you in person. The teacups are amazing. Love you!

Then, because the world provides inexplicable symmetries, a text from Aunt Luca popped up. Hi, Hana my baby! I have a surprise. I'll be in Chicagoland from Christmas to New Year's. Have some big news.

I texted back immediately: Can't wait to see you! Must know the news now.

She sent back a laughing emoji and said, That's no fun. See you soon!

This was followed by a picture of her sitting on a chair near a Christmas tree. I couldn't tell if she was in her own apartment (which I had not seen, since she moved often) or a restaurant or a friend's house. Luca was four years younger than my mother, so about forty-nine years old, but she looked younger than her age, as did my mother. While Magdalena's hair was blonde and wavy, Luca's was dark and straight. For some reason she always reminded me of the pretty female spies from espionage films.

I sent a question mark emoji. My family — always full of surprises.

My next task awaited me at the stove, where I warmed up some *paprikás* that I had made the night before. I packed the hot dish into a thermal container, making sure to get a generous helping of chicken, dumplings, and gravy. I tucked the dish into a tote bag, along with some books I had finished reading and had enjoyed. I put on my coat and scarf, kissed the cats on their fuzzy heads, and grabbed the bag and my purse. I was bound for St. Francis of Assisi, and Runa.

I was nervous on the drive to the hospital, fearing that Runa would look ill or feel depressed. Her appearance was shockingly divergent from those images. She sat up in her bed; her hair, in thick blonde braids, looked glossy and clean, and the smile she sent me was so big it filled me with immediate joy.

"Oh, Hana, I'm so glad to see you!" she said, reaching for me. "Andy has a night class and Thyra is running the store, and my mom left hours ago. I'm lonely."

"Have you eaten?" I asked, giving her a quick kiss.

She shrugged. "The stuff they're bringing me ruins my appetite. It's like gruel."

"Are you allowed to eat solid food?"

A nurse wafted in as I asked the question, and she began efficiently checking the various machines around Runa. "She can eat whatever she likes," she said. "But she needs to eat."

Runa rolled her eyes behind the nurse's back. "Yes, ma'am," she said.

"I brought you something," I told her. I pulled the wheeled table over and pushed it until it jutted over her bed. "Family recipe." I took the *paprikás* out of the bag and popped open the lid. I provided a fork and knife and a napkin.

The nurse spun around. "That smells amazing," she said. "If you don't eat it, I will." She winked at me.

"Thank you, Hana." Runa took a tiny bite of chicken and chewed it obediently. Her eyes widened. "That is very good." She took a larger bite and chewed with some more enthusiasm. "Mmm," she said.

"Good. Now, look what I brought you. All sorts of fun books. I've read them, so I can tell you what they're all about and you can decide which one you want to start with."

"That's so thoughtful, thank you," Runa said, forking up some dumplings. The nurse took Runa's pulse, tucked her blankets around her, and left with the promise that she would soon return.

I looked at the radiator by the window, on which was a giant floral display — a gorgeous thing with red and white poinsettias with sparkling accents and painted-white wheat stalks. "Wow — who sent you that? Andy?"

"No. My poor Andy hasn't had time to do anything but run back and forth between me and the campus. I owe him about three solid days of sleep."

I pointed at the flowers. "So — is that from your other lover?"

She laughed. "It's from my brother Felix. He couldn't come out to see me, and he feels bad about it." She shrugged. "He'll probably be in for Christmas."

"That's good." I pulled a chair up next to her bed. "How are you? You look amazing."

She set her fork down and leaned back. "That was so good, thank you." She closed her eyes for a moment, then looked at me. "I'm great, Hana."

"And our little girl?"

"She's great, too. I talk to her all day. I've been telling her to stay there. That I can't wait to meet her, but she needs to stay in that warm, watery, soothing place and get better. I need her to get strong and be ready when the time comes."

"The operation went well?"

Her smile widened. "My doctor said she could not have asked for better results. So Andy and I are happy. But — we're vigilant, you know."

"Yes, of course. It must be exhausting."

"I'm resting a lot. I know I have to do it. So thank you for the books." She touched the spines of the books absently, then smoothed the edge of her coverlet. "I wonder if you'd do me a favor."

"Sure, what? Do you need me to go out and get anything?"

Her green eyes met mine; they were serious now. "Could you just feel her?"

I knew what she was asking; I shook my head. "I'm not my grandmother, Runa. I don't have — any confidence in whatever uh — gift — I might have inherited. Grandma just knows things. I am not certain. Maybe I can bring her here sometime."

"You don't have to make any promises or tell any lies. Just put your hand lightly above her and tell me if she seems fine."

"Runa, your doctor is the one who should tell you things."

"She will. Please, Hana?"

I sighed. I never should have introduced Runa to my grandmother. But if I hadn't, Runa's baby might have died. Runa might not have known she was pregnant for another month or so. It was Grandma who had told her she had a child in her womb, and Grandma who had told her the child needed to be strong for a "battle" she would face. No wonder Runa was trying to get more information out of me, poor substitute though I was.

Reluctantly, I put a hand on the edge of Runa's blanket. She snorted, then lifted my hand and set it lightly on her abdomen. I closed my eyes, and in an instant, she was there again, the girl I had seen in my hospital vision. The girl with Andy's eyes. She was laughing, standing in between Runa and Thyra, who each held one of her arms and lifted her into the air with every other step. All three of them had blonde braids. The older women were laughing at the child because the child was laughing with pure joy.

"Hana?" Runa asked. "Why are you laughing?"

I opened my eyes. I was laughing still. I felt happy. It was strange . . .

"What did you see?"

I told her about the three of them, blonde and braided and happy. She nodded, contented. "Thank you."

"It might mean nothing, Runa. I might be manufacturing my own images."

"I know. No guarantees. It's fine."

She was serene. She took a few more bites of the chicken, then pushed the container away. "I think I've eaten enough. Thank you for the treat. I'm so glad Erik brought you into our lives."

I had never seen Runa as a sentimental person, but that was how she struck me now. Perhaps motherhood was making her take stock.

The door opened and Andy came in, looking a bit harried. "Hey, beautiful," he said to Runa, leaning in to kiss her. "Hi, Hana! I'm glad you're here. I was afraid Runa would be bored."

Runa pointed at the food. "Andy, eat this."

He did, all of it, in about two minutes. "Oh God, that was good," he said. "Hana, you made this?"

"Yes. Hungarian recipe."

He gave me a big hug, then walked to the only other chair in the room and collapsed into it. "Long day."

"You should go home and sleep," Runa said.

"I will. In a while." They exchanged a look that said more about Christmas love than anything I had experienced so far that season.

"I've got to go," I said. I stood up and packed the empty food carton and the silverware. "Runa, text me if you have questions about the books. Meanwhile, both of you get lots of rest."

They nodded at me, tired but happy.

I peered at them from the doorway; Andy had edged his chair closer to the bed so that he could hold Runa's hand.

With a sigh I moved into the hall and headed for the elevator. A woman walked out of a room a few doors down from Runa's; I recognized her immediately, but she was out of context, and I couldn't remember where I had seen her. She walked ahead of me, her dark hair swinging, a shiny bob that rested on the shoulders of her expensive-looking red sweater.

She reached the elevator and turned to ask me what floor I wanted. "Lobby," I said, and that's when I realized it was Yvonne Yves from the university. "Hello again," I said.

"Yes," she said, nodding at me. "You're the girl from the tea house. The one who was talking with Livia today."

"That's me." We boarded the elevator, and she pressed *L*. "Did you get through your interview all right?"

She shrugged her elegant shoulders. "I suppose. No one likes to be interrogated, do they?"

"I guess not."

"You have a parent here?" she asked.

"Hmm? Oh — no. A friend. She just had surgery."

"Ah." The elevator stopped, and a few more people got on. Yvonne was forced to stand closer to me. The doors closed again, and she said, "My father had surgery, as well. We're still awaiting his prognosis."

"Oh, that's stressful. I hope it's a good one."

"Yes, I, too." She looked as though she should be smoking a cigarette; it would help to complete the indifferent image she seemed to want to project.

The doors opened onto the lobby, and she pulled a phone from her pocket. She stopped just outside the elevator to send a text. "Ugh. The Ubers are making me wait tonight," she murmured.

"Did you need a ride somewhere?" I asked. "Ubers are so expensive."

She looked halfway tempted to accept. For a moment, her guard was down and the ironic look left her face. In that instant she was pretty, almost vulnerable. Then that smile that bordered on a sneer was back in place. "Thank you for the offer. I can wait. But I appreciate your attempt to save me money. Believe me, at this point, that is a welcome gesture."

I nodded and smiled, then lifted my hand in farewell. "Have a good Christmas. I hope your father is better soon."

"Thank you. I'm sorry, what was your name again?"

"Hana Keller."

"Thank you, Hana. And I hope your friend has a complete recovery." Again, that trace of a French accent that gave her a European charm.

I nodded my thanks and went out into the parking lot. It was dark now, and despite the bright hospital lights I could still see a sprinkling of stars.

My car was cold; I locked all my doors and turned on the heater, closing my eyes for a moment while I let the mechanical parts warm up. My mind drifted back to what Yvonne Yves had said to me — that my attempt to save her money was very welcome "at this point." Was she struggling for money? Didn't university professors make good salaries? Perhaps she was a gambler, like Sandor and Tony. Or perhaps her father's operation had cost her some of her savings.

Before I pulled out of the lot, an unbidden question floated into my consciousness: would Yvonne have known how valuable Sandor's collection was? Would she have killed to get some of those pieces for herself?

It was a ridiculous picture, and I frowned into the darkness. And yet, I told myself, someone had killed Sandor, had shot him in cold blood, and the Fisher Woman had disappeared from his shelf. Had it been stolen? Had other things been stolen?

I pulled out of the lot onto the dark road, wondering what guilty person sat in Riverwood tonight, concealing the secret of murder.

CHAPTER 12
THE MAN WHO DIDN'T KNOW

My cell phone rang as I was leaving the downtown area. I poked the button while keeping a hand on the wheel. "Hello?"

"Hey, sweetie, it's Dad."

"Hi, Dad. What's up?"

"I'm helping your grandpa decorate his tree. Your grandmother is at some parish thing tonight."

My grandparents insisted on having a giant, real tree in their home every year, and each year it became more of a chore to decorate it. But my grandfather clung to this tradition, and my father had always been willing to lend a hand. A wave of love for them both surged in me. "That's nice of you, Dad."

"Apparently, Grandma left you some tubs of food. Some for you to eat, some to send to work with your boyfriend."

"If she keeps sending them food, pretty soon she'll be feeding the whole department," I warned. "Erik and Greg keep sharing it around, and people are forming addictions."

My father laughed in my ear. "Anyway, are you all tucked in at your place, or can you swing by and get it? Otherwise I'll try to bring it on my way home."

"I'm out in the car, as it happens. And I want to see the tree. I'll be there in about ten minutes."

"Great. Major misses you, by the way. So you need to schedule a visit to our house, too."

"Will do. I think Mom and Grandma and I will be making *mézeskalács* in the near future at your place. I assume you and Domo will be lurking around to eat the dough."

"Tradition is important," said my father.

"You've outdone yourself," I told my grandfather, and I meant it. This year's tree, fragrant with fresh pine sap, towered to the ceiling in their living room between their fireplace and their television table. They had covered it in white and gold lights and strung it with straw stars, clear icicles, dried red berry garlands, and tiny gold bells. Now they were hanging the family heirloom ornaments one by one, with the utmost care, finding the places that would best showcase each ornament.

"Look at this one. Baby Hana's first year," my grandfather said, holding up a photo of me as a fat infant. "We should show this to your wolf."

"His name is Erik. And, no, you don't need to show him that."

My father was digging around in a box. "Hana, help with a couple of these before you take your food."

I moved to the box and let my hand wade through the ornaments — the history of my grandparents' Christmases. One fragile-looking blown-glass ball said "Budapest, 1956." Another frame ornament, this one featuring three red-clad children hugging one another: Zoltan, Magda, Luca. My mother looked about six years old. Luca was just a toddler. "This is a great picture," I said. I moved across the room to hang it on the tree.

"Yes, my little ones," my grandfather said, untangling some garlands with surprising patience. "They grew quickly. So did you." He looked up at me with his kind eyes, and I moved swiftly over to kiss his cheek.

"Still a baby at heart," I joked.

"Little Zsa Zsa," he said.

I sighed. My family had held on to the

myth that I had a terrible temper and they likened me to the notorious Zsa Zsa Gabor. I went back to the ornament box, and my eyes lighted on a photograph of my grandfather building a shed behind the rectory with some men from his parish. "Grandpa, you knew Sandor Balog, right?"

He finished untangling and started hanging the garland on the tree. "Ya. He and his wife go to my parish."

"Nancy?"

"Yes, Nancy. Nice lady."

"Did everyone know about the two of them separating?"

He looked at me, his brows raised. "How did *you* know?"

"Gossip at the university."

He shrugged. "Not everyone. We did, because sometimes Nancy would come for tea, just to talk, you know. She's not Hungarian, but somehow it helped her to talk to other Hungarians who understood Sandor. We felt sorry for her."

"Why?"

"He left her, for some other woman, she said. A man his age, leaving his wife for someone younger. Shameful, we thought. But also childish. And poor Nancy paid the price for a man who could not decide what he wanted."

"Hear, hear," my father said.

I thought about this. What, really, was Sandor seeking, with his endless quest for expensive porcelain, his dalliances with women, his gambling? Had his life been ruled by his appetite for the next great thing? "Was he looking for peace?" I asked aloud.

My grandfather turned, his garland hung, and contemplated me. "Why do you ask that?"

"People said he was always — looking for more."

My father left, murmuring something about eggnog. Grandpa moved closer to me. "Funny you should ask that. I always felt a little sad around Sandor."

"Why?"

"Because I thought *he* was sad, himself. Not in a way he was conscious of. Deep down, in a way he don't understand."

"Didn't," I corrected automatically. "But — overall you liked him, right?"

"Ya, ya. A good man overall. Born in Hungary, like Grandma and me. And your mama. Some people died in his family, when he was young. A brother, I think, and a parent. This changes people."

I couldn't imagine losing Domo, or my mother or father. Or even aunts or uncles.

"Besides, he came to his senses and went back to Nancy. They were happy again."

"Huh," I said, thinking about this. "Hey! Did you know Luca was coming to town? And she said she has a surprise."

He grinned. "She always has a surprise. From babyhood she was surprising us. She got us all presents when she was two years old — Christmas presents. An acorn for me, and a rock for her mother."

I laughed. "Did you save them?"

"Of course. My acorn is on my desk upstairs."

"A talisman," my father said, handing a glass of eggnog to both of us.

"Thanks," I said. I sipped and thought about that. About love in the form of an object, saved for half a century . . .

"Don't forget about the food," my father said. "It's all stacked up neatly in there."

"Right!" I ran into the kitchen. I took another couple of sips of my eggnog and set it on the counter. I found a plastic grocery bag in my grandmother's bag cozy and started packing up plastic containers of noodles, dumplings, chicken soup, *paprikás,* stuffed cabbage, sausage. "Good Lord! Did she cook all night?" I called.

My eyes fell upon a little plaque that read: "Andras loves Juli." My grandfather had it made once at a county fair, back in the nineties. My grandmother had never seemed to pay much attention to it, but my mother had told me recently that the two of them put it in different places in the house, waiting for the other to find it. Right now, it was sitting on the stove. I wondered if he had put it there, or she.

The smell of the food was making me hungry. I wanted to go warm some of it up in my apartment and share it with Erik Wolf, when and if he came by. I grabbed another sip of eggnog (the holidays in a flavor, my brother said) and went back out with my bag. "Dad, you have to finish my eggnog. It was delicious, though. I hate to take all of your food and run, but I'm going to head out. Grandpa, that tree looks amazing. You're lucky you have such a nice and helpful son-in-law to get it ready so quickly."

Grandpa put an arm around my father and gave a mighty squeeze. "Always a good boy," he said.

When I left, they were back at the tree, hanging delicate ornaments to please the women they loved.

That evening, after a late dinner of my grandmother's food, Erik said he needed an hour or so to do some work; he sat in my kitchen, scrawling notes, looking at his computer, and occasionally murmuring into his phone.

I kept out of his way, sticking to my bedroom and the living room. I knew that he would normally have stayed in his office until late in the night, but he was making an effort to spend time with me while still doing his job. I didn't want him to regret his choice, so I gave him his quiet space. In the meantime, I thought I would clarify my own ideas. Perhaps they could be helpful to Erik.

I got out a notebook and sat on my couch. Antony and Cleopatra jumped up to join me, jutting their heads into my arms for a while until I ordered them to stop, at which point they curled up on a pillow to my left, and Antony washed Cleopatra's ears.

I sighed. What did I want to write down? Perhaps the basic facts would come together into a recognizable shape. I could do it by name. I began with what I thought of as the origin: the boy in the snow.

I jotted "People Who Knew Sandor" and began a list.

Frank Dobos
Took a gun away from the scene because he feared his mother killed Sandor. Why

would he fear that?

His father had assured us that Frank's mother was a gentle, nonviolent person, and her speech at the tea house had seemed to verify that idea. In addition, the police had dismissed her as a suspect, for whatever reasons they had.

May or may not have thrown something into a tree at the end of the alley (beer can, lipstick, other? Again, police know about this, but Frank is not in custody).

Sarah Dobos, Mr. Dobos
Sarah was upset with Sandor when he died because there was a chance he would cut her language program from the department. Doesn't seem very likely, since she teaches Spanish (again, wouldn't Frank realize this, too?). He said his mother was "so angry," but was it really about that?

Don't know anything about Mr. Dobos, except that he washes windows. How exactly did he end up with Sarah?

Falken Trisch
Friends with Sandor. Sold him many of

his treasures.

Friends also with Nancy Balog.

Found the Fisher Woman at a pawnshop.

Nancy Balog
Sandor's wife. Recently reunited with
him after long separation (how long?).

Said she realized the Fisher Woman was
not on Sandor's shelf as of December
2nd.

Livia Parravicini
Dated Sandor Balog during his separation. Liked him, said he was "romantic,"
but said she was never in love with him.
Claimed that Sandor wanted to keep her
on as an "option" even after returning
to his wife.

Potentially at risk of losing the Italian
program?

Wanda Lee
Also dated Sandor. Seemed to have had
genuine feelings for him. Livia insinu-
ated that Wanda had genuinely loved
him and perhaps still did.

Wanda admitted that she was familiar with Sandor's collection and had often polished it. Most likely knew of its value.

Taught Mandarin. Seems most at risk for losing her language program.

Yvonne Yves
Seems to have a negative opinion of everyone.

May be under stress because of a family health issue.

Will replace Sandor as the new department chair. Does not seem popular with the other World Languages professors.

Rumored to have had an affair with a student. Made inappropriate advances toward François, supporting this contention.

Possibly has money troubles. Would she steal to solve them?

Hans Weber
Persuaded Livia to break up with Sandor. Competitor for her love. Was angry with Sandor because the former was cut-

ting his study abroad program. Said that he and Sandor went way back and had always been friends.

Tony Malandro
Loved to play chess with Sandor but owed him a huge amount of money.

Nancy Balog seems interested in calling in the debt. There seemed to be tension between them at the tea house.

Malandro said that his games with Sandor challenged him and stimulated his mind.

Alessandra Spencer-Malandro
Worried about the debt her husband owed to Sandor. Seemed fearful that her husband was a suspect. Was this because she herself suspected him?

Other Faculty?

Other Students?

I set my pen aside. The cats were asleep now. I studied the lights twinkling on my little mantel, wondering how one could possibly narrow a list like this into something specific. Some*one* specific.

Erik walked in and said, "Sorry to come here and cloister myself away. I'm all yours now." He sat beside me on the couch and kissed the top of my head.

"I have some notes for you."

"Oh?" He raised his brows and took the notebook that I handed him. "I mean, obviously I can't discuss . . . What — How did you know about the lipstick and the beer can?"

"I was in Stones by Sparkle, doing some Christmas shopping. We happened to discuss the crime scene outside her window."

"Ah." He read some more, then looked up at me. "You got some good information out of Dr. Parravicini. How did you happen to do that?"

"We're kind of trying out a friendship. Something about her — I just like her. And I think she likes me. I think we're dating," I joked.

He let out a short laugh. "Well, obviously if she offers any other significant information —"

"I will share it with you immediately."

"Good." He took out his phone and snapped a picture of my notebook page. "Some great stuff here," he said.

My cheeks warmed at the compliment.

He had told me once that I should become a police officer, but I didn't really want to pursue that line of work. Still, I did enjoy the challenge of a mystery . . .

He set down his phone and notebook and put his arm around me. "I talked with Runa. She said you came over and kept her company."

"Yes. She looks healthy and good. I'm so glad the scariest part is behind her, and behind the baby."

"She also told me you saw the baby." His green eyes were curious.

"She asked me to touch her. I closed my eyes, and I saw a little girl playing with Runa and Thyra. It wasn't exactly a vision; more like a daydream. I told her it could be just that — me manufacturing images."

"Ah." His hand moved into my hair and massaged gently. "Do you think your insights are, um, *deepening*?"

"I don't know. I'm not like my grandmother. She has such confidence in her feelings. I have none. So I'm choosing to believe that they are not to be trusted."

"Hmm. I don't know if you can dismiss them that easily. At the very least you are an insightful person. That's why you've been so helpful to me."

I put my head on his shoulder. "We need

to talk about Christmas. Your parents seemed to imply that they're hosting something at their place, but we have our big family Christmas at Grandma and Grandpa's. They have a giant tree, and tons of food — I was hoping you could come."

He frowned. "The fact is, I don't think I can be at either celebration. I think I'll be working."

I sat up straight. "Erik, *no*! Not on *Christmas*?"

He shook his head. "We're in the midst of an investigation. It's a very busy time. I'll see you for at least part of the day . . ."

"Oh no. This is — so sad. It's our first Christmas together."

"We'll celebrate a lot. Maybe just not on the one big day. Don't look like that, Hana. There's really nothing I can do."

"I know. I just need some time, I guess. To get over the disappointment."

He shifted on the couch, turning his whole body toward me. "We'll find a special time to do our present exchange. And another time for dinner with your family. It will be like an extended Christmas. We'll have fun."

"Yeah. I guess I'll have to get out the calendar so you can show me the times you'll be available."

"Um — maybe in a week. I'll know better

then. I will get to spend the evening of your birthday with you. I made sure of that. We can go out to dinner — wherever you like."

"Sure." I sighed. "Please don't think I'm a big baby. I'm just a Christmas purist; I like everyone to be together and celebrating. I guess I'm traditional. But it's because we have such nice traditions."

"We'll work it out," he said. He sounded confident.

I wondered, with a plunging of spirits, why I couldn't feel the same.

CHAPTER 13
THE COLLECTIVE
UNCONSCIOUS

If St. Mikulás Day was my favorite Christmas season event, the yearly Brownie Christmas party was a close second. Girls between seven and nine gathered in their charming uniforms to celebrate their troops and to give out some holiday awards. The children were adorable, and when we weren't among them, we were stealing peeks at them from the back room, jostling for a view from the World Tree hallway (as I now thought of it).

I went out with a refresher pot of tea, and little girls politely raised their hands to indicate that they wanted more. One of them was particularly ladylike, and her mother and I shared a smile. "What's your name?" I asked her.

She lifted her teacup (we had gone with a white set with holly berries around the rim) and took a dainty sip. "Chelsea," she said.

"Nice to meet you, Chelsea. Are you and

your friends enjoying your Christmas tea party?"

"Yes!" she said, wiggling in her chair. "I feel like I'm in a storybook."

"That's great! It's the effect we're going for," I said, winking at her mother.

Chelsea's mother put an affectionate arm around her daughter. "Chelsea loves stories. She likes to write them, too."

"Oh? Have you written any Christmas stories?"

She shrugged. "I'm working on a story right now, but not really a Christmas one. But there's a problem. I have two ways the ending could go, and I can't decide which one to pick!" She grinned up at me; she was missing one of her front teeth.

Faint with déjà vu, I said, "Well, I'm sure whichever one you choose, it will be just the right ending for your story."

I moved away with my teapot. Doubleness. The story with two endings . . . Little Chelsea had set something off in me, but I didn't have time to think it out. I took the pot back toward the kitchen and found the father of a Brownie examining the World Tree. "Beautiful, isn't it?" I asked.

"This is Yggdrasil, yes?"

"That's Norse mythology, but, yes, similar to our interpretation, which is the Hungarian *égig érő fa,* or the 'sky-high tree.' It's also called Világfa. I think the World Tree emerges in the folklore of many countries. Are you a historian?"

He shrugged. "I'm an English professor at Riverwood University. But I teach a folklore class once a year, and we've delved into these stories. Fascinating, all of them. Where in the world did you find this?"

"A friend in the antiques business. He keeps his eyes open for us."

"Yes, this is an amazing piece." He ran a gentle finger over the base of the tree — the border between the middle world and the lower world, between life and miserable death. "Some historians have suggested that the reason the tree emerges in so many folktales is rooted in the idea that we evolved from tree dwellers. And that because we were all once primates, the tree was our entire world. Therefore, the notion of the World Tree has remained in our collective unconscious."

"That *is* fascinating. I think I would love to take that folklore class!"

He took out a wallet and reached inside for a business card. "You could audit the class, if you'd like. Just let me know. It starts in January."

I glanced at the card, which read: "Dr.

William Stanton-Briggs, English Department, Riverwood University."

"Well, thank you, Dr. Stan —"

He grinned and stuck out a hand. "Just Bill is fine. And you are?"

"Hana Keller. I was an English major, too, but I never took folklore." I studied his card for a moment, then said, "Did you know Sandor Balog?"

His brows rose. "I — yes, I did. Did you know Sandor?"

"Only slightly. And of course, I read about the crime in the paper."

"It's terrible. Sandor and I were in different departments, but we were on a committee together. We've known each other for more than a decade."

"Is it hard to imagine he had — an enemy?"

He frowned. "I don't know that he did. He struck me as a nice guy, and kind of solitary. He was separated from his wife, and he just hung out in his office a lot. The place was a real museum — fascinating to visit."

So word hadn't necessarily gotten around campus that Sandor had reunited with his wife. "It must be so hard for all of you, just to process this loss to your community."

"Truly." He nodded, his expression somber. "And we had harbored the notion that Riverwood was safe. A safe campus, a safe community. Now our illusions have been shattered. I hope the students are not traumatized by this."

"Do you think someone surprised him in his office? Maybe a burglar?"

He shook his head. "It happened in the morning, didn't it? I don't know the time, but one of my colleagues saw him walking to his office from the parking lot that morning." He glanced behind him, seemingly to check on his daughter. He waved at her, then said, "It's unfortunate that Sandor was in the Ellis Building. It has more than one entrance, and the south door is rather sheltered from view — just in front of the back lot and the forest preserve. Most people come in the front way, but people familiar with the building might come in the south entrance if their destination was closer to that door. Sandor had an office just feet from the back stairs."

"So — whoever did this probably knew the campus?"

"I would think so, yes."

"And could have effectively escaped down the back stairs and out the back door without being seen? Maybe even walking into the woods to avoid detection?"

He looked grim. "Yes. And while we have some security cameras on campus, we don't have them everywhere. Certainly not on the older buildings."

I thought about this as he took one last look at the World Tree. Then he turned to me. "That's another thing in our collective consciousness, I suppose. Awareness of sin."

He murmured that it had been nice to meet me and walked back to his daughter's table. A tall, thin girl with red hair beamed up at him and pointed to François's Christmas cakes. He laughed down at her, clearly happy about her happiness.

One of the troop leaders went to the microphone, where my grandmother helped her flip on the mic and adjust the volume. Then she made a speech about how special the girls were and what good work they had done in the last year.

I grabbed a tray and started collecting empty cake plates.

My phone buzzed in my pocket, and when I got to the back room, I checked my texts. It was from Livia: Hans is dropping me off. He would like to treat us both to a late lunch (or an early dinner) before we go shopping.

That was odd; I wondered why Hans Weber had any interest in my shopping adventure with Livia. Did men usually try to join in on girls' days out? Certainly Erik had never indicated an interest in going out with Katie and me, or even when his sisters invited me out to see a movie.

My grandmother marched into the back room, adjusting her glittery earrings. It made me think of Stones by Sparkle. I wondered if Grandma would ever return to her tradition of reading tea leaves in the tea house; she had not done it in weeks. Sparkle had a display of giant rings just inside the doorway to her shop. I looked at Grandma. All of us — Grandma, Mom, me — we were descendants of Natalia Kedves, my great-grandmother, from whom we had all inherited some modicum of "insight." Perhaps for Christmas I should get us all some chunky fortune-teller rings so that we could truly play our roles to perfection. The rings would make good stocking stuffers, at the very least.

I would go back to the store today, perhaps, with Livia . . .

My mother whisked by, glancing at her watch. "Mom?" I said. She paused, glanced across the room to see if anyone needed her, then turned to me.

"They seem just about finished. We can start clearing in about ten minutes, I would think," she said. Then: "What's up?"

263

"I was going to ask you about that. You seem nervous. Do you have an appointment or something?"

She sighed. "I'm going out for coffee with Alex."

"What? Ugh."

"Yes, I know, but she really does need an ear, I think. She's just so upset over this thing with her husband."

Something softened inside me, against my will. "Is their marriage in trouble?"

"I don't know. They've been married a long time. She wouldn't want to throw it away over nothing, but —"

"A gambling addiction isn't nothing. If he gambled with Sandor, it's likely he gambles elsewhere, right?"

My mother sighed. "I'm so grateful for your father, do you know that? His only addictions are his little food cravings. Oh look, they're starting to leave. Let's go."

She whisked away to clear tables and say farewells; I did the same in the other direction.

Fifteen minutes later everyone had gone. It usually happened that way: one person stood up to leave, and then the rest followed like falling dominoes.

I got a clean rag and began to wipe down tables. Alex Spencer-Malandro wandered in, wearing a big fake smile. I saw the sadness in her eyes now, and it made me want to be kind.

"Hello, Alex! I hear you and my mom are going out for some friend time."

She strolled to me on expensive-looking suede boots. When did she work? "Hello, Hana." So I was Hana now. "Yes, I'm whisking your mother away to Drake House for a meal. She said she's never been."

I wanted to say, *No — most people who make less than a hundred thousand dollars a year don't go to Drake House,* but instead I smiled. "Well, have a great time."

"Thank you." She hesitated, then said, "Does your boyfriend — do the police — have any leads about poor Sandor?"

Poor Sandor. We were all calling him that. "He can't really discuss the case with me. I know they're working hard. They'll be working right through Christmas."

"Oh, what a shame."

I moved toward her and put a hand on her arm. "Alex, are you really worried that your husband had something to do with Sandor's death?"

Her eyes widened. "He wouldn't commit murder, if that's what you're asking me."

"Then why are you so nervous? Is there

265

something else you're afraid the police will learn?"

Her gaze shifted away. "Obviously I wouldn't want people to learn about his gambling."

"They already know — at least about the fact that Sandor and Tony bet large amounts of money. And that apparently one owed the other when Sandor died."

"Oh?" This didn't seem to distress her unduly. There was something else.

"Alex?" I prodded. I saw my mother coming, her coat over her arm. She had changed into a winter-white dress, with a little red scarf tied at her neck.

Alessandra's smile was back in place. "Oh, Maggie, you look chic! All set? Okay, we have to run to make our reservation. See you later, Hana!" She waved, a gesture that said, *Go away.*

I murmured a response, but she was already whisking my mother out the door.

My grandmother stood near the World Tree, and her wise eyes met mine. She nodded once, indicating that she had seen what I saw.

Behind her, Ördög stirred his cauldron of souls, grinning.

CHAPTER 14
ELUSIVE THINGS

The holiday lights flickered up and down Andrews Street; downtown Riverwood had donned its Christmas finery, and my mood lifted at the sight. What was it about light? Somehow it was a tonic for the soul.

I had texted Livia of my arrival, and soon I saw her and Hans waving to me from halfway down the block. They beckoned me forward and pointed to the Druid's Retreat, a fun restaurant and bar that I had occasionally visited with Erik. I walked down the snowy sidewalk and Livia gave me a friendly hug, after which Hans shook my hand. "Hello again, Miss Keller."

"Hana, please."

"And I am Hans. You and Livia seem to have formed a sudden friendship, like a flower that blooms overnight."

That was a very pretty analogy, and I told him so as we moved up the walk and through the entrance. The interior was meant to be cave-like and mysterious, and the walls were filled with sconces that created the illusion of flaming torches against rock. It had an oddly cozy effect. The three of us tucked into a booth, Livia and Hans on one side, my purse and I on the other.

Hans held up a hand. "Please, ladies, this is my treat. Order whatever you wish. I am stealing this time with two lovely women, and then I will let you shop in peace, at which point you can gossip about me and every other man you know."

This was a sexist comment, but in fact I did plan to talk about him after he left, so I shrugged. "I'm sure men do the same," I said.

Hans grinned at me. "I suppose if I had close men friends I would occasionally indulge in talk of women. Namely: what is the best way to please a woman?"

We laughed.

He added, "I'm sure we could fill a whole night in pursuit of the answer to that question." He beckoned a waiter, then turned back. "But I don't really have a male friend like that. I did, in Sandor. Once, at least. We had grown away from those sorts of personal conversations."

The waiter came and handed us menus, promising to return. I opened mine and said, "Why do you think you and Sandor grew apart?"

Hans narrowed his eyes and seemed to study something on the opposite wall. "A good question. We were young when we started at Riverwood, both of us. So we had some high times together, drinking in pubs or staying late on campus, determined to find the answer to every philosophical question."

He took a sip of his water, and Livia rubbed his neck affectionately. "But our jobs grew more stressful. We both took on extra responsibilities. Sandor got married."

"How long ago was that?"

"Oh — fifteen years? Something like that."

"Did it surprise you when they separated?" I asked.

He and Livia exchanged a glance. I wasn't sure if it was about the question or the fact that I was asking it. Hans said, "I wasn't really surprised. They seemed to argue often."

"You heard them arguing?"

Livia said, "No, I don't think any of us ever saw them together that much. We just knew that Sandor spent a lot of time in his office. We assumed that meant marriage troubles. Sometimes he was in there until midnight or later."

"And how would you know he was there at midnight?"

Hans laughed. "You raise your brows at us as though you work for the police. We all answered these things for your boyfriend, you know."

I shrugged. "I'm just curious by nature, I guess. But how would anyone know he was there late unless *they* were there late?"

Livia leaned back against the leatherlike seat. "It was common knowledge on the campus. Someone would come back for a file they forgot, or to set up equipment they needed for the morning — usually an emergency trip made by someone who had panicked in the night — and there they would find Sandor, smiling behind his desk."

"That's odd," I said.

Hans frowned. "It never seemed so. More like he was part of the building. It made people less worried about coming to that hulk of an office in the middle of the night, because Sandor was a sort of unofficial custodian. He loved the place."

Livia looked solemn. "Word on campus is that he was shot with his own gun. He kept one for security; it makes sense, I suppose. Between his odd hours and the fact that he had all that expensive art in his office."

"His own gun?"

I must have looked surprised. Hans said, "I might have made the same choice, if I were routinely alone in the building. I think he kept a gun at home, as well. He was security conscious."

"And yet someone used that security against him. Doesn't that suggest that someone knew him well enough to know that he had a gun in his drawer?"

This thought troubled Livia. "It would, normally. But once we had a scare on campus. We were put into a soft lockdown because police had reports that someone was in the area with a firearm. It turned out later that it was a drunk man who had fired a gun into the air; he never actually threatened anyone or stepped foot on our campus. But at the time we were concerned, obviously, and Sandor got his gun and went down to our main entrance. Everyone saw him; it was rather surreal, seeing a professor holding a gun."

"Yes, yes. I remember. That was last year," Hans said. "So I suppose there were many people who knew Sandor had a gun. On the other hand, the person who came in didn't have to know he had it. If Sandor pulled it out and they wrestled over it, that would also explain how the person got

Sandor's gun."

"Huh." I sat and thought about this while the waiter reappeared and took our orders. I asked for tomato soup with a turkey sandwich, and my companions ordered similar fare. I wondered what sort of meal my mother was having with Alex. "On another note, do either of you know Tony Malandro?"

Hans smiled. "Mr. Handsome?"

Livia laughed.

"What am I missing?" I asked.

Livia shook her head. "No, I shouldn't laugh. And, no, I don't really know him. But he and Sandor would often gather attention, playing chess in that public forum. And they were interesting to watch. But sometimes we got the impression that Dr. Tony played more for the — ah — theatrical aspect of it."

"Meaning what?"

"That he liked being seen," Hans said. "But perhaps that's how life feels when you are good-looking and a doctor, and probably very wealthy. As though everyone just waits for you to walk onto the stage."

"Wow. That bad, huh?"

Hans shrugged.

I sighed and took a sip of my water. "Thank you for taking me out, both of you.

This is a nice treat. I don't eat out that often."

"Surely your boyfriend takes you?" Livia's wide brown eyes were curious.

"When he can. But he works weird hours, and I pride myself on keeping him filled with homemade food, often Hungarian fare. So we eat in my apartment, or his, or at my parents' or grandparents' house. But we've been here a few times."

"Ah."

"I promise not to talk about Sandor the whole time, but, Livia, can I ask something about — when you two were together? Will that make Hans jealous?"

Hans grinned at me. "Hans does have the capacity for jealousy, but he is fairly confident of his companion's devotion." He pointed at her left hand, where a ring sparkled.

"Oh! Livia" — her eyes were smiling now, and fixed on me — "that is brand-new!"

"Yes. Hans proposed last night. Once again. In such a romantic way that I could not refuse."

"Congratulations to you both!"

"Thank you," they said in unison, and turned to smile at each other. I realized that they were quite comfortable together, and that without even looking at each other they had seemed quite connected since we had arrived.

Livia turned back to me. "So what did you want to know about Sandor?"

"Just — on the day of his memorial at the tea house, I overheard you telling Yvonne that he still had feelings for you. But people suggested that he was devoted to his wife. Could his feelings have been a misunderstanding?"

The waiter arrived with three bowls of soup, and Livia waited until he was gone. I got the sense that she had been carefully framing her answer. "I may have read things wrong," she said. "Many people have told me that Sandor and Nancy were utterly devoted to each other since the reunion. Perhaps what I read as overtures were just Sandor being friendly."

"Hmm."

"Sandor was a romantic," Hans said. "He loved romance, and romancing. But his greatest love was, perhaps, not a woman."

"You'll need to explain that," I said, taking a sip of my soup.

Hans laughed. "Let's put it this way. For a time, he was dating Wanda Lee."

"Yes, I had heard that."

"One night he and Wanda were going off to some concert. I remember seeing her in

his office, dressed in a lovely red gown, looking quite attractive. Sandor was slogging
away at something on his computer, some
form he had to fill out as part of his work as
chair. She had to lure him away from his
desk, but she finally did, and then he went
into romantic mode, dancing her around
the room, telling her she looked mysterious
with her red dress and dark hair. Things like
that. I had come in to ask a question, but I
watched them for a while, laughing at
Sandor's antics. Then I wished them a good
night and went back to my office."

Livia and I shrugged. "Why is that so
strange?" Livia said.

"Ten minutes later I looked up and saw
them walking past." He turned to me. "We
have windows on the outer wall of our offices so that everyone can see in, and out.
So I watched them walk past on their way
to the exit. Wanda was chattering away,
excited to be going out. Sandor was listening quietly, but he turned and looked back
at his office, just before they moved out of
sight. Looked back with longing."

I tore a piece of bread off of my sandwich
bun. "So you're saying his true love was his
work?"

"Yes, essentially. And that office that he
turned into a little museum. He loved being

in it. It was more than a home to him — it was his identity."

"That's silly," Livia said. "He loved going out, with Wanda and then with me."

"Did it cause problems between you and Wanda? Being co-workers, and both going out with Sandor?"

They both seemed to realize at the same time that I was firing a lot of questions their way. Livia stiffened slightly, and Hans raised his brows. "Are you here on behalf of the police?"

"No! I'm just very curious. When I'm presented with a puzzle, I have a need to solve it, somehow. So I tend to ask a lot of questions when one big question remains unanswered."

Livia slumped slightly in her seat. "I'm afraid we can't answer the big question. And, no, not really. I think Wanda was sad when Sandor broke things off with her. That was at least two years ago, though. Water under the bridge. Sandor tended to move on. What's that expression? About the moss and the stone?"

Hans made a wry face. "A rolling stone gathers no moss. Yes, I suppose Sandor was a bit of a rolling stone."

Livia nodded, absently stirring her soup with her spoon. "And yet he returned home.

So he rolled in a circle, right? It was more than two months ago that he told me he was moving back to Sycamore Street. He and Nancy have a lovely house there."

Hans lifted a finger of annunciation. "And now, we are finished talking about our poor friend. We must talk about Christmas, and a new year, and bright and happy things."

"Like your engagement," I said.

He smiled at Livia, and again I felt a wave of positive emotion. "Yes, like that," he said.

After Hans bid us farewell and discreetly paid our bill, Livia and I were left to plot out our shopping course. "I can't believe it's already getting dark," she complained. "It's only five-thirty."

"Late lunch and daylight savings," I said lightly. "But it will feel cozier because we can see all the Christmas lights."

We made our way out of the restaurant and onto an Andrews Street that sparkled in the twilight. Livia wanted to visit a woolen shop, and I told her about Ulveflokk and my connection to Runa and Thyra.

"Oh, I love their stuff! I got some of their gloves last winter, and they're the warmest thing I own. I don't have them now because they don't go with this coat. They're a lovely blend of pinks and purples." We walked into the shop called Warm Your Heart, and Livia began studying a rack of scarves.

I was drawn to some earth-toned cable-knit sweaters; I found a cardigan that looked perfect for my father. The price tag was a bit steep, though. A saleswoman material-ized beside me and said, "That's on sale today." Was it part of their training? In any case, it worked. I went dutifully to the counter with my selection, and a young woman named Tessa happily rang me up and wished me a merry Christmas.

I waited at the door for Livia, who ulti-mately bought nothing, and we moved down the darkening street with the fortitude of women who have only begun to shop. A bookstore, an electronics store, a sewing shop (Livia was a seamstress, apparently), and a pet shop where she bought a doggie sweater for her mother's dog, Rodolfo, and I bought holiday scarves for Antony and Cleopatra, and another for Major, my child-hood cat, who lived with my parents. We moved toward a chocolate shop that I very passionately wanted to visit, and I saw a familiar face on the crowded sidewalk. "Hey, isn't that Yvonne?" I asked.

Livia had been smiling at a window dis-play, but her head turned sharply at my words. "Yvonne from RU? My new chair?"

She scanned the crowd and shook her head. "I don't see her."

"No, I've lost her now, too. It's so weird — I saw her just recently at the hospital."

"Why were you there?" Her brows formed a line of concern.

"Long story. I was visiting a friend. But I guess she has a sick —"

"Oh, Yvonne. She always has some sort of drama. That might be why she seems sour to people."

"Sour? You mean unpleasant? Yes, she does seem that way. Are you saying she's not?"

Livia shrugged. "She has had her good moments, yes."

"And are you glad that she'll be running the department?"

Her eyes did not meet mine. "Time will tell. Now we must go into this chocolate shop and breathe deeply, yes?"

I put my hand on her arm. "Livia — do you think everyone in your building was aware that Sandor's collection was worth money?"

"What?" Now she leaned in slightly to study my face. "Well, those of us who knew Sandor — yes, probably. He talked about it often enough. He'd say, 'Oh, come see my newest acquisition.' Once I even saw him showing off his statues to the mail carrier." She smiled at this memory. "You know, he gave me some of those trinkets, too. Not long before he and Nancy reconciled, he gave me a Herend snake. A beautiful porcelain, painted orange with white flowers. It was a garden snake, he told me — not evil or bad luck, but protection for one's garden and home. A good omen."

"I saw that snake in a picture! It was lovely."

"It was. I adored that little thing, and especially the smile on the snake's face. It had a friendly demeanor." I chuckled. Then Livia shook her head. "But I gave it back to him. On the night before he died, it turns out. I didn't think I could keep such an expensive gift; I told him, and I think he understood. He said, 'He's yours whenever you want him back, Livia.' And he gave me such a sad look — oh, I hate to think about it. And the next morning —"

"It's a terrible thing," I said, putting an arm around her.

"Yes. All the more reason that we need chocolate, yes?" She smiled and, my arm still around her shoulders, steered us into the sweetly fragrant chocolaterie.

Eventually Livia and I, weary but satisfied, said our good-byes and went our separate ways. By the time I walked back to my car, I was laden with several bags and feeling that I had just about finished with my Christmas shopping. I was almost at the parking lot and walking past Stones by Sparkle when I saw Sparkle herself in the window. I attempted a wave, and she waved back, but in the dimness, I couldn't tell if she was smiling. I did still want to buy rings for all the women in my family, but I was tired, and I could always stop by Sparkle's after work on another day.

I was about to keep walking when my gaze moved from Sparkle to the pine outside her window — the one where I had seen young Frank standing as though he were about to enter Narnia. It had been a strange moment, watching him hover there, shivering in the cold.

The tree was covered now with a net of tiny white lights. They seemed to grow brighter and brighter as I stared at them, and suddenly I realized why: Frank had lied to the police.

I moved swiftly to my car and bundled my packages inside. I turned on the motor and let the heater warm up; in the meantime, I called my grandmother and asked for Frank's phone number.

"Why?" she asked, her voice suspicious.

"I just want to ask him a question."

"For your wolf?"

"No. Why does everyone keep asking me that? I'm just asking for myself. May I have his number, please?"

My grandmother grumbled in Hungarian but gave me what I asked for. I said I would see her soon and ended the call.

I dialed Frank's house, and, to my relief, the phone was answered by Frank himself. I hadn't relished trying to explain to either of his parents why I wanted to talk to him.

"Frank, this is Hana — from the tea house."

"Oh, hi, Hana. Did you guys need us to do the windows again? We're not scheduled until —"

"No, this isn't about that."

"Oh, okay." He sounded uncertain, so I plunged in.

"It's about the day I saw you in the snow."

"What?"

"The day you hid the gun."

"I already answered all the police's questions. They know everything."

"But there's one thing they don't know, Frank, and I don't know, either. What did you throw into the tree?"

"What?" He sounded genuinely shocked.

"After you dumped the gun, wrapped in

your coat, why did you come out of the alley and throw something in the tree? And what was it?"

"What do you —"

"It was either a lipstick or a beer can, or maybe something that you came back for later on. What was it, Frank? I'm just trying to piece some things together. It's not like it's going to hurt you one way or another; you've already faced the police."

Silence on the other end of the line. "I don't know why you care about this," he said finally.

"I don't, either, except it's been bothering me. Why would you stop at that tree, and what did you throw into it?"

"It was nothing," he said. "Just a lipstick. I found it on the floor by the gun."

My face grew hot. "Why didn't you just throw it in the dumpster with the coat?"

"I forgot I had it. I had shoved it in my pocket before I picked up the gun."

A blank moment. "Why?"

"It looked like the kind my mom uses. She buys the lipsticks with those round black tubes. I didn't want anyone to think —"

"But now you know your mom didn't do it, Frank, and so do the police. That's probably Revlon lipstick. It's relatively cheap and lots of women buy it. It could have belonged to anyone."

"I know, I guess. I got out of the alley and put my hands in my pockets and felt it still in there. So I threw it in the tree."

"Frank. You need to tell the police that."

"I can't! I already lied to them once. I don't want to tell them I left something out!"

I kept my voice gentle. "Why *did* you leave it out?"

"I don't know. I guess I was still protecting my mom. Or I just forgot to mention it; I don't remember."

Frank was still afraid; that made me afraid, too.

"Hana, could you please tell him? That guy who is your boyfriend? Just tell him I forgot. I don't want to go back to the station, where they'll all give me those looks and say I'm in trouble."

I sighed. More evidence taken from the scene, thrown away, and not mentioned to the police. He *was* in trouble. "Frank, I'll tell Erik. I cannot guarantee what happens after that, but I will frame it in the most sympathetic terms. Okay?"

"Yeah, all right. Can you let me know what he says? I don't want to worry all night that they're going to pound down my door."

"They're busy right now, Frank. No one's

going to pound down your door for this, but — they'll be displeased."

"Yeah, I get it. Sorry," he said.

I said good-bye with another promise that I would call him back.

The car was warm now. I pulled out of the parking lot and made the drive home on autopilot; my mind raced with the possibilities, including the idea that the lipstick could have been planted at the scene to make it look as though a particular person had killed Sandor, but that seemed unlikely. By the time I reached my parking lot, one thing felt true: a woman had committed this crime.

I gathered my packages, locked my car, and went inside my warm and welcoming building. There was no sign of Iris or her family at the foot of the stairs; I climbed to my apartment, greeted the vocal cats, and put down my things.

I set my hands on my hips and surveyed the room. "We need light, we need tea, we need cat food, and we need Hana's notebook," I told the cats. I fed them first, to stop their singing, and then I turned on all my Christmas lights. I decided to save the present wrapping for another day, so I put my bags in a corner of the kitchen, but I did retrieve some chocolates that I had bought to share with Erik.

With a flick of the wrist I turned on the flame under the teakettle, and then I got the notebook in which I had made all of my notations for Erik, including long lists of suspects and their connections to Sandor. Now I crossed out the names of the men and wrote this reduced and pointed list:

"Yvonne Yves; Sarah Dobos; Wanda Lee." After a moment's thought, I added: "Livia Parravicini; Nancy Balog." And then: "Alessandra Spencer-Malandro."

Erik Wolf was not pleased to hear about Frank's omission. I let him verbalize some threats in a loud and aggrieved voice. I set a bowl of chicken soup in front of him, along with a sandwich on beer bread. He started eating, still grumbling in his throat, and I massaged his shoulders. Finally, I peered around to find him wearing a wry expression. "A carefully calculated plan of attack, Hana Keller."

"I just wanted you to have time to process it. Frank was afraid, Erik. He was afraid about the lipstick, and then he was afraid of you."

He drummed his fingers on the table. I felt him relax slightly under my massaging fingers. "It didn't have prints on it. It might have, when that young idiot picked it up, but there was nothing usable when we found it."

"There's something else you should know, by the way."

"Oh?"

"I had lunch with Livia and Hans Weber. They just got engaged." I stopped massaging and sat down across from him. "They said that Sandor was always in his office, even at midnight. And that everyone knew he was a fixture in the building. That they knew, too, that he kept a gun in his drawer."

"Is that so?" asked my boyfriend, widening his green eyes.

"Yes. And Hans said that Sandor's true love was his work, and his office."

"Hmm."

I gazed at him for a while. A gentle green-gold light hung around him like a vague halo. He was feeling cranky and tired, but as always, he was beautiful to me.

Eventually he felt my admiration and managed a grudging smile. "Despite all your efforts, Frank is not off the hook."

"No, of course not. You can worry about that tomorrow. Tonight is your time to relax. Crime will still be there in the morning."

He was laughing now. "Hana, you are transparent, but somehow effective anyway."

"It's magic," I said.

"What else did you learn from Livia and Hans?"

There was more, but nothing that couldn't wait until the morning. "Just some more campus gossip. No big red flags. But a certain friend of yours has brought you a mouse."

Erik looked down at Antony, who had sidled in with his toy to impress the visitor. Erik laughed and bent down to get it, then threw it out of the room. Antony gave chase; meanwhile Cleopatra, who normally didn't show off but was learning how to do it from her brother, jumped into Erik's lap and began butting her head into his stomach.

"It's a conspiracy," he said softly.

Erik eventually went home; he had to sort through his mail and do some work, but he promised me that he would get a good night's sleep. After he left, I turned off my lights and went into my room, where a string of white lights lined the large window and glimmered like a celestial frame around the moon. I had put a couple of strands of tinsel on the top branches of Isabella, my Norfolk pine, and they, too, glittered on my windowsill, making my bed seem like some magical portal. I climbed under my covers and looked out at the last of the snow, which clung to tree branches and frozen grass.

My phone buzzed on my bedside table; I had three texts. The first, from Erik: I'm home. I miss you. The second, from Runa: Feeling good. We're thinking of naming her Anya. The third, from my uncle Zoltan, a response to my thank-you: You're welcome, dear Hana. I hope you enjoy them. Even when you were eleven you told me that someday you were going to live in a giant mansion and collect beautiful things.

"Got it half right," I murmured. I turned off my light and unplugged the white lights so that only the moon illuminated my bedroom.

I closed my eyes. The cats tucked against me and purred.

Zoltan in the snow. The image was before me again, behind my closed lids, reminding me of something I had forgotten . . . but then the snow grew into a flurry, and then a storm, and then darkness.

CHAPTER 15
GYPSY RINGS

We were busy all the following day with a
huge Christmas event at the tea house; my
new friend Henrik Sipos at the chamber of
commerce was hosting a party for all Riverwood merchants and employees. It was a
bustling affair, and we three tea house ladies
were running at what felt like twice the
usual speed to see to everyone and to greet
the people we knew. François had been a
bit overloaded with the holiday schedule
and had received our permission to bring in
Claire for a day to help him in the back
room. I had feared they would spend it
mooning around and stealing kisses, but
they were both far too professional for that,
and they turned out an amazing array of
sandwiches and tea cakes for Henrik's event.

After two hours I found a moment of
quiet, hiding near the World Tree so that I
could escape both François's clipped com-
mands and the guests' rather voracious

desire for conversation. Henrik wandered past and found me there. His face brightened, and he lunged in to give me a hug. I always responded positively to Henrik: he had a long and beautiful history with my family, and a fascinating personal history, as well.

"Hallo, Hana! Are you enjoying this Christmas season?" he asked, smiling into my face. I always felt a warmth coming from Henrik, as though he had found a way to house joy permanently in his tall, thin body.

"Yes, yes. It's busy, but I have many things to be grateful for. I'm enjoying the beauty of the holiday."

"That's the spirit," Henrik said. He was still holding my hands in his and didn't seem to have plans to let go. This was classic Henrik: lots of beaming and joyful clasping.

I was about to pull my hands away when I had a thought. "Henrik. You know many of the Hungarians in town, right?"

"Oh yes."

"Did you happen to know Professor Balog, at Riverwood —"

"Oh, poor Sandor. Yes, yes. We planned many events together. And we shared seats on the board of the Hungarian-American Heritage Center."

I became lightheaded at the thought of Henrik and all the information he might have. He was peripheral yet important; I doubted the police had even spoken to him. He was like untouched snow . . .

"Is there something you needed, dear?"

"Yes. Can you sit in back with me for a moment? I just wanted to ask you a couple of questions."

He finally let go of my hands. "In back? Oh, of course! I would love to see this hidden room where all the magical treats are made," he said, following me into the kitchen and earning surprised glances from François and Claire, who were putting the final frosted touches on some tiny lemon cakes.

"François, you remember Henrik Sipos?"

François nodded; even he, with his perpetual disdain, could not dislike Henrik. "How are you, sir?" he asked.

Henrik nodded. "Very well. Everything is delicious!"

I met François's gaze. "We'll just be a minute. We want to talk in private."

"Sure, sure," François said, and then he began a quiet conference with Claire about something on their pastry tray.

I sat down with my guest and said, "First of all, what did you think when you heard

Sandor had been killed?"

Henrik looked mournful. "I said a prayer, of course. And I wondered — an angry student? An angry co-worker? Who had done this?"

"Why didn't you think it was a stranger?"

He pondered this question. "I suppose — things he had told me. Occasional discord at his office, you know. Things that stayed on his mind. People came there for help, but also to complain. I suppose this is the norm, yes? But lately, so many complaints. And he was going through stressful things, trying to sell his house, trying to deal with changes in his department."

"Oh, yes. Because he and his wife had gotten back together. But what sorts of changes? Do you mean the reductions in his department?"

"He didn't go into detail. Just, I knew he felt rather sad about it all. It weighed upon him, you see. Because ultimately he was a good man."

"What do you mean, ultimately? Was he not always good at first glance?"

Henrik leaned toward me and studied my face. "You are very exacting, very precise. If I didn't know better, I would think you were a policeman."

"No, just Hana."

He sighed. "Sandor was like any one of us. Sometimes very selfish. Other times altruistic. It depended on the moment."

"Henrik."

He nodded, waiting for my question.

I leaned in. "Tell me something selfish that Sandor did."

Later, from my kitchen, where the cats sat in the window and watched the wind blow the dust of snow into tiny whirlwinds in the corners of the parking lot, I talked into Erik's ear. "One of the reasons he and Nancy broke up was that Sandor would use their savings for his 'discoveries.' Money they had saved together, and which he would wipe out with the promise that he would return it soon, perhaps after a game of chess paid off, or after he sold something that no longer enthralled him. Sometimes he did sell things, Henrik said, but he bought far more than he sold, and his wife lived in fear that he would bankrupt them."

"Ah," Erik said.

"Also, I guess he really was being selfish about his Hungarian program. It was a distinctive program on campus, but not as popular in terms of numbers as any of the other languages. So the fact that he was lobbying to keep it suggested he wasn't really going to bat for his department members."

"Right." He was rustling papers on his desk, but I could tell he was thinking about my words.

"So I wonder — who else did Sandor victimize with his selfishness? Because it seems the man didn't always realize how unacceptable his behavior appeared from the other side."

"Blinded by his desires?"

"Perhaps. I don't know. There's something we're missing here, something important."

"We?" he said. He was smiling; I could hear it in his voice.

"Yes, we. It's your job, but it's my *puzzle.* I want to know what happened. I knew the man. He was likable. But there are so many different views of him, it's like a kaleidoscope."

"Welcome to my world."

I sighed. "Are you coming over tonight?"

"Probably not. Tomorrow for sure, though." He paused. "I bought you a birthday present on my lunch hour."

"You don't have to worry about that stuff when you're this busy."

"That *stuff* is finding a token of my esteem for the woman I love. Nothing is more important."

Something melted inside me; I feared I

would slide right off my chair . . . "That's nice," I managed. "Maybe come over to-night."

He laughed and sounded young. "We'll see."

"How's Runa? She sent me a text and seemed really upbeat."

"My dad was with her today; he told me that she and the baby are getting strong. The doctor is very happy."

"She said her little warrior might be named Anya."

"So weird to think of Runa with a daughter. I still think of us all as kids, despite our professions."

"Time for the next generation."

"Yeah." He cleared his throat. "Much as I love talking to you, I have to go."

"Okay."

"Keep working on your puzzle. And call me with any epiphanies." His voice was growing distant as he began to think about the tasks that awaited him. Erik Wolf, when working on a case, could be as elusive as the solution to the puzzle that tormented us both.

I made a batch of cookies and thought again about dualities. I decided to list any that came into my mind; since I was busy stirring batter, I recited them into my phone's recorder.

"Okay, things that happen in twos: at least two views of Sandor. Two entrances to his building. Two possible outcomes for every event: example, Runa's baby could have died, but she lived. Two sisters, Runa and Thyra. Two brothers, Erik and Felix. Two women in Sandor's life when he separated from Nancy. Two ways of viewing each person — those who liked and disliked Sandor. Same for Tony Malandro. Same for everyone, I guess."

I finished flicking rounds of dough onto a pan, and I slid the pan into the oven.

I grabbed my notebook and began to write a more concrete list:

TWOS
Alternative views of everything:
— Two lovers: Livia and Sandor — finished, or at least Livia believed they had been, and she returned the snake Sandor gave her
— Two proposals: Hans had to propose at least twice. Why?
— Two male friends: Hans and Tony — claimed they had been close to Sandor
— Two women who were not his wife: Livia and Wanda

— Two department chairs: Sandor and Yvonne

— Two Malandros: Tony and Alex — why was she so worried about his involvement?

— Two views of Tony: the selfish gambling egotist, and the man Alex loved

— Two guns: one at Sandor's office, one at his home. Why?

— Two pictures: one in the yearbook, which included the Fisher Woman; one in the crime scene photo, which did not

— Two purchases: Falken bought the World Tree and the Fisher Woman. How did he afford all of these things? Did he allow a certain amount for purchases, or was he like Sandor, buying things he couldn't really afford?

— Two houses: Sandor would certainly have been saving money when he moved back home with Nancy. Didn't that help alleviate his financial burden?

— Two pieces of evidence found by Frank: both removed from the scene. What had convinced Erik that Sarah Dobos wasn't guilty?

— Two other guns: the one Frank removed, and the one that his father said was safely locked up at home

— Two companions to St. Nicholas: one

good, one evil

— Two destinations for a human being in
the World Tree: heaven or hell

I sighed, realizing I was getting nowhere.
Then I looked up at my glass cabinet and
saw Zoltan's gift. I added:

— Twin lizards

This reminded me of the night of my tea
party, when the image of Frank in the alley
had seemed so monumental. Something
about the path he had taken; there were two
ways he could have gone, and two ways to
view the situation. That had stayed with me,
as had the image of Zoltan in the snow.

It also reminded me that I had promised
to call Frank back, and I had promised to
show my teacups to Falken.

I dialed Frank's number, and his mother
answered. I introduced myself and asked to
speak with her son. He said hello a moment
later, sounding nervous. "Hi, Frank. I
promised I'd call you back. Have you heard
from the police at all?"

"No. Am I going to hear from them?" His
voice sounded higher than I remembered.

"If you haven't by now, probably not. I
told Erik a couple days ago. He wasn't

pleased, but I think the lipstick is water under the bridge at this point. If for some reason they do call, just tell them you forgot you had done that. You told me that, right? That you thought in the chaos of being questioned that you focused on Sandor and the gun, and forgot about the lipstick."

"Yeah, pretty much."

"But I think you're in the clear. Erik hasn't said any more about it."

"Okay. Thanks, Hana." His voice was relieved.

"Have a nice Christmas," I said, and we ended the call.

I scrolled through my phone, looking for Falken's number. I thought that maybe if I talked the case out with him he would help me see something I had missed. After all, Falken was my connection to Sandor. Those times that we chatted at Timeless Treasures, Sandor so friendly and erudite, holding a purring Inspektor . . . Yes, Falken was a key. And he was friends with Nancy; perhaps I could get him to bring her along. With the soothing effects of tea and cakes, perhaps she would reveal more about Sandor's actual financial state. Hadn't she just been to a meeting with the executor of Sandor's will?

I dialed Falken's store and he answered

right away. "Hello, Hana!"

"Caller ID has taken all the fun out of phone calls."

"Some of it, for sure," he agreed.

"Hey, remember when I said that you should see my uncle's gift? The Herend Yellow Dynasty cups?"

"I do, and I intend to hold you to that offer!"

"How about tomorrow morning? A quick little tea party, maybe around ten? I have a three o'clock event, and I know you open at noon tomorrow, right?"

"Sounds like a plan. What should I bring?"

"Nothing. I'll have tea and cakes for you and Elise if she's available. But there is another *who* you could bring."

"Ah?"

"Nancy. I feel like I didn't get to say much to her at your store, and everything was so awkward because I had called the police."

"That did make things awkward," Falken agreed with a laugh.

"Hey, speaking of that — did you get your money back? Or will you? That's a lot of cash."

"I did in fact receive a refund from the pawnshop owner. The police are investigating him, and he didn't want to appear shady by withholding funds from the sale of stolen merchandise. I lucked out. Hopefully he'll somehow get reimbursed, too. He's a good guy."

"You think everyone is a good guy." I paused, then said, "How do you have the money, anyway? To buy all those things? For thousands of dollars sometimes, especially if a sale isn't guaranteed?"

"Good question. Believe me, if I invest a large amount, it's because I'm confident I can sell it for more. My instincts have served me well so far. They have been lucrative, shall we say? I rarely make the wrong decision these days. When I first started out? Yes. But then my wife threatened to divorce me, and I learned my lesson."

"Ah. Maybe that's what happened with Sandor and Nancy."

"I think it very well may be. I shall ask Nancy if she would like to attend the tea party. Elise will be thrilled to be invited."

"Good! It's been too long since I chatted with your lovely wife."

"Terrific. I'll text you tonight to let you know whether it will be two or three."

"Thanks, Falken!"

Cleopatra wandered past with a look of cat contentment. That made me think of Inspektor, who had essentially led me to the Fisher Woman at Falken's store. Really, if

302

Inspektor had not been sitting just under it, would I have seen it at all? I had been in a hurry that day . . .

I shook my head. I was doing too much random surmising. What did I think, that a cat had helped me solve a mystery? I laughed and looked at my tea set. "Tomorrow you get your second show, guys! I have to tell Zoltan how much attention you're getting in just over a week."

Then I noticed the bags I had stuffed in one corner because I had been too tired to wrap presents. I checked on my cookies, found that they were done, and set them on the stove to cool.

I went to my pantry and removed wrapping paper, tape, and scissors from the drawer where I kept them and returned dutifully to my table, the wrapping station at every holiday. "Wrap and stash," I murmured to the cats, who strolled in to watch. "That's the secret, guys."

Since Erik couldn't come over, I decided to brave the cold night for some more shopping in pretty downtown Riverwood. I waited until my car warmed up before venturing out of my parking lot, fiddling with the radio dial until I heard some classic Christmas music. Bing Crosby crooned in my ear as I piloted the car beneath a clear dark sky dotted with glittering stars. A burst of wind slammed into the side of my car with a low howling sound. This pleased me. I liked cold winter weather — the flip side of warm and cozy, and the thing that made warm and cozy such a pleasure. I thought about this: another duality. Because of the cold, I found joy in my flannel sheets and warm blankets; in the soft fur of my cats, and the sight of them cuddled together; in the warm touch of Erik Wolf when he rested his hand on the back of my neck; in the bracing heat of the tea we served each day; in the warmth of my grandmother's chicken soup, which filled a soul with love.

I turned onto Andrews Street with a pleasant feeling; it would be fun to do a dose of shopping again, if only to look at all the pretty decorations. The first store that caught my eye, of course, was Stones by Sparkle. Ah! I could get my gypsy rings. The more I thought about it, the more I felt my tea house ladies would really enjoy this gift.

I parked near Sparkle's store. A sign on the meter assured me that I needn't pay for the spot, and "Merry Christmas from Downtown Riverwood!" "Nice," I said. I made my way to the store, with its twinkling windows and glimmering garlands. I could see through the front pane that it was a bit more crowded this time. Indeed, when I walked into the shop, greeted again by the lovely scents of candles, especially a balsam-scented one that Sparkle had burning in the window, I saw at least three different groups milling through the store: a group of sisters, based on their resemblance to one another, was closely studying the precious stones. A tall, elderly man was peering at the snow globes, while a young couple stood at the counter, chatting with Sparkle as she wrapped their purchases in her pretty tissue paper.

The room was warm and full of good vibes. I caught Sparkle's eye and waved, then moved slowly up and down the aisles, absorbing the Christmas spirit and soothing myself with the sight of lovely things. I ended up at the snow globe table. Sparkle had put out some new ones; the man I had seen earlier was holding one with the Chicago skyline inside. He looked at me and said, "A little cliché, huh?"

I shrugged. "Someone might love it, but if you're going for pure beauty, I think this one is the nicest." I pointed to a replica of the one I had gotten for my grandmother — the one that reminded me of her tales of her childhood town. The snow within it had a lovely, silvery quality that could provide many hours of joy for a snow globe fan.

He nodded. "You know, that was the first one I looked at. Then my brain kept showing me other options."

I shook my head. "This one is the best, hands down. I would love to open it on Christmas."

"You sold me, young lady. Now — how are you at selecting the perfect earrings for an eighteen-year-old girl?"

"It depends on the answers to several questions."

He perked up. "I'm ready. Let's see how well I know my granddaughter. Shoot!"

"Okay. Does she have pierced ears?"

His face fell. "Ah, dang. Lost on the first one. Hang on, let me text my wife." He sent a text to his wife, using one finger and perching his glasses on his nose so that he could better read the message on the phone. He waited a moment while I played with a snow globe that had a white ceramic puppy inside. Then he said, "Okay, yes — she does."

"Great. What color are her eyes?"

He looked a bit depressed, then perked up. "They're definitely in the brown family. Maybe touches of gold."

"Good, good. How much jewelry does she

tend to wear?"

He took a deep breath. "Well, let's see. She doesn't drape herself in it. I mean, she's not dripping with jewels. But I think she usually has a necklace and some earrings. Wait, I have a photo."

He scrolled around on his phone and then showed me a cute picture of a brunette girl with dimples and a pixie cut. Her earrings were small rhinestones, her necklace a delicate silver fawn with painted-on spots. "Is that Bambi?" I asked.

"Yeah. We got that for her when she was a little kid, and she still wears it."

"So she's sentimental," I said. "That's good to know, too."

"Okay."

"Here's another one: only child, or sibling?"

"She's got two sisters."

"Ah. Look what Sparkle has over here." I led him to a side table, where the three sisters were still staring down at the stones. I led the man to the necklaces; he still clutched the snow globe that I had recommended. I pointed down to some necklaces suspended on delicate silver chains. "See the sign? These are called 'family jewelry.' You can pick the one that represents your whole family, or just choose sibling groups.

Here's a three-sisters necklace."

It was a lovely piece, depicting three sterling silver women with simple dresses, holding hands in a way that suggested there was strength in numbers. On the bosom of each gown was a carved heart. "It's only twenty dollars," I said. "I don't know your budget, but you could potentially get one of these for each sister. A sign of their bond with one another. Something they can wear all their lives."

He studied it for a moment, then said, "Do you mind holding this up, like you're wearing it?"

I did, and we both contemplated it in a little mirror that Sparkle had there. It was quite attractive; it made me wish I had a sister. But then I saw the two-sisters necklace and realized it would be perfect for Runa and Thyra, who shared such a strong bond.

"I want it," he said. "You're really good at this. They should give you a commission."

The couple who had been ringing up walked past us and went out into the cold darkness, and Sparkle appeared beside us. "Why should I give you a commission?" she asked brightly.

"She just sold me on four things. I want three of these sisters necklaces and this snow globe."

Sparkle brightened. "Oh, that is a popular choice this season! Let me take those up to the front and start wrapping them for you."

I handed her two of the dual-sisters necklaces. "And I want these for a beautiful pair of twins I know. What a cool idea for jewelry. Such a great way to show solidarity with your loved ones."

"Yes, it's a distinctive gift. They look great with casual or elegant outfits. Okay, wow, what a haul here," she said, laughing. She moved up toward the front, and the man with me stuck out his hand.

"Young lady, you have made my job very easy."

"Well, of course I have to know how they like the gifts," I said. I dug in my purse for one of our Maggie's Tea House cards and handed it to him. "I'm Hana. Maggie is my mom, and I work at the tea house. Bring your family sometime."

"I would love that, dear lady. Perhaps a New Year's event."

"In any case, give me a call, or shoot me a note at that e-mail there."

He nodded with a sage expression. "I will do that. Look for a note from Harry Wilde."

"Have a wonderful Christmas, Harry!"

"You, too, Hana. I guess I'll go pay the

piper," he said, and I laughed. He went to the front desk and began to use his charm on Sparkle.

I moved to the ring table and scanned over the possibilities. The stones varied from small, unobtrusive things to large, glittering baubles. "Bingo," I said.

Held up to the light, the largest stones seemed to possess a fiery inner glow. I especially liked the amber, the purple, and the red. They were essentially tiny crystal balls; I knew the drama of the stones would appeal to my grandmother, who had always enjoyed glittery things. The bands were adjustable, one size fits all. I selected my three favorites and held them loosely in my hand. Sparkle was ringing up the sisters, and they enjoyed some happy holiday conversation. I paused at the candle wall on my way to the register, sampling the various scents and indulging my senses: spicy aromas, glimmering lights, happy chatter, smooth, sculpted wax in my hand — and a sudden strange taste on my tongue. I stood still, gathering awareness, and felt the last people move behind me and open the door. A gust of cold air cooled my cheeks; the shoppers bundled down the stairs, laughing and jostling, and then were gone.

Sparkle appeared at my side. "Ready to

ring out, hon?"

"Yes, sure. I have these three rings. The rest you have up at the front."

"I do, and I've already started boxing them. Come on over and we can talk while I do it."

Something odd, disjointed, was making it hard for me to come up with conversation. "How are sales?" I managed.

"They're great! I'm not sure what it is, but December sales have exceeded expectations."

"Good, good."

Sparkle chatted happily, working her magic with curling ribbon and scissors, then tucking everything into her pretty store bags.

"There. All the jewelry is boxed separately, and I've removed all the price tags, okay, hon?"

"That's great. Thank you, Sparkle."

"Unless I see you here again, have a wonderful Christmas."

"You, too."

I started walking toward the door, and she followed me. "I have to admit, I'll be glad when I can close up in an hour and put on my pj's. Maybe have some hot chocolate and a Netflix movie."

"Sounds good," I said, not really hearing her.

When my hand touched the door latch, she covered it with hers. I turned in surprise; her eyes had widened, and her smile had disappeared. "Hana," she said.

Something vibrated in the air around us. "Yes."

"I think — everything is about to change for you."

"I know," I said.

When I walked out into the deepening cold, I felt her eyes on me, fearful or concerned.

CHAPTER 16
COLD AND DARKNESS

The strange feeling persisted, but I realized it wasn't fear. Something in the darkness was calling to me; or perhaps I really wanted to solve the puzzle of Sandor's death.

I started my car and sat while the heater warmed up. I wasn't far from Sycamore Street, where Sandor had lived. The street, I knew from my chats with Livia, was informally called "Professor Lane" because so many of the Riverwood faculty lived on it, and on several of the streets surrounding the university. Many of them walked or biked to work. Livia said she loved it because it "had a European feel."

Suddenly curious, I drove to Sycamore, which was only three blocks long. It was a cozy little street, dotted with muted Christmas decorations and tasteful lawn ornaments. The street was full of parked cars; everyone was home for the night. I took the first spot I could find and pulled up behind an SUV with a vanity plate that read "RWLWPRF2." I stared at it for a while. RW was probably Riverwood. What was LWPRF? Lower Prefect? Last Week Perfect? Law Professor? Ah. That was it. Riverwood did have a respected law school.

I climbed out of my car and walked through the parkway to the sidewalk. A man was out in front of his house, doing some night shoveling. He said, "Evening," to me as I walked past. I didn't recognize him, and he didn't seem professorial, but then again, was there only one type? The people who had come to Sandor's event at the tea house had been a diverse lot, to say the least.

The street seemed dark after the intense light of Andrews Street, with its Christmas bulbs and bright shop windows. Here it was subdued, quiet. The sound of my feet crunching along the icy sidewalk was all I could hear, aside from the occasional dog bark or train horn sounding from the Metra tracks several blocks away.

A figure walked down a driveway two houses ahead of me, carrying bags of garbage. By the time I reached the driveway she had put the bags into a can near the street and turned back, and that's when I saw her face under a lackluster streetlight; it was Yvonne Yves.

"Oh — hello," I said.

She wore a huge black sweater, and she burrowed into its warmth as the December wind gusted into us both. Her expression was somewhere between surprised and suspicious. "Hello. It's Hana, right? What brings you here this evening? Do you live on this street?"

"No." I grasped for an answer that wouldn't sound weird. "I was visiting a friend."

Her eyes narrowed slightly. "Every time I see you, you're visiting a friend. You must have a lot of friends." A wave of loneliness wafted from her, a palpable thing. I understood now why she had come on so strongly to François. The dark hulk of a house behind her felt empty; no companion, young or old, awaited her within. I wondered if the "boy toy" rumor was even true.

"Yes, well. I like to think so." I plunged my hands into my pockets and looked up and down the street. "This is a nice street. So close to the university. Do you walk to work?"

She nodded, looking annoyed. "Usually. Most of us do, or we bike. It would be rather ridiculous to start up a car and drive it two blocks, wouldn't it?"

"I suppose so. Oh, and congratulations. I

heard you are the new department chair."

"Yes. How wonderful for me. I shall inherit all the resentment people felt for Sandor, along with his unsolved problems. Uneasy lies the head that wears a crown. Who said that?"

"I think it's Shakespeare. One of the king plays."

"Of course." She yawned and looked at her watch. "And I suppose I'll get that giant office of Sandor's, with the floor-to-ceiling shelving. God knows what they'll do with all his expensive toys."

Her voice was wry, but underneath that tone was something else; it sounded almost smug — or excited? Could it really be that special to move from one office to another, from one title to another?

I cleared my throat. "Did Sandor live on this block?"

She nodded and gestured with her sharp chin. "That's his, up on the corner."

I followed her gaze and saw a dark shape with a string of white lights outlining three-fourths of the front door.

"Anyway, I've got to get going." Yvonne lifted a hand and started back up her walk.

I called, "I hope your father is feeling better!"

She stopped for a moment and turned to

look at me. "I'm sorry?"

"Your father. When we met at the hospital, you said he was recovering from surgery —"

"Oh yes. Yes. He — he didn't make it, actually."

"Oh my God. I'm so sorry! I didn't —"

"It's all right." She waved vaguely. "Thanks for coming by." She said this as though I had come to visit her.

I would have offered further condolences, but she turned back and disappeared up her driveway and into the shadows.

Disoriented, I looked up and down the street. Who else lived here on "Professor Lane"? Hans Weber, with his charming smile? And would Livia move into his house with him? Had she already? Did Wanda Lee live here? And what about the Dobos family? Were they also within walking distance? If so, why didn't Frank walk the other way on the morning he disposed of the coat, the morning of the snow? Why wouldn't he simply walk home, just a couple of blocks away?

And what of Tony Malandro? To hear Alex talk, one would think the two of them lived in some sort of amazing mansion, not in a modest house on Sycamore. Besides, Tony was a surgeon, not an academic. *A surgeon who played chess with a professor of Hungar-*

ian. There was something odd about that picture, and about Yvonne's casual announcement that her father had died. Why had she sounded so surprised when I mentioned him?

Shocked and saddened, and suddenly unbearably cold, I returned to my car and waited for the heater to warm up again. Whatever I had expected to experience on Sycamore Street had not come to fruition, and I had no particular desire to walk its icy sidewalks anymore.

I pulled away from the curb and drove to the end of the block, where I paused in front of Sandor's house. I couldn't make out much detail except for the asymmetrical Christmas lights on the door, which also bore a slightly scraggly wreath, and the outline of a "For Sale" sign pounded into the frozen grass. There was a small beam of light in one of the windows, indicating that someone was probably within.

A burst of loneliness rose within me; how sad, how disorienting it would be to lose someone who shared your home, who sat beside you on the couch each night. How joyless the holidays would feel.

Whatever his failings, Sandor had been a nice man, a tall and jocular presence who had stood beside me, holding a purring

Inspektor, as we admired Falken's latest arrivals on the Timeless Treasures shelf. And if I felt his loss — I, who had been a mere acquaintance who sometimes saw him in a shop — how much greater the loss for his family, his colleagues, his friends! Once again John Donne was in my head, as he had been the day of the murder: "Every man's death diminishes me, because I am involved in mankind."

As I drove away, though, I couldn't help but think of Yvonne Yves, and her barely concealed excitement at the thought of getting Sandor's title and his office — winning, essentially, the life that had once been his.

CHAPTER 17
THE STORY WITH
TWO ENDINGS

In the morning I got a text from Erik. I miss you. Will come by tonight for sure.

I texted back a joke: Why wait until tonight?

I smiled, first at the phone, and then at the fuzzy faces of my cats, who were sitting closer than was polite. "Time to get up, you two. You get breakfast, and Hana gets a shower."

They followed me into the kitchen, and I fed them some soft food and replenished their water. Then I took a quick shower and dressed in faded jeans and a jade-green sweater — a casual look for my impromptu tea party.

Within half an hour I had set out my beautiful yellow Herend cups and put some coffee cake on the matching serving platter. I brewed some tea while I checked my texts: one from Grandma, telling me to stop for sugar on my way in, and one from Livia, asking me to call her.

I considered calling right away, but a peek out my window showed me that Falken had pulled into the lot. I watched him fold his lanky body to get it out of the car; then, gentleman that he was, he held open the back door for Nancy Balog, then jogged around to open the passenger door for his wife, Elise, who seemed to be digging for something in her purse. This made me smile, because Falken had once confessed to finding women's purses an absolute mystery: "What is in them, and how do they consume so much of your time?" he had asked.

Now Elise and her purse emerged from the car, and the three companions walked cheerfully toward my door. When the doorbell rang, I was there at the buzzer to let them in.

I went to my apartment door and opened it wide; Antony and Cleopatra had disappeared into my room. They generally waited there until they could decide whether the visitors were friends or foes.

"Hello," I called, as three figures, wrapped in coats and scarves, came marching down the hall. "Oh, my goodness! What's the temperature out there?"

"Frigid," Falken said.

"I think the thermometer said fourteen

degrees," added Elise. Her voice always had a bright and positive quality, even when she was complaining. She had wrapped her scarf around her feathery white hair, and it made her look nunlike.

Nancy's ensemble was a bit more elegant — a black coat with a white mohair scarf and matching gloves — but she looked colder than Elise.

"Come in. I think you all need some nice hot tea. How are you, Elise?" I gave her a quick hug. I'd known Falken's wife for several years, but I didn't see her very often.

"Just fine, thanks." Elise crossed my threshold first and said, "Your place is lovely, Hana! Oh, look at this tree!"

The other two came in and admired my decorations. "Let me take your coats," I said. They handed them to me, and I hung them in my tiny hall closet.

When I returned, Nancy Balog smiled at me. "Thank you so much for including me in your gathering. I told Falken this would be a nice distraction."

"I hope it will be," I said. "Well, you must all come in the kitchen to see the star of our show."

We traveled together to my tea table, and I received three gratifying "Ahs."

Falken moved forward and lifted one of

the cups to examine it. "Wonderful," he said. "Such large cups, and these curved saucers are perfect. Look at the artistry, the color!"

"Exactly. I keep having tea parties because everyone should experience these dishes. Please, sit down. I'll get the teapot."

They arranged themselves around the table, and I poured the still-steaming tea.

"You're right, Hana — this is perfect after that frigid weather," Nancy Balog said, tucking a strand of blonde-gray hair behind her ear. "And these are stunning cups. I suppose they have the maker's mark." She flipped over her saucer and nodded. "Oh, yes. Sandor has many Herend pieces."

"Will you keep them? Or do you think you'll sell some things?" I asked.

She shrugged. "Falken said he'll help me work through that when the time comes. It seems overwhelming. My husband had quite a collection."

"An amazing collection," Falken said.

Elise was eyeing the coffee cake; I found a knife and sliced the pastry into pieces, then used a pie server to put a piece on her plate. "Enjoy," I said. "It's from the bakery on Elm Drive."

"Wonderful, thank you, Hana! So, are you all ready for Christmas? Last time I saw you there was some young man in your life. What was his name — Adam?"

I stared at her for a moment, nonplussed to hear a name from the distant past. "We really need to see each other more often. Adam is an ex. A year and a half gone, at least. I'm with someone else now," I said, trying not to sound smug. "His name is Erik."

Nancy Balog said, "Oh yes. Hana is dating a policeman. Falken must have told you about the Fisher Woman. Her young man came to the store and whisked it away."

"Ah! Now I'm putting it together." Elise forked up a piece of her pastry with an interested expression. "Did you ever get that piece back, Nancy?"

Nancy shook her head, studying the lizards on her cup handle. "Not as of yet. The police said they'll keep me updated. But I certainly have a wealth of other Hungarian treasures to keep me company."

Falken laughed and patted her shoulder. "We'll go through them with you. You can keep what you like and sell the rest. I'll find fair prices for them, and you'll be a wealthy woman."

"That will be a first," she said with a grin.

We laughed again, and my phone rang. I glanced down to see the name "Livia

Parravicini."

"Excuse me for one moment," I told my guests. I walked to the doorway and swiped the phone on. "Hello?"

"Hana! How are you today? Did you enjoy our shopping adventure?"

"Yes, it was fun. Thanks for going with me."

"Meanwhile I've been practicing my Hungarian. I can say *Boldog ünnepeket.*"

"That's pretty good! And I can say *Buon Natale.*"

"Wonderful. Oh, Hans told me he enjoyed our time out. He wants me to invite you to the wedding."

"You have a date?"

"Yes. We think probably March. Nothing really to wait for — it won't be a big affair. Neither of us are youthful and we've both been married before."

I had not known this, but this wasn't really the time to ask questions. "Listen, I have people here so I have to run, but you should know something."

"Oh? Do tell."

"I was talking to Yvonne Yves. I mean, I ran into her last night. I found out that her father died. It's very sad, and she seems to be alone. I thought you might want to — reach out. She seems like she could use some support." I stared at the winter sky through the window over my sink.

"You're very sweet, Hana. But I think you got something turned around. Yvonne's father died long ago. I think she was still in high school when it happened."

"What — but she told me — I saw her at the hospital. She was visiting him in the hospital."

"It must have been someone else."

"Uh — okay, I have to run. Talk to you soon." She said good-bye, and I hung up. The room had a crooked feel, as though the building had tilted slightly sideways. What was I to think? There had been no confusion. She had said it was her father — twice.

"Hana? Are you all right?" Falken asked.

"Hmm? Oh, I — just something is confusing me. I guess I misunderstood something Yvonne said to me yesterday."

"Yvonne Yves?" Nancy asked. "How do you know her?"

"Well, I don't really know anyone from the university, but at the same time I met several of them when they came to the memorial at the tea house. And then I kept seeing one or another in town — funny how those things happen. I even went shopping with Livia."

Nancy's smile disappeared, and I realized

she must have known about Sandor's other relationships. Or did she? Everything was confusing me now.

"Anyway," I said. "Can I get anyone some more tea? And I made a batch of cookies that I can share when we're finished with the coffee cake."

Falken was studying his teacup. "Hana, not to talk shop, but do you have any idea what your uncle paid for this? It's a truly impressive set."

"I don't, no. I've been wondering that myself. Either he got a steal from someone who didn't know what he had, or he paid too much for a birthday present. I don't really like either possibility," I said with a half smile.

"I suppose there's some Hungarian legend to go with this," Nancy said, touching the lizard handle. "Sandor was full of those Hungarian stories."

"No legend that I know of," I said. "But this tea set, the whole Yellow Dynasty thing, is an homage to Chinese art, so maybe it's based on a Chinese legend."

"Ah," said Nancy. "Perhaps we could ask Wanda Lee." Another frown on her face: so she knew. About Wanda, and Livia, and — had there been others? That knowledge must have been hard, in the face of their reconciliation. Not to mention the lifestyle changes.

The twin lizards looked at me with their tiny black eyes.

Twin lizards.

Wanda and Livia.

The two sides of Sandor.

Two Herend dragons on his shelf.

Two pictures of Sandor's office, one with the Fisher Woman missing.

Two houses.

Domo and me, throwing snowballs at Zoltan . . .

I shook my head, then took a sip of my tea and smiled at Nancy. "I happened to see Yvonne at her home last night, and she pointed out your house. It looks like a lovely place." I had barely seen it, but the street was pretty, and Livia had said the house was beautiful.

Nancy brightened slightly. "Oh yes, I love my house. We've been in there almost fifteen years. Made a lot of improvements along the way."

"So — do you still have to sell it?" I asked, taking a slice of coffee cake and setting it on my plate.

I looked up and saw that she looked upset. I had touched a nerve.

"No, I absolutely don't! It's my home, and

I'm happy there. And I said as much to Sandor's Realtor!"

Falken looked shocked. "Wait — Sandor arranged to sell the house without consulting you?"

"Yes. Can you believe it? My home."

Elise shook her head. "That's silly. It was his home, too! And he had moved back in, right? So why sell it? He could just sell whatever other place he'd been living in."

"Yes, exactly. He had only just come back to Sycamore Street."

I heard Livia's voice in my head: "He told me he was moving back to Sycamore Street." Not, "He was going back to his wife."

Nancy was still frowning as she added sugar to her tea; her hand shook slightly. She was genuinely angry. I recalled Frank Dobos telling me that his mother had been angry the day before Sandor's death; she had been talking with someone on the phone. What had she said? That "if he was going to be like that, he didn't deserve his life." Frank had thought she meant that he didn't deserve to live. But what if she meant he didn't deserve his life with Nancy? Had she been on the phone with an angry Nancy Balog?

What had Sarah said at the memorial,

when I had thought she was worried about offending Nancy? She had said something like "no matter how angry we were with Sandor." I had thought she was apologizing for the other professors, but what if she had been talking about Nancy and herself?

A sudden image flashed in my head: Zoltan in the snow. Why had Zoltan gone back to his wife? My parents had said he needed to apologize for whatever transgression he had committed. He had gone home and presumably done just that, and he remained married.

I was still thinking, but I heard my voice say, "Nancy, did Sandor apologize?"

Her eyes, red with some emotion, met mine. "Sandor wasn't the type to apologize."

"Not for the house? Or for — whatever split you up?"

Nancy shook her head.

Elise said, "Well, how in the world did he get you to take him back if he didn't say he was sorry?"

She fingered a doily under her plate. "He said we belonged together."

"Well, you did," Falken said brightly. "Elise and I could never imagine one of you without the other."

"If he hadn't come back, would he still have wanted to sell the house?" I asked.

Nancy's flashing eyes met mine. "It doesn't matter," she said. "I wouldn't have let him divorce me and then sell my house out from under me! When that Realtor showed up with the sign, I told her as much. And then I marched to Sandor's office one morning and told him the same." She sniffed, still indignant, and I realized that Sandor's thoughtlessness had created a great deal of unnecessary trouble.

"I told him," Nancy continued, "that if he didn't find some other way to get his funds, he was no better than the snake on his desk." She smiled at me. "One of those precious Herend figures, I meant. I thought it was poetic justice that I compared him to the snake made of porcelain, since it was those figures that made him a snake."

"The Herend snake?" I said, surprised. "But if that was on his desk, you must have been talking to him the morning he died!"

The room went silent. It is said that Ördög hides in the walls of his victims, and that one can hear him there, making soft sounds and high-pitched noises. Ördög was here; I could feel it.

The misery rose in me, nauseating me and making me almost blind. Falken saw it and sat up straight. I think he sensed it, too, then: that Nancy's anger had pushed her into an irrational and dangerous place.

I forced myself to breathe calmly. "I mean, I just happen to know that someone only brought him the snake the night before. Have you told the police you saw him that morning? It's important information." I wanted to downplay the implication of my words. It wasn't Livia's revelation, after all, that had the room feeling crooked, off balance. It wasn't Yvonne Yves' lie that had made me picture Sandor in the snow.

Nancy stared at me for a moment, her face blank. Then she stood up so abruptly that her teaspoon clattered to the floor. "I have to go," she said, her voice toneless.

Elise gasped, and Falken said, "Oh, Nancy . . ." in a voice of deep despair.

I had to keep her talking, long enough that I could find a way to text Erik or dial 911. But Nancy's eyes had a glazed look, and a sense of danger permeated the room.

And then she pulled a gun from her purse.

Sandor had two guns, one at work and one at home. Who had told me that?

Falken sounded almost annoyed. "Put the gun down, Nancy. You don't want to kill us."

"But I don't want to be caught, either," she whined. "This is all Sandor's fault. First he left me alone; then he threatened to take the very house I lived in. And all the while he flaunted those women in my face, those beautiful, exotic women he worked with. All just to torture me, for what? Being boring? Not liking his spending habits? This is *not* my fault."

My fingers found my phone in my pocket. "You used the gun in Sandor's office, right? Did you go there with the intention of killing him?"

"No! I'm not a killer." But the gun was steady in her hand. "I went to fight about the Realtor, the sign. He wasn't there, but all those pieces of porcelain were. His expensive collection. I decided I would take one and sell it. Give Sandor a taste of his own medicine. So I went behind his desk and grabbed that ugly green thing —"

She meant the Fisher Woman. That artwork of astounding beauty. "And he came in?" I said. My eyes darted to Elise, who looked so pale I thought she would faint.

"Yes, he came in. And we fought. You know what? He was more concerned about the thing in my hand than about me. He was afraid I would drop it. So I set it down on his desk and opened his drawer to find something to throw at him — and there was his gun. I don't even remember shooting him. I was standing there with the gun in my hand. I dropped it. I just — grabbed everything — my purse, the statue. I needed spending money, and something to pay bills. And I ran out the back way. I didn't see anyone. I walked to my car and drove away, and that was it."

"You dropped a lipstick," I said. I had managed to turn my phone on and tap the button for the main screen. But I needed to see it to select a phone number. I couldn't count on calling some random number; this was an emergency.

"What?"

"You dropped a lipstick on the floor. Poor Frank found it when he found Sandor. He thought his mother had done it — had killed Sandor. But *you* did."

"I didn't kill him," Nancy said, her eyes filling with tears. "I loved him. I was just mad at him, so mad at him, for so many things . . ."

"I understand that, Nancy. Please put the gun down; you're frightening us."

She looked at Elise and Falken, helpless. "But I can't. I don't want you to tell on me. I don't want anyone to know." I heard a noise in the other room: the cats? Ördög, coming to claim our souls?

The worst thing about the situation was that I understood why Nancy would have to kill us. If she didn't, we would tell the police what she had done. She would go to jail. All her friends and family would learn that she had committed murder. Her reputation, her happiness, her life were at risk. This, then, was how people brought themselves to pull the trigger.

I forced myself to breathe. Erik had told me that in a situation with an unstable person, it was crucial to remain calm. "You're a good person, Nancy. A good person who did a bad thing. And you regret it. You can't compound that by hurting three other people."

Nancy Balog looked me in the eye, and I saw that I was wrong: she didn't regret what she had done, and she was willing to do it again. In that instant, I saw Ördög, grinning at the base of the World Tree. I saw the pair of lovers in the lower world, their hands wrapped tightly around each other's throats. Sometimes people embraced evil.

"I'll do it if I have to do it," she said. "I don't think there's any other way to keep you quiet. You would all go to the police."

"Nancy," Falken said. "We have been friends for years. You obviously need help, psychiatric help, and we can get it for you."

She shrugged. "I'm sorry, Falken. Every-one kept taking things from me, and after a while I just refused. I still refuse. You can't take away my future. I won't let that happen."

She lifted her gun, and I screamed.

A voice said, "Lower your weapon, or I will shoot."

Erik's voice. Erik! Somehow, he was in my house. Had my longing for him made him materialize? Had he found his way out of the Land of Darkness? I thought of Katie's story about her kitten, Charlie, and Margie saying that people could sense the distress of others. Had Erik sensed our distress? Shocked, disjointed thoughts bounced around in my head as I stared at him, looming large in the doorway and holding a gun that looked both utilitarian and frightening, then turned to look at Nancy, who still had her gun trained on poor Falken.

"If I put my gun down, I lose," she said, her voice gloomy but determined.

"If you try to pull that trigger, I will take you out," Erik said. "Put it down, last chance."

If even I was afraid of his face, grim and unwavering, surely Nancy must have been. We all knew in that moment that he would shoot her. "Nancy, please," I said. "Please. There's only a chance for you if you live."

Her blank eyes moved to me, and I feared she would shoot and take the consequences. Two seconds, perhaps, but it felt like a hundred years. And then she lowered the gun, her arm collapsing in sections, like an accordion. Falken lunged out of his seat and wrested the weapon from her hand. His face was as white as one of my grandmother's Christmas doilies, but he was more composed than I would have been if someone had held a gun on me for a full minute.

Erik moved in quickly with a pair of handcuffs and secured Nancy's hands behind her back. I couldn't look at her; my eyes moved to the table and the remnants of our tea party, now a disquieting sight. Erik started to lead Nancy out of the room; she passed very close to me, and I felt her jumble of emotions.

I said, "Nancy, I know a woman who killed. She's in jail now, but she's happier than she was." Nancy looked at me, and in her eyes I saw anger and hate, but also misery and a gleam of hope. "She's happier," I said, "because she's begun to redeem herself. Every day, her load lightens. Her granddaughter told me so."

Nancy shook her head; she didn't believe me. But the words had been said, and there was a chance that one day they might take root inside her, help her wherever she was going.

They left the kitchen; I heard the squawk of Erik's radio and his voice, firm, authoritative, as he spoke to other police. And then he and Nancy were gone.

I turned back to Falken and Elise, my hands suddenly shaking uncontrollably at my sides. "That was terrifying," I said.

Elise buried her face in her hands and began to cry. Falken put an arm around her shoulders; he and I exchanged a dismal glance. I dropped into a chair across from him and said, "How could people not have seen it? Her resentment, her anger. Sandor's mistreatment wearing her down bit by bit. She must have found someone to sell the Fisher Woman for her; Erik would have known if it had been her at the pawnshop."

Falken nodded. "Hana, I could actually use some very hot tea."

I poured him some, and he took a bracing sip, then sighed. "I am having trouble believing this. Nancy has been our friend for years. She is a kind woman."

I pointed at the handle of his cup — the identical lizards, side by side. "We are all dual creatures. Something bad can turn us."

"Sandor wasn't bad."

"No, but he was selfish. He hurt his wife,

338

again and again, and he didn't consider that it might be hardening what was soft inside her." I poured some tea for myself, and for Elise, my hand shaking slightly. I patted her other shoulder. "Elise, drink this. It will help a little. In a minute Erik will come back up here and he'll need to question all three of us."

Elise wiped her eyes and nodded with a courageous expression. Her husband pulled her against his side. "What a morning," he said. Then he pointed at me. "Nancy had a nephew she was very close to; he did odd jobs for her. A likely candidate for the pawnshop. I think you're right, Hana."

We sat in silence for a time, drinking tea and calming ourselves. In a burst of insight, I realized why I might have seen, over an over, the image of Zoltan in the snow. He had been separated from his wife, and my parents hadn't been sure whether she would take him back. It must have made an impression on me, that dissonance within his marriage. All this time I had remembered images of him and wondered how anyone could be angry at my dear uncle. Like Sandor, Zoltan had been charismatic, charming, lovable. But that had been only one side of the man. Zoltan had been forced to acknowledge his wife's suffering, to apologize. It was something Sandor had never done, and he had died because he could not see his wife's pain.

Sirens sounded outside. I could tell, without looking out the window, that cars were congregating, officers swarming. Greg Benton would be there, along with anyone who had been close to Abbott's Lane when they got the call.

"They'll be here soon," I said. "Take a deep breath."

We all took my advice; between the tea and the deep breathing, everyone's color looked a bit healthier when Erik came back; Greg Benton stood beside him.

Greg moved into the room and nodded at us. "Mr. and Mrs. Trisch? I'd like to ask you a few questions."

Erik touched my shoulder. "Hana? You come into the living room."

I followed him into the next room and walked straight into his arms. He clasped me tightly and kissed my hair.

"Erik, thank God. I was scared. Really scared. I didn't know. I didn't sense her guilt, maybe because I thought my miserable feeling was about Yvonne Yves. I found out she lied to me about something, and I wondered if she could have somehow —"

"It's okay. Nancy Balog is under arrest

and on her way to the station."

I looked up at him. "How did you know to come here? Did you read my mind?"

He shook his head. "I don't think we're at the mind-reading stage. But I did read your text. You said, 'Why wait until tonight?' And I thought, yeah, why not? I figured I would come and steal a quick kiss before things got crazy. I let myself in quietly, thinking I'd surprise you. Instead, I heard you trying to get someone to put a gun down. That was more than a shock."

"Oh God. That could so easily not have happened. You could have gotten busy, or not read my text, or just laughed at it and gone back to work."

His arms tightened around me. "I wanted to see you. Maybe I did sense something after all."

"I was so relieved when I heard your voice I almost slid down onto the floor like a puddle of water. But then I was afraid I was going to see someone die in front of my eyes."

He grew solemn. "I was, too. I would have killed her, Hana. I've never killed someone before, but in about five seconds I would have done it. I'm glad I was spared that choice."

I hugged him and kissed his cheek. "I am,

too." Then I pushed him away. "You probably have to ask me some questions."

Erik studied me with his green eyes and saw that I was feeling better; he got out his notebook. "It won't take long," he said.

I only got to call my family about half an hour later. My mother and grandmother were shocked and horrified, and they insisted that I not come into the tea house at all. "We can handle this," my mother said in my ear. "You sit there and relax, and we'll come to see you after the event. We'll bring you dinner."

"Thank you," I said. "I love you."

"I love you, too, my little Haniska. I guess your grandmother was right: your wolf watches over you. She read that in your leaves, do you remember?"

She had done that. And it did in fact seem that, fairy tale–like, my wolf protector had appeared just when my friends and I were in danger. He had faced peril and risked the misery of murder on our behalf.

I recalled being troubled by the idea of a story with two endings. When I had heard things about Sandor and his wife, it had felt odd that she had taken him back and all was well when it seemed that many things pointed to an alternate reality. I had seen that, unconsciously, but I hadn't realized it was Nancy that troubled me.

Now I was troubled again by the way random choices could change the course of a life. Erik Wolf could just as easily not have seen my text. As a result, Nancy might have made three more terrible choices.

But as it happened, we would all see another Christmas.

CHAPTER 18
GIFTS AND GOOD WISHES

I spent the morning of my birthday, December 18, as I always liked to do: in quiet contemplation of a new year. Sleepy and happy, I cuddled with Antony and Cleopatra under warm covers and stared at the frost etched on my window, its lacy patterns almost obscuring the gray light beyond.

I had gotten up early to eat breakfast with Erik before he ran to work. He had given me a card and told me that he would bring presents to our dinner that night; he had made reservations at Evening Light, an upscale Riverwood restaurant that I had only been to once, when my parents took me there after my college graduation.

His card sat on my windowsill, under Isabella, my Norfolk pine. On the front was a small red heart with a ribbon tied around it.

Inside he had written, "To Hana, who already has my heart. So I'll just follow

344

Domo's advice and get you 'glittery things and toys.' " Next to this he had drawn some hearts, and then, "Hopefully you'll have a hundred birthdays, because that means I'll get to spend the majority of them with you. Love, Erik."

I smiled at the card, and the memory of his kiss good-bye. I smiled at the cats, and at the wisps of snow outside. I was still smiling in the shower, and as I donned the blue knit dress I'd bought for the occasion. I slipped on knee-length black boots and a jet-black necklace, gave the cats some extra food, and bundled into my "good" coat and out to the car.

On the way to my parents' house, Perry Como crooned to me, assuring me that there was no place like home for the holidays.

"I know," I told him.

My childhood home was full of family: Grandma and Grandpa, bustling around the kitchen (she with food, and he with drinks); Domo and Margie, holding hands and sipping eggnog; and my parents, greeting me with bear hugs and calling me their little girl, as was tradition. Major strolled in to greet me, and I wrapped his new Christmas scarf around his neck. It was red and white, a beautiful contrast with his gray fur.

"He looks so regal with it, Hana! I think he even likes it," my mother said, laughing. "Now, come and have some treats. Mama says her dinner will be ready in an hour, so we can munch on little things until then. And you can open presents!"

"Sounds great," I said.

Domo stepped away from Margie, who looked alluring in a white blouse and black velvet skirt. "Han, can I talk to you for a minute?"

"Sure." I shrugged at my parents and followed Domo into my mother's sewing room; he closed the door and turned to me, his face pale.

"Oh my God, what's wrong? If you have bad news, don't even tell me. It's been such a nice day so far —"

"I don't have bad news. I just want to ask for — your permission — I mean — I don't want to steal your thunder . . ."

"What thunder?" I had never seen Domo look so serious.

"It's your birthday. Your special day. But I suddenly realized I wanted to do this when everyone was around, and — you know — everyone's here."

I stared at him, my mind blank. "Do what?"

He pulled a tiny box out of his pocket and opened it. A diamond ring sat inside. A *lovely* diamond ring. "Oh, *Domo*! You're going to propose to Margie!"

"Do you care if I do it on your birthday? Because by Christmas I kind of — already want to be engaged."

"Of course I don't care! This is the best present ever! I'm getting a sister!"

"If she says yes," my brother said, looking about ten years old.

I gave him a hug, then looked into his face. "Of course she'll say yes. She loves you."

"You never know. Women say no sometimes. For all sorts of reasons."

"She wants you, Domo. She loves you."

"Yeah." He smiled briefly.

"Let's go, before they think we're plotting an uprising."

He followed me back out; my grandmother studied us with narrowed eyes. "Stay away from that one, or she'll figure everything out," I said under my breath.

Domo nodded. "Hey, let's watch Hana open presents!" he said.

My mother clapped and pulled me toward the "seat of honor," which was simply the head of the table. She had set out a red place mat, along with a fat white candle surrounded by pine branches, and a variety of neatly wrapped packages. I proceeded to unwrap them with the abandon of a child. From my grandparents, a fleece blanket, a cinnamon candle, and a jar of paprika. From Domo and Margie, several mystery novels and a Budapest bookmark. From my parents, a lovely white sweater with silver beaded snowflakes, three pairs of woolen tights, and a pair of jade earrings.

"Thank you, everyone! These are all wonderful, and I'll get tons of use out of them."

My family clapped, which was our birthday tradition, and then we cleared away my presents and began to set the table, spurred by the wonderful aromas that were coming from the kitchen.

No one talked about the crime, or about the trauma I had suffered in my apartment, because we had been through that, and we all wanted this day to be free of care or sadness.

Half an hour later we were eating our first course: Grandma's chicken soup. I sipped at my spoon and watched Domo out of the corner of my eye. When exactly was he planning to do this?

He clearly couldn't stand the tension, either. When my grandmother gathered our soup bowls, he said, "Grandma, I'll help you bring in the main course, but hold on a minute."

"Vat?" she asked.

"Just — go ahead and put those down. I just want to say something, before we eat any more."

Her eyes narrowed again, and she walked out of the room with our bowls, the skirt of her dress making a swishing sound as she turned the corner into the kitchen. My grandfather went in to help her, and I heard them talking softly in Hungarian.

She returned, empty-handed and expectant, and sat back in her seat. "So? What do you want to say? A prayer?"

"No, no." Domo looked pale again. "I just wanted to point out that this is Margie's second Christmas season with our family. I started dating her a year ago last September. And she fits right in with our family." My parents and grandparents clapped. We really were a clapping family. Margie blushed and laughed.

Then Domo was standing, and his hands were shoved into his pockets. "I guess that's why I wanted to say this — to do this — here today."

I got out my phone and turned on the camera. Domo got on one knee, and my mother gasped. My grandmother looked smug.

Margie's mouth opened slightly, and her eyes grew wide. She was genuinely surprised. I held the camera surreptitiously in my lap.

Domo said, "Margie, I love you. You put up with me even when I'm annoying or lazy or obnoxious. You have embraced my family, and they all love you, too. I can't imagine you not in my life, not in this house with me at every holiday. You are my future, if you will say yes." He took out the ring and gulped some moisture into what was probably a dry throat. "Marguerite LaSalle, will you marry me?"

Margie put a hand on Domo's shaggy head. "I would love to marry you, Domo!"

I snapped pictures of the whole scene. Domo on his knees, Margie's face when he proposed, Domo standing up to embrace her and put the ring on her finger.

Margie smiling the most beautiful smile I had ever seen.

And my family clapping.

Erik had obviously been dressed by his sisters; he wore black pants, a maroon button-down shirt, a gray tie, and a gray tweed jacket. They had even mussed his hair into some fashionable style, most likely with a ridiculously expensive mousse or gel. "You look very handsome," I said.

We were seated in a cozy booth at Evening Light, and Erik had just ordered champagne. "And you look lovely. Blue is a great color on you." He leaned forward and touched my hands. "Every color looks good on you."

"That's sweet."

"Happy birthday, Haniska."

"Thank you."

He studied me with his green eyes. The gold-green light around him was muted in the dimly lit booth. "You're in charge this evening. What's on the conversational agenda?"

"Well, first off I need to show you this." I got out my phone and went to my photos. I handed it to Erik. "Scroll to the left," I said.

He did so, his eyes widening as he went. Then he looked up. "Domo proposed?"

"Yes. And she accepted his proposal."

"Your big smile tells me this was well received."

"Oh, by everyone. It was great."

He nodded. "Good for Domo. I wondered when he was going to make things official."

"We all did." I smiled down at my menu. "I had my grandma's cooking a few hours ago, so I will not need an appetizer."

"Your call."

I stole a glance at him. "Since I get to choose our conversation, I wonder — could I ask a couple things about the case?"

He stiffened slightly, then shrugged. "It's your birthday. Fire away. I'll answer what I can."

"Okay. First of all, why was Frank Dobos so convinced his mother committed the crime? That never seemed to make sense. It was all so extreme — removing evidence, keeping secrets even after talking to the police. All from mild-mannered Frank."

He nodded. "We've had some more discussions with the whole Dobos family. It wasn't just that Frank overheard his mother on the phone, talking about Sandor not deserving his life (and as you suspected, Sarah had been talking to Nancy, who had been complaining about Sandor's selfishness). It was also because he normally walked to campus with his mother, but she left him a note that day, saying she'd had to go in early. By the time he arrived on campus, she had been there for more than an hour. He went to the foreign language department, where he expected to find his mother conducting office hours, but her office was closed.

"He moved on toward Balog's office, where he was expected for a meeting with Sandor. The office was the last one in the hall. He opened the door and found Balog on the floor in front of his desk. The rest of what he told us was true. He saw the gun, the lipstick, and panicked. He was in shock, of course, from seeing the body. His parents are sending him to a therapist so that he can talk the whole thing out."

"Well, that's good." I thought about what he had said. "And where was his mother?"

"Making some copies in the resource center. All very innocent."

I thought for a while. "And so it was actually pretty easy for Nancy to escape undetected? Even walking out with that big porcelain statue?"

"Oh, absolutely. Sandor's office was at the end of the hall, and the exit was just beyond his door. She went out, down some stairs, through the outer door, and to the parking lot. She has assured us that no one saw her, and we can't find anyone with information to the contrary. Not that it matters, since she has confessed."

"Is she — repentant?"

"Yes, mostly. She's also defensive. That's pretty natural, though. I don't think it's sunk in fully, that he's never coming back.

That she committed murder. That will come with time."

"And Sandor's gun, that he kept for protection — he would have been better off without it, wouldn't he?"

He nodded. "People's guns are often turned against them. I wouldn't want you to have a gun in your home. Pepper spray, maybe."

I wrinkled my nose. "I think I'll just keep you in my home at all times."

This earned a smile. "I'll certainly stay in your home tonight. I have a special birthday present for you."

I laughed. "Besides the ones in that bag?" I pointed at a large gift bag with wrapped presents inside that sat next to him on his side of the booth.

"Some of those are from Runa and Thyra. One is from my parents. They said they're sorry they won't see us at Christmas, but they want to host us soon."

"Ah."

"They're not too bad."

"No, they seem very nice. A little intimi-dating, but —"

"Not as intimidating as your grandma, back when she hated me."

I giggled. "She didn't hate you. She just thought you were bad luck."

"And I won her over with my charm."

"Yes, you did." We looked at each other for a while. Then I said, "What about Yvonne Yves? Why would she lie if she didn't have something to hide?"

He nodded. "I had another interview with Professor Yves. She did in fact have a family member who died in St. Francis Hospital. He was her stepfather, but she had called him 'Dad' since she was about eight years old. She had been in touch with her actual father, as well, before he died years ago, but apparently in a more distant fashion. It was this other man that she felt close to."

"Huh. Well, that's sad."

"Yes. But apparently her mother is going to sell her house and move in with Ms. Yves. She seemed quite happy about that; she had been concerned about the mother's finances, and with the sale of her house and some of its contents, they'll be able to pay off all debt and live quite comfortably in Yvonne's home. There was some talk of her mother applying for an administrative assistant position on campus."

"Wow — you really are thorough. She implied she had money worries when I saw her at the hospital. That's good for her, then. I'm glad. I think Yvonne is misunderstood."

"Hmm." He stretched in his seat and peered into the bag. "Are we finished with crime? Shall we open presents?"

"One more thing."

"Okay . . . ?"

"The Fisher Woman. If she's worth close to ten thousand dollars, why did Nancy sell her so cheaply?"

"She needed to stay under the radar. That piece would have attracted attention at its full price. Falken only found it because he's vigilant. He pounced before other collectors even got a peek."

"And the pawnshop owner —"

"Was insured. He'll be fine. You really want loose ends tied up, don't you?"

"Yes, as you know. And Tony Malandro — he'll get away without paying the debt, right?"

"Of course. They had no written contract. Only a gentlemen's understanding. As far as Tony was concerned, that was between the two of them, not between him and Sandor's estate. And at least some experts might agree with him."

"Do you think he'll learn a lesson? San dor's gambling was partly why he lost his life."

"I don't know." Erik's expression was growing stern, and I laughed. "Okay, fine. I would like to open a present, please."

He brightened. "Good. We'll start with Runa's."

The waitress came with our champagne. I ordered a chopped salad, and he ordered a steak. She left, and he handed me a little box with an attached envelope. I opened the card first. It was a reproduction of a painting by Joan Miró called *Portrait of a Young Girl.* It depicted a child with thick blonde hair and green eyes.

I flipped open the card and read, "Hana, you have been a godsend. Thank you, and happy birthday." It was signed, "Runa and Andy."

I opened the little box. A silver lapel pin, shaped like a sitting cat, was tucked into the cotton wool. The cat's eyes were bright with some green stone, and the collar was made up of single tiny topaz circles. It was striking, elegant, and clearly expensive. "Wow. I love this," I said.

He smiled. "Runa asked me what you love best. I said you loved your family, your cats, the tea house, and me."

"Not in that order, but yes. And chocolate."

"Thyra's got you covered there."

"Nice! I hope your mom and dad didn't spend too much money."

"I think they probably just picked out a nice Trekker item for you."

"I will love that! Trekker is a great store. And a bit out of my price range."

"It all works out." He reached into the bag and placed another box in front of me. "Hurry, before they bring our food."

"Okay, okay."

"I happened to stop in that store, Stones by Sparkle."

I looked up. "Really? What a coincidence."

"I asked her for advice, and she said she needed to know what my girlfriend did for a living. I said you worked at a tea house —"

"So she knew it was me," I said, grinning.

"She did. And she led me right to this, which did seem perfect."

Intrigued, I opened the box and pulled out a delicate silver chain, on which hung a silver key, into which was embedded a red heart.

"It means you have the key to my heart. She said it was perfect for you because you're a romantic."

"She's right," I said, fastening it around my neck and then using my phone's selfie feature to study it. "Oh, Erik — it's enchanting."

"It accentuates your beautiful neck," he

said. "And it's you providing the enchant-ment."

When we arrived at my apartment, I felt that my birthday could not have been more perfect in any respect. But I was wrong. A tiny figure in the hallway, wearing red long-john pajamas, elf slippers, and a determined expression, turned as we opened the door.

"Hana! I was just going to tape dis on your door," Iris said, holding up a construc-tion paper card.

Paige and Paul were standing in the doorway, looking stern but indulgent. "Yes, because it's way past your bedtime," Paul said.

Paige pointed at me. "Give the card to Hana and tell her good night."

Iris pranced toward me and handed me the card. "Happy birthday!" she said.

"Thank you so much, Iris! How nice of you to remember me. And is this Antony and Cleopatra on the front? What a terrific drawing!"

"They're waiting for Santa," Iris said.

"Aren't we all," Erik said solemnly, and held out his hand for a high five. Iris slapped it, and Erik looked pleased.

"I appreciate the birthday wishes, Iris. I'll see you tomorrow!"

"Good night!" She rushed forward, and I bent to hug her sturdy little body.

Then she skipped over to her parents, who waved to me and said happy birthday. "We left a gift at your door, too. Then Iris had the idea to make a card, so here we are," Paige said with a smile.

Erik and I thanked them again and walked up the stairs to my place, where another present sat on the mat.

"I'm spoiled," I said, putting my key in the lock.

"No, you're loved." He slid his hands around my waist and kissed my neck.

"Oooh. Wait until we get inside," I said, laughing.

We walked in to the familiar feline complaints; Erik fed them while I flipped on my Christmas lights and read Iris's card. Paige had written a message lightly in pencil, and Iris had drawn over it, very neatly, in crayon: "I was trying to pick a color of paper, and I thought this red one had Hana Keller written all over it."

CHAPTER 19
MAGYAR BABÁK
(THE HUNGARIAN BABIES)

On Christmas Day, my grandmother connected with Zoltan on Skype. There he was, handsome, graying slightly, but exactly the same. His family stood around him briefly, saying their pleasant hellos. I hadn't seen them in years. His children, my cousins, now young men, waved at us and said hello to my grandparents in Hungarian, which clearly earned points with Grandma and Grandpa.

My mother told all of them that they were welcome to visit us in Riverwood, and they seemed genuinely interested in staying with us, perhaps touring Chicago. Zoltan's wife, Paula, looked less grave than I recalled; clearly that had been a childhood impression based on limited evidence. She was friendly, almost playful, and she kissed Zoltan before she waved at us and led the children away so that "Dad can speak to his family in peace."

Then Zoltan let loose a stream of Hungarian, interrogating his parents and his sister about their lives in the language they all loved best. Finally, his eyes on Domo and me, he switched back to English.

"Hana, I'm glad you liked the teacups!"

"Oh, Uncle Zoltan — I love them! I've been showing them off to everyone. And they sort of indirectly helped us solve a mystery."

"Intriguing," he said.

"But I'm afraid you paid too much."

He waved a hand. "I have Hungarian friends here. One was going through her parents' estate. She asked me if I would like to look through. She promised a motivated price on anything I wanted. I got a few things, including your set. Not much money at all. She knew they were worth more, but she didn't really care. She just wanted to finish sorting through it all, save the few pieces with sentimental value, and move out the rest. I told her how much you would love them, and she was happy to hear it."

"Well, that's a relief. I'll send her a note."

"Good." He nodded, then studied Domo and me. "So, my young friends. Since I saw you last, you both fell in love."

"Yes," I said. "I'm dating a man named Erik; he's a police detective. He had to work today, or else I could introduce you."

"A hardworking man, and one who serves his community. A good thing," Uncle Zoltan pronounced. Then his sharp eyes moved to Margie, who stood shyly on the outskirts of the group.

"Domo, is this your young beauty?"

"It is," Domo said, pulling Margie against him. "We're engaged, Uncle Zoltan."

"Congratulations! We will all drink some champagne to you here in California. You'll be jealous, but today it is sixty-eight degrees. We're going to dine outside."

Grandma sniffed. "Christmas should be cold."

Zoltan laughed, and I was transported to my childhood. Zoltan in the snow.

"Uncle Zoltan, remember the snowball fight you had with Domo and me?"

He grinned, looking momentarily like Ördög. "As I recall, I won."

Domo was indignant. "No way! Hana and I had to forfeit because Mom called us inside."

Zoltan held up a hand. "Clearly, a rematch is in order. I happen to have business in Chicago in February. Will there still be snow then?"

"Yes," we all said, and we laughed. I couldn't imagine anything more wonderful than reliving that long-ago carefree snowball fight. And judging by Zoltan's expression before he said good-bye, neither could he.

Aunt Luca came at lunchtime. Her cheerful little blue car pulled up, and I thought I saw someone sitting in her back seat. I turned to my grandmother. "Does Luca have a new boyfriend?"

She shook her head. "She didn't say so."

My mother leaned toward the window. "What in the — ?" Her phone buzzed, and she checked her texts. "Luca wants me to come out alone for a minute." She looked at us, her blue eyes wide, then donned her coat and went outside.

I stared out the window as Luca spoke animatedly to my mother. Watched my mother stiffen, her arms fly up and then around her sister. I couldn't tell if she was laughing or crying. They talked some more. Then, to everyone's surprise, my mother climbed into Luca's car, and Luca came to the door.

"Hello! Merry Christmas," she said.

"Aunt Luca," I cried, running to greet her. I hugged her and enjoyed her familiar scent — fresh roses.

"Hello, Mama, Papa, Domo," she cried, and they all embraced her, talking at the same time, creating a familiar family chaos.

"Luca," I said, bursting with curiosity. "What's going on?"

"Okay, sit down," she said. "I need to tell you my surprise."

We sat around the kitchen table with Luca, who looked pretty and rosy-cheeked. "You all know my friend Sasha, right? We worked together at the paper company before I left."

We nodded. Luca had all sorts of jobs.

"She ended up living in my building, and we were basically best friends. When Sasha decided to become a single mom, I was supportive. I knew she would do a great job; she loved kids, and she just never found the right guy for her. So I helped her fill out the adoption papers, and I signed on as godmother and all that, and she adopted Jia two years ago."

"I think you told us," Grandma said, her face troubled. "But Sasha —"

"Yeah, I called you a few months ago about her. The car accident, the hospital. But she didn't make it. We were all hoping, but —" Luca looked away for a moment, tearful at the memory of her friend.

"Anyway, I was executor of her estate. I've been super busy. And of course there was Jia. My focus was on her, and her well-being. I needed to make sure the transition was relatively smooth and as painless as possible."

"Transition?" Domo said.

"I was her godmother. I signed on to take her if anything happened to Sasha. Jia is my daughter now."

We stared at her. Luca with a daughter.

"So that's who Mom's meeting out in the car?"

She nodded. "She's a wonderful girl. I love her. You will, too. It was good for her, that she already knew and loved me. I told her she could call me Mama Luca for now, and if she ever wants to just make it Mama, that's up to her. That obviously neither of us would ever forget the mama who brought her here and loved her more than anyone on earth."

"How old is she?" I asked.

"She's six. Sasha adopted her from China, and she's special. She's got a lot of love in her."

My grandmother looked at my grandfather. "We have a grandchild," she said. Her face was triumphant. "First Domo's engagement, now this!"

He grinned, then turned to his daughter. "Luca. When will you bring her inside?"

Jia was exactly as Luca described her.

Sweet, loving, affectionate, adorable. She took to the idea of an extended family with such enthusiasm that she climbed into every lap that was available. First Domo's, when he sat down to read his texts. He looked utterly disarmed and put his phone away to look into Jia's little face and tell her jokes. Then my grandfather's, when he sat in his chair to take a midday nap. Jia curled up against him and closed her eyes, too, and his arm slid around her in a protective circle.

She climbed in my lap when I sat down to read a recipe. "You are such a wonderful surprise, Jia. I didn't even know I had a cousin, and now you're my best Christmas present."

"You, too," she said. "I like your hair."

"I like yours! It's very straight and smooth."

"Yes." She accepted the compliment as her due, and I smiled. "What are you reading?" she asked in her little voice.

"I'm double-checking a recipe. We're all making some food and bringing it over to the police station, where men and women are working hard, even on Christmas. We're going to treat them all to a Christmas dinner."

"That's nice," she said. "Can I help?"

"Yes, we'll absolutely need your help.

Especially when we get there. We'll need to carry plates of food to various busy people. Do you think you'd be comfortable doing that?"

She nodded. "Like a waitress. I play waitress all the time. I wait on Mama Luca when I make spaghetti."

"That's wonderful. Do you know — how long are you and your mama Luca going to be in town?"

She shrugged little shoulders. "We're not sure of our whole itinerary."

Hilarious. She sounded like Luca already. "Well, if you have time, there's a little girl named Iris who I know would be your immediate friend. You two seem like peas in a pod."

"Oh?" She thought about this. "I guess I could meet her. I'll ask my mama. I could show her some toys I brought."

"That sounds great." Suddenly I remembered Runa telling me, back in October, that you began to love a child the moment you knew that child existed. Gazing down at Jia's adorable face, I realized it was true.

Our busy Christmas Day ended at the River-wood Police Station. Erik let us in, and we walked through a main lobby into a vast back room filled with phones and offices.

368

We were shown to a kitchen, which was to be our center of operations, and a receptionist named Shawn made an announcement: "Detective Wolf's girlfriend and her family have brought an authentic Hungarian dinner for a holiday treat. Come to the first-floor kitchen to fill a plate, or buzz me if you need a plate brought up to you. Thanks for serving Riverwood, and merry Christmas!"

Shawn was the first to be served by a tiny and careful Jia, who brought a giant plate loaded with a little of everything: chicken *paprikás, pörkölt, Székely gulyás,* beer bread, mashed potatoes, and cranberry sauce. She made a second trip with a plate of *kiflis:* cherry, cheese, and almond, and Hungarian apple slices. Shawn looked so happy after one bite of food that she almost forgot to answer the phone when it rang.

Erik and Greg started leading people to the kitchen as though it were a lifeboat and these hungry-looking people were the survivors of some vast shipwreck. Hearty policemen and women loaded up their plates and said gracious thank-yous. Several who had obviously heard of my grandmother from the ever-admiring Greg Benton actually stopped to hug her. I saw my grandmother's new gypsy ring flashing on her finger; my mother had worn hers, as well, and I was wearing mine.

Erik finished off his first helping and cornered me in the kitchen, giving me a resounding kiss. "Thank you for this," he said. "You wouldn't believe how much this is boosting morale. Even if I have this day off next year, maybe we should think about doing it again, for the ones who have to work."

"A new holiday tradition," I said. "I like it. I'll bet I could get my family on board."

"Who is that little girl?"

"Long story — but she's my cousin. And I only learned of her existence today. The dark-haired lady is my aunt Luca."

"Ah! So that is Luca."

"Yes! Look at my grandma. She's so happy. She got to talk to Zoltan this morning, she's got her Luca and Magda together, and now she has a grandchild. I heard her say *'Magyar babák'* to my grandpa. It means 'Hungarian babies.' All her babies together in one day. I tend to forget how much she misses them."

He nodded. "I'm going to grab some more food before it runs out."

I laughed. "Erik? It's not going to run out."

Greg Benton happened to be walking past;

370

he tried to look casual as he asked, "So —
you think there will be leftovers?"

CHAPTER 20
SNOWFALL

The day after Christmas I received an e-mail from someone named Harold Wilde. I didn't recognize the name; I clicked on it to see a graciously written note:

Dear Hana Keller,
I hope that you recall the help you gave me as I struggled with my Christmas shopping at the Sparkle Store. I wanted you to know that my wife absolutely loved the snow globe you selected, and I know this is the case because she put it in her picture window display, which is what you might call Prime Real Estate in our house.

My granddaughters loved their sisters necklaces so much that they wore them last night and today, and I got extra kisses for my efforts. So I certainly owe you a note of thanks, because I was what my wife calls the Big Man on Campus this Christmas.

I told all of my girls that I intend to take them to the next Maggie's Tea House tea event open to the public, which seems to be something called "Spring Fling." We look forward to seeing you there.

Best wishes for a Happy New Year,
Harry Wilde

This was a day brightener, and I showed it to both my mother and grandmother. We were back at the tea house, scrubbing and cleaning for some post-Christmas events.

My grandmother nodded. "You are good at gifts. It's because of *bepillantás*. The insight." She pointed her duster at me. "Didn't your Wolf girls love their gifts?"

They had loved their necklaces a great deal; in fact, they seemed genuinely moved by them, perhaps because Thyra had been so worried over her twin. As a result, I, like Harry Wilde, got lots of affection in the form of scented hugs from my tall, elegant friends.

My mother wandered past. "Oh, but gift giving is exhausting. I'm glad to have a reprieve until next Christmas." Her phone buzzed in her pocket, and she said, "Hang on, I have to take this." She picked it up, clicked it on, and said, "Alex? Thanks for calling back." She walked away from us to take her call in private.

I turned to my grandmother, brows raised.

She shrugged. "She's being a counselor to her old friend."

I stared. "I can't believe that woman! She just doesn't stop, does she? Showing up here during events, monopolizing Mom's time —"

Grandma shook her head. "No, your mama called her. She reached out, because she had a feeling."

"A feeling — you mean, a psychic feeling?"

My grandmother looked proud. "Yes. She understands that the girl needs her help, her guidance now. Magda wants her to lay down the law with this husband, who is vain and selfish."

That sounded about right. "So — Mom is advising her to do what?"

"Therapy. For couples. Your mama says he owes that to her."

"She's right! He does. Alex is annoying, but she does deserve better than a gambling Narcissus who takes her for granted."

My grandmother had become distracted by something outside. "It's snowing," she said.

I turned to look out the window, and it was true: a lacy snow was falling, gentling the landscape and bringing a sense of quiet.

"Looks like the snow globe you gave me," she said dreamily. "The one of Békéscsaba."

"It does. It's beautiful." I rested my chin on her shoulder, and we watched the snow for a moment. "I have that box of tea in the car," I said. "I'm going to grab it before it snows any harder."

I jogged to the entrance, threw on my coat, and went outside.

The world is silent in a new snowfall: life is dull and distant from the immediacy of ice crystals on hair, in eyelashes, on the tongue. I stuck out my tongue to catch some memories in the form of snowflakes.

In the parking lot, halfway to my car, I stood looking upward at the magic of falling snow, and I realized that my grandmother was right. Snow *is* friendlier than rain.

Rain makes us run and hide, fearing the soaking it will give us.

But snow makes us pause, look upward, and contemplate miracles.

We smile, and then we laugh.

Yes, Grandma, snow does tell us the truth. Because this is a world where people often choose the wrong action, the lower world, the place of suffering. They choose evil, and evil feels contagious sometimes.

But then snow falls and reminds us of beauty, and beauty reminds us of the upper world, the possibility of goodness, the transformative power of love.

I let the snow bathe my face, and I held some precious flakes in my hands for a sacred moment, a moment of what the nun in the tea house had called grace.

By the time I went back into Maggie's Tea House, my footprints had disappeared.

Magdalena's Stuffed Peppers
(Töltött paprika)
Eight helpings

8 medium-sized green or red peppers
1 large onion
3 Tbs shortening
1/2 lb ground beef
1/2 lb ground pork
1 cup uncooked rice
1 Tbs salt
1/2 tsp black pepper
1 large can tomato juice (46 oz)
1 cup sour cream

Prepare peppers by carefully removing tops and seeds.

In a large pot, mince the onion and sauté in the shortening.

Mix in the meat, dry rice, and seasonings. (You may wish to drain the grease from the

377

meat before adding the other ingredients.)

Using the meat mixture, stuff the peppers until they are three-quarters full.

Place the peppers upright in a baking pan.

Cover with tomato juice, making sure that the peppers do not tip over.

Bake at 350°F for an hour.

Your kitchen should now smell divine!

Make sure that rice is soft before removing peppers from oven.

For a truly Hungarian dish, add a cup of sour cream, then shake pan gently until the cream is mixed into the sauce.

Enjoy!

JULIANA'S CHRISTMAS MÉZESKALÁCS

Adapted by Francois

4 Tbs butter
1/2 cup honey
1/2 cup sugar
1 Tbs brown sugar
2 1/2 cups flour
1/4 tsp salt
2 tsp baking soda
2 tsp cinnamon
1 1/2 tsp powdered ginger
1/2 tsp cloves
2 eggs

To start, melt the butter and honey in a small pot.

Eventually mix in both kinds of sugar, but don't boil.

Let the mixture cool before moving to the next step.

In a bowl, stir together 2 cups of the flour, salt, baking soda, cinnamon, ginger, and cloves.

After cooling butter, honey, and sugar, beat the eggs and add them in.

Add the ingredients in your pot to the dry ingredients.

Mix dough well. If need be, divide into pieces for easier storage.

Seal in plastic or foil and refrigerate chunks of dough overnight.

Taking one chunk at a time, roll out your dough on a floured surface and cut with cookie cutters of your choosing.

Line a cookie sheet with parchment or waxed paper and bake at 350°F for about 8–10 minutes.

Let cookies cool.

Now the magic begins! It is time to decorate the Mézeskalács. Perhaps check Pinterest or baking sites for some patterns that you can paint (with frosting) onto your cookies to make them look truly like the traditional Hungarian treats.

Make sure to take pictures of your works of art before people eat them!

Boldog ünnepeket! Boldog Karácsonyt! (*Merry Christmas!*)

ACKNOWLEDGMENTS

As always, I am grateful to my dad, Bill Rohaly, for his help as both editor and cultural advisor. Thank you to Michelle Vega and Kim Lionetti for their interest in this series. I am grateful to my late beloved mother for showing me how to set a holiday table, and to my siblings and my husband for providing me with my best snowball fights. Thank you to all the wonderful readers of my series, especially those who helped with promotion by posting reviews or telling other readers about my books. I am grateful for all of you! Finally, thank you to the great Dylan Thomas for opening my eyes to the poetic nature of snow.

ABOUT THE AUTHOR

Julia Buckley is the author of the Undercover Dish Mysteries and the Writer's Apprentice Mysteries. She is a member of Sisters in Crime, Mystery Writers of America, and the Chicago Writer's Association. She has taught high school English for twenty-nine years.